ARAPAHO
LANCE

Other novels by Alfred Dennis

Chiricahua
Lone Eagle
Elkhorn Divide
Brant's Fort
Catamount
The Mustangers
Rover
Sandigras Canyon
Yellowstone Brigade
Shawnee Trail
Fort Reno
Yuma
Ride the Rough String
Trail to Medicine Mound

To see more books by Alfred Dennis visit
www.alfreddennis.com

ARAPAHO LANCE

Crow Killer Series - Book 1

by

Alfred Dennis

WCP

Walnut Creek Publishing
Tuskahoma, Oklahoma

Arapaho Lance: Crow Killer Series - Book 1

ISBN: 978-1-942869-23-8
First Edition, Paperback
Published 2017 by Walnut Creek Publishing
Front cover: derivative work of Karl Ferdinand Wimar/The Captive Charger/ Wikimedia Commons/Public Domain
Library of Congress Control Number: 201795268

Books may be purchased in quantity and/or special sales by contacting the publisher;
Walnut Creek Publishing
PO Box 820
Talihina, OK 74571
www.wc-books.com

This book is dedicated to my beloved United States of America, the grandest country any true American should be proud to live in.

CHAPTER 1

Dark clouds formed to the west, carrying with them far off claps of thunder causing the ground to rumble and shake with a vengeance. Flashing bolts of lightning seared across the western sky electrifying the air, causing the skies to light up in the distance. The immigrant's heavy-laden Conestoga wagons lumbered slowly over the rough ground that gradually sloped down to the wide North Platte River. The river lay hidden from view by the heavy timbered banks that appeared ahead. Winding back and forth like a snake across the Nebraska landscape, the Platte was normally a peaceful stream that could be crossed with little problems, providing the wagon leader kept a sharp lookout for quicksand or sharp drop-offs hidden beneath the muddy water. Now, under the darkening and perilous looking clouds, the peaceful river had already risen slightly from the heavy rain upstream, but for now the Platte was still passable. Two men sat their horses at the river's edge, carefully studying the murky water as it rolled slowly past.

The larger of the two shook his head doubtfully, then looked across at the slender buckskin clad man waiting beside him. "Well, Lige, what do you think?"

Rubbing his grizzled face, the older of the men shook his head as he looked up at the swirling clouds. "I think if you're planning on crossing this week, you best be moving them wagons and your back sides right now, and I mean right now."

"You figure it's fixing to get bad?"

"Ain't no figuring to it, it's already bad enough!" Lige Hatcher looked up again at the dark billowing clouds moving toward them. "Those clouds are talking, Chalk. We're fixing to have us a bad blow with plenty of rain, and that little old river out there is already on the rise as we sit here chewing the fat."

"You figure we can get all the wagons across before it hits us?" Chalk Briggs took another dubious look skyward. "We sure don't want the train separated on both sides of the river, considering there could be hostiles all around us."

"We should be able to, if we hurry them up a bit." The thin wagon guide shook his head as he studied the sky again. "Mister Wagon Master, we best be getting on with it, and fast."

"Let's get to it then."

Three young boys, almost men, walked beside the last wagon, prodding the slow moving oxen with their long whip handles, making them lean heavily into their wooden yokes. Two of the boys laughed and joked while the third worked steadily, saying nothing as he kept the big oxen moving. A head taller than the tallest of the other two younger lads, this one was completely opposite in looks; coal black hair and dark eyes encased a strong dark complexioned face. The other two had red hair, their faces totally covered with freckles and they had the bluest of eyes.

The smaller of the redheads tossed a small pebble, hitting the taller lad in the backside, and laughed as the boy turned and looked hard at him. "That'll be enough of that, Billy Wilson. Don't be deviling your brother, keep your mind on them ox."

"Yes, Pa." The smaller redhead grinned over at the other redheaded boy, and winked. "But, he ain't really our brother, is he?"

"Same as, boy. I married his mother, that made her your ma and Jedidiah there your brother." Ed Wilson upon hearing the remark looked stonily down on the boys. "Bless her, she's gone now, but he's still your brother. Now, leave him be and pay attention to your work."

"Stepbrother." Billy spat on the ground as he popped his long whip over the back of the oxen. "And that's all."

"You best let it go, Brother Billy, before you get yourself a flogging from Pa."

"Stepbrother is he? Come supper time, we'll step on him alright."

The shorter of the redheads winked again over at his brother. Both boys were sturdily built and had the rowdy, quick tempers that normally accompanied the red hair and ruddy complexion that went along with Irish heritage.

"We tried that several times in the past, but it sure hasn't worked out too well, so far." Seth the oldest rubbed his chin. "Last time, he hit me. He danged near took my chin off."

"When we water the animals, come sundown, we'll both jump him." Billy insisted.

"You heard Pa, he'll wallop us good if'n he catches us." Seth shook his head. "And I happen to like my backsides."

"We'll catch him away from the wagon." Billy grinned. "You know he won't say a word."

"Yeah, you're right there, he's too dang proud to go crying to Pa." Seth shook his head doubtfully. "Sides, why should he tell, we're the ones that always come out the losers."

"You mean, like you told the last time he tossed you head first into the hog trough back home."

"Very funny, Brother." Seth frowned at his younger brother. "I done no such thing. I didn't tell Pa, he just heard me telling you about it."

"Yeah, right."

"I'll get him for that, one of these days." Seth scowled.

"Well, tonight's the night. The men will be busy as usual with their meeting after the crossing." Billy grinned. "Then we'll get him."

"You never learn, Brother." Seth shook his head doubtfully. "Why do you dislike Jed so much? He's never done a thing to you 'cept whip your bottom every time you forced a fight."

"He's like his mother, haughty and uppity acting." Billy glanced at the teams, then looked back at his stepbrother. "Sides, you dislike him as much as I do, and you know it."

"His ma wasn't that bad a mother." Seth shook his head. "I don't dislike him; it's just that, he's so proud and sure of himself."

"She was an Injun, at least half." Billy spat a stream of tobacco making sure his pa didn't see him. "I'll say one thing, she was a good cook."

"She wasn't no part Indian." Seth shoved his brother sideways playfully.

"Was so, she was sure dark."

"Yes, she was for a fact, but she was from someplace far away across some ocean." Seth glanced up at his pa. "I heard Pa tell Uncle Cletus, she was from Italy, Russia, or somewhere like that."

"She was Injun. Look at him with those black eyes, dark hair, and skin." Billy spat again. "He's Injun I tell you. He can outrun, outjump, and outwrestle anybody back home anywhere near his age."

"That don't make him no Indian."

"Yes, it does, everybody knows how good Injuns are at things like that." The little redhead glanced slyly over to where his stepbrother walked beside the oxen. "He's a heathen, I tell you, pure blood."

"You're nuts, Brother." Seth laughed and shook his head. "He's all white, Billy Boy."

"Yeah, and I'm green." Billy frowned. "You seen how easily he whipped the tar out of old Fred Abbot last week, and poor Freddie's two years older and twenty pounds heavier."

"Maybe you are green. Leastways, I seen you turn green once when you hid out in the corn crib and smoked that cigar you stole from Pa." Seth laughed again. "But you're right, he did put it on Fred for a fact, whipped him to a frazzle."

"That he did." Billy laughed. "And little Sally Ann Duncan standing there watching it all."

"Old Freddie shouldn't have insulted her."

"He only told the truth, she's skinny and ugly." Billy spat again. "Why, she's ugly enough to stop an eight-day clock, dead in its tracks."

"Maybe so, but you sure don't tell a girl that to her face, especially not in front of Jed." Seth shook his head. "Man, I thought Jed done did for him, the way he hit the ground."

"It'll be different next time, Fred will be ready for him."

"Won't be no next time, you couldn't melt Fred and pour him on Jed now." Seth grinned. "I'd bet my best marble on that."

"I'll just take that bet, Brother." Billy was already figuring how to get a fight started between Fred and Jedidiah. "I've always had a hankering to own that shooter of yours."

Seth stepped out and looked down the wagon train. "You know, fact is, she really ain't a bad looking girl."

"Who?" Billy brought his attention back to where Seth was.

"Sally Ann, she's actually kinda pretty."

"Yeah, and so is Pa's old mule, if'n you look at her long enough."

"Well, I think she is."

Billy thought on it a minute, then shrugged. He knew Seth was right, old Fred showed his yellow when he wouldn't get up and fight. Billy liked a good fight, and he had been in a hundred in his short lifetime. Nevertheless, he knew old Freddie was under hack and would avoid Jed like castor oil. One dose of Jed is about the same as a dose of that awful stuff, enough to last a lifetime.

The wagons rolled to a stop with the yoke of oxen pulling the lead wagon, standing barely ten feet from the already rising Platte. Waving his arms, Chalk Briggs summoned all the men from the train forward to the banks of the river.

Waiting until the crowd of men gathered closely around him in the rising wind, the wagon master motioned toward the river. "There's a storm coming men. Lige here says, if we don't get across right now, we may be held up for at least a week on this side."

"Or more!" The wagon scout added looking up at the boiling clouds. "This is gonna be a bad blow, boys, or my name ain't Lige Hatcher."

"So we're crossing, right now." Briggs shook his head. "Lash down your wagon beds, see to your families, and above all keep them oxen moving, don't let them stop midstream for any reason."

"You plumb sure we can make it, Mister Briggs?" A stout man spoke up. "I've heard bad things about the Platte."

"We'll make it, Mister Brown. Me and Lige along with several other riders will flank each wagon as it crosses."

"How high is the water in the middle?" A small immigrant raised a question, looking nervously at the river. "How deep, I mean?"

Chalk Briggs studied the foaming water. "I doubt it's over your hubs yet, so let's start moving because it's gonna start rising fast."

Ed Wilson walked back to his huge Conestoga where the three boys held the placid oxen in line. "You boys will help me drive them to the river's edge. I want all of you to climb in the back of the wagon and stay there until we get safely to the other side."

"Yes, sir."

"And boys, I want no horsing around back there while we cross." Wilson shook his finger. "You boys hear me good, now pay attention, that current could get pretty swift and downright dangerous, and ours will be the last wagon to cross."

"Yes sir, we hear you, Pa." Billy Wilson grinned, the sneaky little smile he was known for. Seth was ornery in his own way, but Billy was downright mean-spirited and when he disliked something or someone, he would devil the poor thing for any reason. One thing could be said for the redhead, he'd tangle with anything smaller or bigger than he was, it didn't matter a bit to him. He didn't know the meaning of fear. Other boys on the train, the recipients of Billy's bullying said he'd fight a grizzly bear with only a willow switch.

The Wilson's wagon rolled slowly down the sloping grade, stopping then waiting their turn to move forward as the advanced teams moved slowly into the murky waters of the Platte. The powerful span of oxen, owned by Ed Wilson, had crossed many streams on their trek to the west; they had been tried and tested. Several of the rivers were much larger than the Platte, but this was scarier. The murky water was littered with all kinds of debris from upstream. The debris stirred up the water, making it so muddy a driver couldn't see the bottom, or what the oxen were fixing to walk off into. With the thunder, darkening clouds, and roaring wind a man's vision and hearing were strained to the limit. Several heavy cracks of the whip and heavy prodding were needed before the oxen would plod slowly forward into the moving water. Flicking his whip with its loud popper over the ox as they started across, Wilson motioned at the three boys.

"Now, quickly into the wagon with you three." The farmer studied the foaming, muddy water worriedly. "And get a good hold back there; this could be a rough ride."

All three boys climbed nimbly into the tall wagon as the rear wheels rolled forward entering the Platte. Two outriders had already tied their ropes onto the wagon to help steady the Conestoga and to pull if they were needed. The six big oxen were powerful animals, under normal conditions they could pull the big wagon easily, but the river was on the rise. The current was pushing and tugging at them, becoming more powerful by the second.

The wagon was almost halfway across when one of the outriders hollered a warning. "Look out Wilson, there's a pretty good-sized log bearing down on your wagon."

"I see it. I believe it'll miss us." Wilson watched as the tree trunk turned and upended as one of its protruding limbs snagged the bottom of the river. "You boys get a tight hold back there."

"Yeah, Jedidiah. You get yourself a good hold like Pa says." Billy Wilson grinned at his dark-headed stepbrother from where he settled himself on a heavy box. "We wouldn't want you to fall out and drown."

Jedidiah Bracket looked over his shoulder to see where the redheads were while he held on to a wooden overhead hoop that held down the heavy canvas of the Conestoga. His mother had married Ed Wilson only three years before, then when she died of cholera on their way west, far from civilization, he had no choice but to remain with the wagon train and the Wilsons. Since his mother's passing, his stepfather treated him like his own son, but his two rowdy stepbrothers were causing trouble and torment every day and almost every mile of their westward journey. Casting his eyes over his shoulder again at the redheads, the dark youth shook his head. Jed refocused his attention on the muddy river as the wagon passed into deeper water, causing the heavy wagon to lift and rock slightly. From where he stood at the back of the wagon, he could tell the river was rising fast and they had yet to reach the deepest part of the crossing. Both outriders had their ropes tied to the quarter beams of the wagon and were helping to steady the heavy wagon as the oxen labored forward.

"Sure hope you don't fall in, Jed." Billy grinned and looked out at the muddy water. "You might get yourself all wet for sure."

Ignoring the comment and not seeing the ornery redhead wink at his older brother, Jed leaned out and looked around the wagon at the nearest outrider who was completely engrossed in keeping his rope tight and the wagon upright. As the heavy wagon neared midstream, the current was becoming more powerful, pulling at the wagon as it bumped over the rock and mud bottom, threatening to capsize the Conestoga.

The huge floating log, Wilson had been warned about earlier, touched the rear of the Conestoga lightly. The log almost cleared the wagon when a long limb completely submerged underwater lodged against the tailgate, causing the wagon to lurch dangerously.

Up to his usual antics of bantering Jedidiah; Billy was caught off balance and slung backwards into the taller youth, knocking him loose from his grasp on the wagon bow, toppling him out of the wagon onto the log head first. Scrambling to keep from falling out of the wagon, Billy felt Seth's strong hands pulling him back from the rushing water that started to lap into the back of the wagon. For several seconds, their attention focused on their close call with death, neither boy realized Jed was not in the wagon.

"Where's Jedidiah?" Seth looked out the back of the wagon and hollered at the outrider. "Hey, Jim Baker, I think Jedidiah fell out of the wagon."

"Pa, Pa." Billy Wilson scrambled to the front of the lunging wagon as it started its way up the west bank and out of the water. "Jedidiah has fallen out. We can't see him anywhere."

"We can't stop now, boy. You and your brother get yourselves a tight hold. We'll go back for him, soon as we get ourselves safe on land."

"Might be too late, Pa. We ain't seen hide nor hair of him since he fell out, when that old log rammed us."

"Jed's a good swimmer; he'll get out. Now, heed me, and set yourself down."

"Suppose we don't find him?" Billy flashed his devilish grin at Seth, who gave up looking and slogged his way to the front of the wagon. "That would be just awful."

"Then, Billy Wilson, I'm gonna have me several pounds of your hide, boy. Cause I figure, you're behind this in some way." The older Wilson heard the comment and frowned.

"Not me, Pa, honest." Billy's face turned pale at the threatened whipping he knew might be forthcoming. "I didn't do anything this time. I didn't even see him fall out."

"That's true, Pa. We were too busy trying to hold on ourselves." Seth backed up his brother's words. "Honest Injun."

Ed Wilson shook his head, as the boys were his pride and joy, and he had loved their redheaded mother dearly. He knew both were ornery and wild as a peach orchard boar, but even they wouldn't go so far as to push their brother from the wagon. "Well, like I said, he's a strong swimmer. He'll swim out somewhere downstream, and we'll pick him up."

"That would be great, Pa." Billy grinned viciously at Seth. "Just great."

Blood seeped into Jedidiah's eyes as he clung feebly with his right arm to the floating log as it swung and lurched every time the dragging limb snagged something on the bottom. Almost knocked unconscious from the heavy fall against the log, all he could do was hang on as long as he could, at least until he got his strength back enough to try for the bank. He didn't understand how he got in the middle of the roaring surge of water on a log or why his left arm wouldn't move. At least, with the limb dragging the bottom, the log remained upright so he wouldn't be flung from it. Touching his face gently, he felt the deep rip that ran across his forehead and down his left cheek. His eyes were blurred from the collision with the log, and unable to focus as they filled with blood and river water. Even the heavy rain against his face couldn't prevent the blood from gushing out from the gaping wound, down his forehead and into his eyes. His head was groggy, but still he fought to remain conscious and his will to survive gave him the strength to fight the surging beast, the river. Finally, his eyes focused on the near bank. He knew he had to get clear of the log and onto land as quick as he could before he passed out and slipped unconscious beneath the strong current. As the river filled and deepened from runoff water, it grew in strength, carrying the heavy log faster and faster, racing along with the strong current, taking him down the river, bobbing and lurching like a bucking horse every time the dragging limb hit bottom.

His head cleared slightly with the heavy rain splattering against his face as he straddled the slippery log, trying to maintain his grip. The heavy blow he received when his head impacted the log addled him, and he couldn't think clearly or understand what was happening.

In his delirium, Jed felt the limb grab deep into the riverbed again causing the log to swerve and turn, pushing it in a straight line toward the west bank. Seeing his one opportunity, as the log floated toward the muddy shore, Jed loosened his grip on the log and paddled hard for the nearest bank with his one usable arm. The bank where he worked his way to was steep, far too steep and slick to climb with only one good arm. Easing back into the water, Jed worked his way downstream grabbing onto grass, brush, and limbs until he found a buffalo track leading up and out of the river. Pushing and pulling himself painfully with the last of his remaining strength, Jed crawled up the game trail, rolling exhaustedly into the tall grass only inches from the raging river that pulled at his feet. Blood from the ragged cut covered his face and chest as he lay battered and half conscience in the muddy trail, unable to move. Rousing himself slightly, he tried to inch away from the raging river. Finally, with no strength left, he closed his eyes, trying to shield them with his good arm from the fierce pelting rain.

Hearing a slight sound, Jed held his arm above his bloody face and focused on a pair of legs covered in leather breeching and moccasins standing above him. Raising his eyes slowly, he looked up into the dark broad face of an Indian. Long black hair, sprinkled with gray, hung from the broad shoulders, wide, deep-set eyes of a warrior peered out of a broad forehead. The straight nose and thin lips gave the warrior, staring down at him, an aristocratic look. Jed blinked the water and blood from his eyes as he tried to focus on the man before him. Rising slowly and painfully to his feet, he tried to wipe away some of the blood from his face and eyes with his wet sleeve before pitching forward into blackness.

Words emitted from the older man were words Jed couldn't have understood even if he was conscious. Several other warriors stepped up behind the older warrior and peered down at the blood and water soaked body of the unconscious boy.

"He has dark skin like one of the people." A slender bandy-legged warrior knelt beside the unconscious Jed.

"No, he is a white eye from the wagon train ahead." A tall, muscular warrior pointed off toward the wagon road. "He is an interloper, enemy of the Arapaho."

The older warrior shook his head. "He is brave, he stood straight before me. He showed no fear."

"Maybe, my Chief, but he is a boy, a white boy." The muscular warrior spoke up. "I don't think he was brave. I don't think he knew we were here before him."

"No, Walking Horse, he looked into my eyes unafraid. He knew I stood before him."

Another warrior rolled Jedidiah over and looked at the hole in the youngster's back. "He has been stabbed and his arm is broken."

"He is, as I said, very brave." The older man nodded. "A young warrior bloody and hurt such as he, was trying to stand with all of his wounds."

"What will you do with him, my Chief?" The tall warrior spoke again. "I say, kill him."

"Tell me, Walking Horse, what honor is there in killing an unconscious boy?"

"He is our enemy."

Kneeling down beside the prone body, another warrior pulled the already torn shirt back from the ragged hole. "Look!"

"What does Big Owl see?"

"Look." The warrior pointed at Jedidiah's back, then pulled his hand back quickly. "It looks like the medicine mark of the Arapaho Lance."

To the staring eyes of the Arapaho warriors gathered around him, the birthmark Jedidiah carried on his back, did resemble the War Lance of the Arapaho Tribe. The lance was the totem of the Stake Bearer Clan, the Warrior Society of the Arapaho that only the greatest and bravest of the brave were permitted to belong to. Only the Dog Soldiers of the great Cheyenne Warrior Society had such warriors in their Clan Lodges.

"Yes, it is the sign of the Arapaho Lance on his back." The muscular warrior, Walking Horse, stared in awe. "But how could this be?"

"The medicine people put our totem on him. The river has belched him from its stomach. Now, they have placed him here for us to find." Slow Wolf shook his head. "It is an omen, a sign from the ancient ones."

"Why, my Chief? I do not understand."

"He is Arapaho. He has come home to help his people, in a time of need, when our enemies are running everywhere across our hunting grounds." Slow Wolf stared down at Jed in awe. "I say it is a sign from the sacred ones, it must be."

"With respect, my Chief Slow Wolf, he is but a white boy lost from the wagon train of the whites." Walking Horse argued. "It is just a mark, not a sign."

The older warrior, called Slow Wolf, raised his hands toward the west and the heavens, then stood for several minutes before turning.

"My medicine has spoken, your Chief has spoken. This young man is wounded. We will take him to our lodges where White Swan's medicine can heal his wounds."

Walking Horse hated whites and knew the wounded boy before him was a white. He wanted to protest further, but Slow Wolf had spoken. As head chief of the Northern Arapaho, his words carried much weight in council. This chief had led his tribe for many years and counted many coups on their enemies the Pawnee, Shoshone, and Crow. No warrior had been mightier in battle in his youth and kept his people safe and well fed, so Walking Horse held his tongue. It was not his place to argue against his chief, it could even prove fatal if he angered Slow Wolf into a fight.

A younger warrior rode into the gathered group of warriors and whirled his small horse, pointing off to the north. "Whites come down river this way."

"How many?" Bow Legs clutched his war lance tight.

"This many." The young warrior held up four fingers. "They have long rifles."

"We will hide and kill them when they approach." Walking Horse spoke up. "We could count many coups."

Slow Wolf looked up into the eyes of the tall warrior. "Does Walking Horse now give the orders when I lead a war party?"

Dropping his eyes, the warrior shook his head. "No, my Chief."

"Go quickly; build a travois to carry the wounded one on." Slow Wolf barked out orders. "We will only fight if we are attacked."

"I think they come looking for the white one." The young warrior, Little Weasel, added. "They ride along the bank and search every place."

Watching as Jedidiah was laid across the travois, covered with stretched deer hides, the Arapaho Leader mounted and motioned the warriors to follow him. "Walking Horse will stay behind. He will watch to see if the white men follow us."

"I will watch, my Chief."

Slow Wolf nodded as the young warrior had been put in his place without embarrassing him or making him lose face. Walking Horse was still young, and he was a brave warrior loved by his people. Someday, he would be a great leader, but first he had to learn humility and patience.

When the raiding party returned to the village, Slow Wolf would have words with his nephew. In the village each warrior was his own master, doing as he chose, following who he chose, but on the war trail each was sworn to follow the leader of the war party without protest of any kind.

Lige Hatcher and three others from the wagon train followed the west side of the Platte, searching out the rain soaked banks, looking for any sign of Jedidiah. The river was swelling out of its banks and crossing to the other side would be dangerous. If the lad was on the east side, then that's where he would have to stay for now.

Hatcher knew the Platte, he had come west with the early mountain men trapping the South Platte and surrounding waterways for the valued beaver pelts that lived there. He had survived countless attempts on his life by the wild tribes, wild animals, and the elements. For the last four years, with the fur business gone, he had been leading immigrant trains west to the gold fields of California, and into the fertile lands of Oregon. No longer a young man, Lige Hatcher hired out to scout for the trains, hunt buffalo for the army, or work at anything else he could do to eke out a living. Nevertheless, there was one thing for certain, he and everyone that knew him would swear, no man knew and understood this wild country better. The old trapper could track like an Indian, he was completely fearless, and most important of all, the wild tribes liked and trusted him.

Walking Horse waited, obscured behind the tall cane and scrub brush that bordered the raging river. The rain slacked off from the torrential downpour to a steady drizzle, but still rushing water from the heavy runoff raced down into the river. The Arapaho watched closely, his eyes sharp as a hawk, as the four whites sat their horses, studying the river and rain soaked ground. One of the men dismounted and studied the tracks the hunting party just left in the wet ground, then the man bent down momentarily. Three of the whites seemed to be discussing the river as the man on the ground remounted and studied the riverbank momentarily. Finally satisfied, he waved his arm and all four turned their horses back to the north toward the immigrant road.

Lige Hatcher rode through the damp afternoon, his mind mulling over the tracks he had found. The drag marks were faint from the heavy washing rains, but to the old tracker who could read sign like others could read a letter, they read plain enough. The drag marks lay along the riverbank with a few unshod pony tracks leading off to the southwest. Saying nothing to the men with him, Lige looked down at the muddy knife he had found earlier in the mud. He had heard the ring of metal as his horse's front shoe had struck the blade, burying it in the soft ground. He had felt around in the gloom and picked up the hunting knife before any of the others spotted it. The initials L.H. was deeply burned into the bone handle identifying it as his own knife, the same knife he had given to Jedidiah for helping him skin the many buffalo that he had killed to feed the wagon people. He read the signs plainly; the boy was alive. The fresh cut branches scattered about and the tracks of the travois moving away, showed the boy had been hurt badly enough that he couldn't walk. It was the custom of the tribes to shame a prisoner by making him walk back to their village, but they had built a travois for this prisoner, apparently they wanted Jed alive. Studying the knife once more, Lige dropped it in his saddlebag, and led the men back through the dark, damp night toward the wagon train. Just before turning back to the north, his blue eyes stared at the stand of river cane fifty yards across the clearing. His uncanny senses, built up by years of scouting and trapping from a necessity of survival, had become sharp as a knife's edge. Now, the hair on his neck stood up, he could sense something or somebody was sitting in the cane watching them.

Walking Horse scowled as he knew the white man, Lige Hatcher, who the Arapaho called Rolling Thunder from the noise his long rifle made, smelled out his hiding place in the brush. The white had lived with the Arapaho many years, had even taken his mother, an Arapaho woman, for a wife until her death from a Pawnee arrow. On the war trail, he was like a wolf smelling out danger. Many tales were told around the fires of the Sioux and Arapaho, tales of the many times Rolling Thunder had saved the white soldiers from riding into the traps laid by the tribes. Watching the whites retreat toward the wagon road, he nudged his sorrel horse and started after the other warriors.

Hatcher glanced once more over his shoulder and spotted the retreating warrior who had emerged from his hiding place where he had been watching the four white men. His sharp eyes knew this warrior, the way he sat his horse, the set of his shoulders, and yes, he knew the Arapaho. Lige had ridden on many a hunting party years ago with the warrior when he was just a boy. Walking Horse was actually his stepson by marriage. The scout smiled slightly as a twinge of loneliness clutched at his heart. He missed his dead wife, his stepson, the Arapaho people, and the wild and free spirit he had enjoyed while living with them. He was forced to abandon his freestyle living among the Arapaho when word had come from a passing buffalo hunter that his dying mother had beckoned him; Lige had left the boy with his uncle, Slow Wolf, and had ridden away from the village without a backward glance. Hidden behind a lodge, Walking Horse had watched as the white man, he had loved and respected, rode away. Once again, the young Arapaho felt abandoned, and hate for the whites had grown in his chest.

Over the years, his memory of Lige Hatcher had dimmed, but his hatred for the white and other whites had become stronger. Even the words of Slow Wolf, who had become Chief of the Arapaho, had fallen on deaf ears as he tried to defend the white hunter's reasons for leaving the tribe and returning to the east.

"You okay, Lige?" A thin rider spoke up. "You're sure quiet."

"I'm okay." Hatcher nodded slowly. "No, I'm not okay." The words were thought, but not spoken.

Riding into the circle of wagons, Hatcher rode directly to the huge Conestoga of the wagon master and dismounted. Chalk Briggs walked from under the heavy canvas rain tarp and approached where Lige was pulling his wet saddle and blankets from the tired gelding.

"Find anything, Lige?"

"Maybe, maybe not." The old scout placed his saddle under a tarp out of the rain. "Didn't find the boy, but I found some drag marks heading southwest."

"Hunting party?"

"Reckon it could be, but something was weighing the drag poles down pretty good."

"Was it the boy or meat they had killed?"

"There's no way of knowing for certain, Chalk." Lige shrugged, omitting to acknowledge finding the knife. "I'll do some looking when the rain moves out, but I think the only way we'll find the boy is if he comes walking in by himself."

"That ain't likely." The wagon master shook his head. "We're pulling out come sunup."

"No, sir. I agree, it ain't very likely." Lige nodded.

"Get you some grub while I walk over and speak with Wilson." Chalk turned. "He set a store by that young fella."

"I understand the boy was just his stepson."

"He was, but just the same, Wilson thought a lot of the lad."

Lige dropped his bridle and empty rifle scabbard across the saddle. "You know the lad helped me with the skinning, and even shot a couple deer and a buffalo for the fires. He had the makings of a real man."

"He did, for a fact." Chalk nodded. "I sure hope the river didn't take him under."

"Somehow, Chalk, I have a feeling we'll see the kid again." Lige tethered his horse on the tall grass beside the wagon, and walked back to the fire. "Yes, sir, we'll see him again one day."

"I hope you're right."

Hatcher neglected to tell Briggs about the knife for fear the wagon master would send him on a fool's errand to look for the lad. With the heavy rains, the trail would be washed out, and his chances of tracking the hunting party would be slim to none. If the hunting party that took him went to the trouble to keep him alive, then he would be safe. Indians were funny people; they wouldn't build a travois, save a prisoner, just to kill him later. Also, Hatcher knew exactly which tribe had him, the Arapaho, and their villages were a long way from the immigrant trail. When the train was safely delivered to Oregon and the time came for him to go looking for Jedidiah Bracket, then he would go.

CHAPTER 2

The Arapaho Village lay in a large forested basin along the banks of the Laramie River. With the extra burden of pulling the travois across the rough ground, it had taken the hunting party four full days of steady riding to reach the village. With the exception of a few stops for water and to feed the injured boy, the hunting party never slowed their fast pace to the west.

The head Chief of the Arapaho, Slow Wolf, studied the ashen face of the white boy as the drag bounced roughly along the game trail they were following. He was in awe of the boy, he must be the omen. Why else had the medicine people placed the mark of the Arapaho Lance upon the youth and put him in their hands? He did not fully understand, but the older medicine men of the tribe would have to see the mark and they could possibly translate its meaning. This is why he hastened to reach the village where their great Medicine Man, White Swan, could treat the boy's wounds and perhaps save him. If it was as Slow Wolf thought, the white youth could bring good fortune, and he would be big medicine to the Arapaho people.

Villagers gathered curiously around the travois and its injured burden as the hunting party deposited Jedidiah in front of a large hide tepee decorated with several buffalo skulls.

An ancient one, his face lined with ageless seams, exited the lodge when beckoned. He walked slowly to where the travois was laid flat on the ground. Looking down at the injured youth and over at Slow Wolf, the old man nodded slightly, then motioned toward the lodge. "He is white."

"Perhaps, Grandfather, but I do not think so." Slow Wolf watched as several squaws carried Jedidiah into the lodge. "Examine his wounds, White Swan. Study the mark on him and tell me what medicine he possesses to have such a mark."

The old eyes of the ancient medicine man studied the chief for several seconds, but then turned back into the lodge without speaking, dropping the flap behind him as he disappeared inside. White Swan was like most Arapaho, he hadn't had many doings with other white men, only the early trappers and traders. The filthy white men with their hair faces hadn't impressed him. The old one had little use for the treacherous, pale-skinned men from the east. Now, Slow Wolf asked him to take one into his lodge and care for him. Turning to where the squaws placed the injured one on a bed of buffalo robes, the old man frowned, and ordered the women to remove the bloody clothes from the boy.

The mark on the boy's back and its resemblance to the mark of the Arapaho War Lance immediately grabbed White Swan's attention and raised his curiosity. Since the beginning of the Stake Bearer Clan, only two babies had been born into the Arapaho Nation with such marks that he could remember. One, the great, courageous Strong Bear had such a mark and it was he who had become the first Lance Bearer, the bravest of the brave. He had made the Arapaho warriors great fighters, feared by all their enemies. The War Society of the Lance was always at the forefront of any fight. The Lance Bearer would sink his lance deep into the ground, never to retreat in the face of an enemy. If the others didn't show their bravery and charge forward to save the stake bearer, he would perish. The other warriors must fight or they would lose face and dishonor themselves before their people. The Arapaho people were fewer in numbers than other tribes, but the Society of Lance Bearers made them fierce. Other enemy tribes feared the strong medicine of the Lance Bearers and mostly stayed away from Arapaho hunting grounds and horse herds.

Now, before him lay only the third person to carry such a mark, White Swan nodded his head slowly. What could it mean; a white with the mark of the Arapaho? He now knew why Slow Wolf wanted to know more of the youth. The mark could be an omen from the ancient ones, but was it a good omen for the people or bad? First, he would work and try to heal the wounded one. Perhaps, the smoke and stones of his medicine would give him his answer.

Billy Wilson looked worriedly across to where Chalk Briggs stood talking to his father. Switching his gaze over to his brother, the smaller redhead spat. "We could be in trouble, Seth, big trouble. That danged nosy wagon master might have learned what happened."

"Maybe so." Seth nodded. "But this time, it really was an accident. You said you fell into Jed when the wagon lurched sideways."

"I'm glad he's gone." Billy spat again. "I wasn't lying, it was an accident."

Seth looked at his brother doubtfully as he hadn't actually seen Jedidiah fall from the wagon. He just took Billy's word and he knew how mischievous his brother could be. "Honest Injun, Billy? It happened like you said, didn't it?"

"It happened like I said, Brother." The redhead grinned. "It was an accident, but like I said, I'm glad he's gone."

"He could be dead."

"Nah, he'll show up, it's just my luck." Billy shook his head. "You know what they say about a bad penny."

"Jed wasn't bad, Billy." Seth shook his head. "You know he wasn't, we were the bad ones."

"I don't know anything of the kind. He looked down on us and treated us like beggars of some kind."

"That was all in your mind, Brother." Seth held up his hand. "Shh, here they come."

Chalk studied the faces of the two brothers for several minutes before nodding at Wilson. Something in the smaller one's face seemed to be laughing at him, taunting him with something he wasn't telling. He had never taken to the younger brother. The boy was mean and cruel, and he had been into it with everyone on the train at one time or another. Nodding again, the wagon master turned and walked away.

"You boys sure you didn't see Jed fall from the wagon?"

"No sir, Pa." Billy swallowed hard. "Like we said, he was gone when we turned around."

"That right, Seth?"

"Yes, sir. That's the way it happened alright." The older boy nodded. "That old log rammed us and the wagon lurched sideways, next thing we knew we were thrown around back there like spilt beans."

Ed Wilson truly loved his boys, but still he knew they were mischievous, even downright ornery at times, and they hated Jedidiah. However, to drown him on purpose, he just couldn't believe that. "Alright boys, right now all we can do is pray that he'll turn up, down the trail a piece."

"Yes, sir." Billy grinned relieved. "We'll sure do a powerful lot of praying for him alright."

"You bet we will, Pa." Seth chimed in.

Slow Wolf looked up as White Swan stepped through the opening of the chief's huge lodge. Motioning for the medicine man to take a seat across from him, he waited politely as the older man made himself comfortable on a folded buffalo robe.

"These old bones have passed many winters, my Nephew, and they do not bend as easily as they once did." White Swan crossed his withered legs slowly. "Perhaps, I have been on mother earth too many moons."

"You talk foolishly, my Uncle. You have many years left to heal and help lead our people." The chief studied the old one. "You must, the people need your wisdom, more now than ever."

"Now, my Nephew, you are the one talking foolish." White Swan laughed lightly, the toothless gums showing when his mouth opened slightly. "You have been a wise, strong leader and the people are lucky to have one such as you."

"Tell me, how is the wounded one?" Slow Wolf changed the subject. The subject of dying was one he did not like. His words were true as the Arapaho needed the wisdom and guidance of the old medicine man more than ever. There were many problems facing the Arapaho people; the coming of the lodges with wheels, the influx of many whites into their hunting grounds, and their enemies becoming stronger and bolder as they obtained the white man's rifle.

"You worry much about this one, a white." White Swan shrugged his bony shoulders. "Why?"

"I wish to know how he acquired the mark of the Lance upon his back." Slow Wolf slowly removed the parfleche covering from his pipe and held it out to the old man. "We will smoke. Perhaps you will find the answer in the smoke."

"Sometimes the smoke that floats on the air has strong medicine, sometimes the smoke just blows on the wind, saying nothing." White Swan spreads his hands and watched as the chief took a glowing ember from the fire. "I do not see how it is so important to know about one injured white."

Smoke curled slowly upward as Slow Wolf pulled hard on the long pipe. The chief was a nephew of the old medicine man from his mother's side. Over the years, even before his father's passing, Slow Wolf had marveled at the strong medicine and healing powers that White Swan possessed. Many things the old one had foretold and predicted had come true, exactly as he had seen in his visions. Passing the pipe across the fire to the older man, he noticed how gnarled and bony the old hands were as they reached for the pipe. The medicine man was probably right; the chief knew the old one's time before going to meet his ancestors was short. He knew no one lived forever, but still he worried as losing one as White Swan would be a great loss. He would be missed greatly as the tribe depended on his medicine; his ability to foretell how the hunting would be or when the tribe should move into the protected canyons, back in the mountains, away from the fierce winter storms that would rage down from the northwest. Many a time, the old one had predicted rain on a hot humid day, and the rain would arrive as foretold. Slow Wolf would miss his uncle too, it would be hard to lead the Arapaho Tribe without the old one's remarkable ability to tell the future or warn the tribe of danger.

"You are deep in thought, Nephew."

Slow Wolf nodded slowly. "I must know about the injured one. Tell me, Uncle."

The old eyes squinted, focusing sharply on the dark inquiring eyes of his nephew. "I will tell you what I have seen."

"This is good, tell me."

White Swan shifted slightly on his robe and passed the pipe back across to his nephew. "We will talk of this only once, my Nephew, and then we will speak of it no more."

Slow Wolf nodded. "Yes, it will be so."

"I fear evil things could come of this."

"Speak."

"My Nephew, Slow Wolf, lost his youngest son to the Pawnee warriors when he staked himself to the ground on the banks of Little Muddy River. No braver warrior ever lived, none as strong, and none were as dedicated to his people."

"None." Slow Wolf nodded. "He was a great warrior, a great Lance Bearer."

"The others begged him to pull his war lance from the ground and retreat, but he just laughed and turned to meet the mighty Pawnee. Fast Wing lost his life on the banks of the Little Muddy. Before he gave his life that day, he won a great victory for the Arapaho, giving our young men courage and great pride, never will he be forgotten." White Swan looked across the fire. "I have looked into my medicine, into my fires, and I have looked deep into the eyes of the wounded one."

"What have you seen, my Uncle?" Slow Wolf leaned forward eagerly. "I know that my son, Fast Wing, is forever lost to me and the Arapaho people."

White Swan nodded slowly. "I have looked into the smoke, into my powers and the signs of the great ones that have walked on the earth before us."

"What has White Swan seen?" The chief was annoyed, why did his uncle hesitate? "Speak, Uncle."

"From the great hunting grounds in the sky your son, Fast Wing, has sent me a sign, he has spoken." White Swan stared hard into the small flame that lit the lodge. "I have also seen the injured one, in my powers, and he has been sent to the Arapaho. The mark on his back is the same mark that Fast Wing carried; he will someday be a great leader, always a great defender of the people."

"White Swan has seen this?"

"Yes, he has taken the place of Fast Wing even though he does not know it yet." The old medicine man nodded. "Soon the whites will cover the land like the locust in summer. Our enemies from the west outnumber us and they are getting the white man's rifle. Soon they will be strong enough to invade our hunting grounds and attack us."

"Then he will survive his wounds?"

"He is young in years and he will grow strong quickly. When he reaches the status of warrior, he will have great strength, and he will be the bravest of the brave." White Swan nodded. "I have seen this in my visions."

"Will he be Arapaho, or will he wish to return to the whites?"

"This I do not know." White Swan shrugged. "I believe he is already Arapaho, he must be if the ancient ones have sent him to us, but I cannot force one such as him to stay, if he does not wish to."

Slow Wolf looked curiously at the old medicine man. "I do not understand your words, Uncle."

"I have seen the look in his eyes. Does Slow Wolf remember when the young warrior, Red Bird, received the hard blow to his head when he fell from his horse?"

"I remember, for many moons, he could not remember who he was."

"I believe it is the same with this young white." White Swan nodded. "It is early yet, but this could be."

"Are you sure of this, Uncle?"

"We will know soon." The medicine man passed the pipe back across the fire. "Time will tell us."

"Red Bird regained his memory, along with the things he had forgotten."

"I believe this could happen to this white, but for now, I believe he will remember nothing."

"He did take a hard blow to his head and he bled much."

White Swan nodded. "All things will be known in time, Nephew."

"Little Antelope, the woman of Walking Horse knows a few words of the whites." Slow Wolf looked out from the lodge. "She will be instructed to use what words she knows to talk with the young one."

"Walking Horse will not like this." The old medicine man's tongue clucked. "You know, he hates all whites."

"I have banished my nephew from the village for six moons." Slow Wolf frowned. "He would not take her with him. He fears she could be in danger from our enemies who roam these hunting grounds."

White Swan was curious as he hadn't heard this news. "Is this punishment for questioning his chief on the war trail?"

"Walking Horse is a great Lance Bearer, a great warrior, but it is I, Slow Wolf, who is Chief of the Arapaho. I will be obeyed." Slow Wolf straightened and looked across at the old one. "Any who question me on the war trail will be banished."

"As it should be, my Chief." White Swan watched his nephew's face as it relaxed. "Do you wish me to tell the woman?"

"It would be good." Slow Wolf looked at the old medicine man. "Tell me, Uncle, why do you fear this one?"

"This I am not sure of, but I fear the people will perhaps come to depend on him too much." The old shoulders drooped. "I've seen the greatness, the courage in this one."

"Or is it because he is white?"

The old medicine man stood unsteadily, and turned to the entrance of the lodge. Stopping, he turned and nodded before disappearing into the night.

Two figures strolled slowly along the banks of the small stream passing mares, colts, and stallions protecting their brood bands. Women and children bathed in the stream while further downstream older boys fought mock battles while enjoying the water. Curious bashful glances followed them as Jedidiah and White Swan passed by. The younger girls smiled shyly, whispering to one another as they took in the tall straight figure of the younger man. The white scar that ran down the left side of his face showed plainly in the afternoon sun. Most of the Arapaho thought the scar only enhanced his looks, making him look prouder, even fiercer for one so young. Word spread quickly throughout the Arapaho Nation, and everyone knew he carried the mark of the Arapaho Lance upon his shoulder. Even though he was still young in years, legend and prophecies from their great Medicine Man, White Swan, destined the young one to become a great warrior and one day a Lance Bearer.

"You have been in our village for over two seasons, young one." The old medicine man studied the many horses absently as they passed through the small groups. "You have healed from your wounds, learned the words of the people quickly, and you have tried to learn our customs and ways."

"Yes, thanks to Little Antelope." Jed nodded. "But, I still have much to learn, Grandfather."

"Tell me, my son, do you like it here with the people?"

Jedidiah remembered the yelling and squabbling among the people of the wagon train. Here, no voice rose against another, and no child was whipped or punished. "Yes, I do. Here with the Arapaho people it is a peaceful life.

"Do you wish to return to your people?"

"This I do not know, I have enjoyed my stay among the people." Jed looked toward the river. "Am I a prisoner? Tell me, if I wanted to return to the white people, would Slow Wolf let me go back?"

White Swan shrugged. "This I do not know, our chief thinks much of the prophecy, and his mind thinks much of you. He believes you will bring our people good fortune."

"Because of the mark I carry on my back?"

"At first this was so, the mark told of a prophecy of the Arapaho. Now, he has grown to think of you as a son." White Swan nodded slightly. "Our chief had been saddened, he had lost all his sons, but now he has you to lift his spirits once again."

Jedidiah nodded. "Little Antelope has told me of this prophecy. I would like to hear more, Grandfather."

"Many, many moons ago, it was told a great leader and warrior with the mark you carry, would come from the east, arise from the deep waters, and lead the people in times of need."

"Does Slow Wolf think of me as this one?" Jed shook his head. "Surely this cannot be so."

"It has happened as the prophecy was foretold." White Swan looked over at Jed. "Exactly, you came from the east, from the raging waters, and you carry the mark."

"I owe Chief Slow Wolf my life. He saved me from the river, bound my wounds, and stopped Walking Horse from killing me, but even so after two years, I still feel I am an outsider."

"When you first came to us, I thought maybe your mind had forgotten your white life." White Swan slowed. "I was wrong, you do remember the past. You are wrong, young one, you are no longer an outsider."

"Yes, I remember." Jedidiah looked over at the old man. "I do not remember exactly how I got into the river, but I do remember the train and my life with the whites."

"Was that a happy time for you?" White Swan queried. "Living with the whites of the train?"

"My stepfather was a good man, although I did not feel I belonged with him after my mother died." Jedidiah studied the river they neared. "Here it is different, I feel content. I would be content, except for Walking Horse glaring at me all the time."

"Walking Horse will someday be your friend." White Swan nodded solemnly. "Perhaps, he is jealous of the time his woman, Little Antelope, has spent teaching you our language."

"We are just friends, Grandfather. There is nothing more between us." Jed felt his face turning red.

The old one smiled slightly. "Walking Horse is a jealous husband, and Little Antelope is very pretty, is she not?"

"I don't know, would it be right for me to leave my own people?" Jedidiah looked down at the wrinkled face, wanting to change the subject. At nineteen years old, the youth was already a head taller than the older man walking beside him. "I am happy here, Grandfather. Happier here than I have ever been before, and for now, I would like to remain with the people."

"Who is to say who your people are really?" The old one smiled sadly. "Red, white, or even brown is only a color of a man's skin, underneath we are all the same. The thoughts in our heart is what matters most."

"Perhaps, Grandfather. Perhaps, you are right."

"It is what is in here that counts." White Swan tapped his chest. "A man's pride, courage, and most of all his generosity to the people is how he is valued."

"I will remember your words, Grandfather." Jed nodded.

White Swan smiled as it was not enough to be grateful just for his life, but this young man actually felt at home with the Arapaho. He enjoyed the people and their way of life. He had made many friends among the younger warriors and showed courtesy to all. He never failed to treat the elders, even the old women, with great respect. The old medicine man knew he had been wrong about the young man not remembering the past. Since regaining his strength, he remembered everything; Slow Wolf standing above him at the raging river, Walking Horse wanting to kill him, and the long painful travois drag back to the village.

"The Arapaho people will soon need strong leaders." White Swan changed their direction toward a wooded draw that sat beside the creek. "I see many difficulties ahead for our people."

Jedidiah studied the medicine man as he slowed down his long strides to match the older man's slower pace. "What does White Swan speak of?"

"The Arapaho are a strong and brave people, but compared to the Arickaree, Crow, Pawnee, or the many other tribes, we are few." The old man shrugged and pointed a bony finger. "Now, the whites are coming into our lands, another dangerous enemy, and they bring the fire rifle with them."

"The whites move on westward, to the lands of Oregon and California." Jed shook his head. "They will not stop here and they surely won't let Indians have the rifle, they fear the warriors of the red men."

"Our enemies already have the white man's rifle." White Swan shook his head. "The white traders are the ones who gave them power over us with this weapon."

"I did not know this."

"Soon, when the western lands fill up, they will stop here in our hunting grounds, here among the people. Our friends, the Sioux and Cheyenne of the far north, fear this as well."

"The whites on the train feared Indians." Jedidiah remembered how Chalk Briggs would severely browbeat any man he caught without his rifle. "We lost a few horses, but we were never attacked."

"Indians value horses and it is like a game for them to take them from their enemies." The old man smiled. "To us it is not stealing. Did not the old ones put the horse here for all to use, the same as the buffalo and elk?"

"Tell me, Grandfather, if you were me what would you do?"

"I cannot speak for you, for you alone know what is in your heart, what it tells you to do."

"I am content here with the people." Jedidiah repeated as he looked over the grazing herd of horses belonging to the Arapaho. "I will stay with the Arapaho for now."

"Your words make an old man happy."

"I am a young man, Grandfather, and you are wise. Tell me, can a man walk the path of two races?"

"Here a man can walk any path he wishes." White Swan nodded. "A warrior of the people is his own person. Our customs say no leader can tell him what to do, or who to follow."

"This is a good custom, for now I will stay with the people."

"Yours will be a difficult path, my son." White Swan smiled. "The sign of the Lance on your back marks you to become a Lance Bearer of the people, and the Arapaho warriors will expect this of you. The Lance is a very dangerous burden to carry. You will have to gain the respect of the warriors. You will always be expected to be at the front, with the bravest of the brave, fighting our enemies."

"I have heard many speak in awe of the Lance Bearers of the Arapaho." Jed looked over at the old man. "Tell me, Grandfather, why do these warriors stake themselves to the ground in such a way? It seems like they wish to die."

"They do not wish to die, my son. A warrior can gain no greater respect and love from his people than by giving his life for them." White Swan spoke quietly. "Many have died young, but they were very courageous and will always be remembered with honor."

"The whites are the same, they will fight and die to save their loved ones, but they don't look or seek death." Jedidiah shook his head, unable to comprehend the words. "Is honor and respect alone worth dying for?"

"You are young yet." White Swan smiled. "In time, the love for your adopted people will answer these questions."

"Perhaps you are right, Grandfather."

White Swan turned to the far lodge and pointed. "The choice is yours, my son. Stay with the Arapaho, or I will ask Slow Wolf to let you return to your own people."

"This I do not understand. Tell me, why am I a captive, a prisoner, but treated like one of the people?"

White Swan looked into the dark eyes of Jedidiah. "Because, young one, the prophecy and the mark on your back prohibits any Arapaho from harming you."

"How can this mark be such a powerful thing?"

"It is the prophecy of the ancient ones and if it is fulfilled, the future of the Arapaho people will be a long and happy one." White Swan nodded. "For this, my son, the Lance Bearers will be needed, but remember this, theirs will always be the path of war and death, but glory and honor will be theirs also."

Jedidiah studied the old medicine man's words for several minutes before answering. He could remember he never actually felt at home, really at home, while living with Ed Wilson and his sons. Wilson had treated him fair and tried to make a place for him, but with the Arapaho for the last two years, he had been happy, like he really belonged. Walking through the village as he recovered and regained his strength, all the people from the youngest to the oldest treated him like one of their own, like an Arapaho. The old one's warning words of death didn't scare him, instead he felt warm and wanted. "I wish to remain with the people."

"Good, then you have much to learn to become a Lance Bearer." White Swan pointed at a lodge nestled under the far trees. "In that lodge you will stay with the warrior and his woman who are there."

"Who is there?" Jed studied the far-off lodge. He never remembered seeing a lodge by the river before.

"Walking Horse and his woman." White Swan nodded. "He is a hard man, but he is also a great warrior, and a Lance Bearer who will teach you the customs and ways of the Arapaho warrior."

"Walking Horse!" Jedidiah sputtered. "But he's the warrior that wanted to see my scalp on his war lance."

"He is also the warrior that Slow Wolf banned from the village to live alone." White Swan nodded. "For six moons, he was banished from the village. He had to stay away from the people and away from his woman, Little Antelope. He could not join the other warriors in war, or gain the spoils of the warpath."

"Why was he banned from the village?"

"Because, he challenged the word of his chief." White Swan stopped and turned to Jed. "This is not allowed on the war trail, remember it, above all else."

"It was on account of me, wasn't it?"

"Go now, Walking Horse and his woman wait for you to come into their lodge, our chief has spoken to him."

Jedidiah looked at the lodge and whispered to himself. "I bet that tickled him."

"Walking Horse is one of our bravest and best warriors. Learn from him and return to us as a Lance Bearer after you have learned the way of the Arapaho." White Swan motioned with his arm. "Walking Horse is older than you, but still young himself. He is a Lance Bearer, brave in battle and generous to his people. Learn all you can from his wisdom and listen to his words. If you are deserving when you return to the people, you will become a warrior."

"This I will do."

"You will be welcome here, young one." White Swan studied Jed's face. "One day though, I have seen in the smoke, you will see a sign and that day you may wish to leave us to live where this sign calls you."

"What kind of sign, Grandfather?"

"That was not revealed to me. It is for your eyes only to see, but you will know it when it appears to you, if it appears." The old medicine man nodded. "Go now, make an old man proud."

White Swan watched as the tall, straight youth walked to the lodge. Now, he knew Slow Wolf's reasons for taking such an interest in the young one. The ancient prophecy of one day a warrior showing up from the east with the mark of the Lance on his back had come true. The Arapaho people were superstitious and they didn't dare insult the old ones by turning away their gift. Disregarding the prophecy could not be done, as it would bring misfortune down on the tribe.

Jedidiah stopped before the entrance of the lodge and waited. He sensed whoever was inside, already knew he was there. In his two years among the people, he had learned many things. He knew he could not approach this lodge or any other in full daylight, without being noticed. Silently, he stood outside the lodge, waiting until summoned inside and he would not shame himself by bringing attention to his presence.

White Swan had slipped behind a small stand of willows that bordered the creek, watching while Jedidiah waited before the lodge. He knew Walking Horse was inside, and he knew the danger and hate the warrior felt toward all whites. However, Walking Horse was a proud Arapaho, his people always came first and he would never harm one who carried the mark, nor would he dishonor Slow Wolf. Watching, the old medicine man nodded as the white was young, but he already spoke and acted with confidence, one who was too proud to lose face by speaking first, so he stood waiting. The old man still worried about the greeting Walking Horse would give him when he finally exited the lodge.

Slow Wolf had warned, his nephew, the white was not to be harmed, but Walking Horse was young, proud, and full of hate for the whites. His hatred started many years ago, when a white buffalo hunter killed his father. Later on, another white took his mother as his woman, and then deserted both the woman and her young son. They were both forced back to the Arapaho in what he thought was shame, but then the dreaded Pawnee raided the village and his mother was killed. All these things had burned a deep hatred into the young Arapaho's memory for anything white.

From inside the lodge, the familiar voice, Jedidiah recognized spoke. "Will you stand out there all night, white man?"

"Only until Walking Horse invites me into his lodge."

A tall warrior stepped from the lodge, his eyes glaring at the tall youth. Standing just feet in front of Jedidiah, the dark eyes of the muscular warrior smoldered with hate. While both men were the same height, Walking Horse was heavier with huge arms and torso. His muscles rippled across his broad chest as he breathed deeply. Jed has seen this warrior many times in the village after he was allowed to return from his exile, but he has never been this close or had the opportunity to look into the dark eyes. "Slow Wolf has ordered for you to stay in this place with me and my woman until you have learned the ways of the people, and earned the right of becoming a Lance Bearer."

"Do you blame me for being put out of the village?" Jed looked straight into the warrior's eyes. "Do you resent your woman, Little Antelope, teaching me the Arapaho tongue? Tell me."

"No, I do not blame you, white man." Walking Horse stepped around Jedidiah. "I speak from the heart. I say this; to me, you are white, and I hate all whites."

"I am as dark as you are."

"Maybe on the outside, but inside you are white." The warrior looked Jed up and down. "I think you are weak, too weak to become an Arapaho Lance Bearer."

Jedidiah pulled the long skinning knife Slow Wolf had presented him as a gift and sliced his arm, causing a thin trickle of blood to flow. "Tell me, Walking Horse, if you bleed will it not be the same color as mine?"

White Swan stiffened as he watched the younger man pull his long blade, but smiled and nodded as he watched Jed cut himself. "Yes, you have done well, young one."

"Save your blood, white eye, you may have need of it if our enemies catch us in the days to come." Walking Horse nodded slightly, he felt this youngster had no fear. Perhaps he deserved his respect, time would tell. "We will hunt near the land of our enemies in the coming days."

"I have told the old one of my wishes to stay with the Arapaho." Jedidiah looked at the tall warrior. "Slow Wolf has ordered that I am to learn from you, this is what I will do."

Walking Horse waited momentarily, and then nodded. "I have been asked to teach you the way of the Arapaho Lance Bearer, this I will do."

"I would like to become friends with Walking Horse."

"This will never be, but I will teach you the ways of the Arapaho." The warrior looked over to where White Swan waited and watched. "The old one watches, is he afraid for you, white man?"

Jed did not know the medicine man waited. "I don't think so, he says you are too proud to do me harm."

"I will teach you what I know, no more." Walking Horse shrugged. "It is my chief's wish; do not ask more of me."

"For this I thank you." Jedidiah nodded. "I will ask for nothing more."

Walking Horse grunted. "Do not thank me too quick, you have much to learn, and I wonder if your white blood is strong enough to follow the way of the Arapaho."

"We will see." Jed nodded.

"Yes, that we will."

Jedidiah sat on a soft buffalo robe as Little Antelope placed a bowl of buffalo meat and wild onions in front of him. Kneeling beside Jedidiah as Walking Horse watched, she smeared bear grease across his face, rubbing the foul smelling mixture onto the scar.

"My face has healed many moons ago." Jed tried to duck away from her. "It is good."

"I have told you before; the scar will get smaller if you will keep grease on it." The woman scolded him and continued to rub the mixture onto his face. "The young women will smile upon you even more."

Walking Horse scowled and grunted. "The scar makes him look strong, ferocious."

"Thank you, Little Antelope." Jedidiah took the bowl from the beautiful woman, and looked over at Walking Horse embarrassed. "I wish to thank you for the clothes and for teaching me your language."

The lodge was big, consisting of at least twenty skins, making it very large inside. Jedidiah looked to where the woman pointed at what was to be his bed. He was surprised, figuring he would be sleeping outside with the stray dogs and horses. All sizes of parfleches and baskets, along with Walking Horse's personal items of an Arapaho warrior, hung from the rawhide thongs that dangled from the lodge poles. The lodge was surprisingly clean, warm, and comfortable as the small fire gave off its heat. Smoke drifted lazily skyward into the draft hole in the middle of the lodge where it was drawn outside. Raising his hand in protest, Jedidiah rubbed his stomach contentedly as the woman offered him more to eat.

"No, thank you. I'm full, it was delicious."

Walking Horse leaned easily against his backrest and studied the youngster. His hatred for the whites had made him bitter, he couldn't help himself. However, this youngster has an easy grin and a likable way about him. He could see the muscles ripple under the doeskin shirt every time the white moved his arms. He figured this young man could prove to be powerful and agile.

"Tomorrow we will hunt. Do you know the bow or lance?"

"No." Jed shook his head. "I shot a bow a few times as a kid, but we had nothing to compare with the ones I have seen here."

"Then maybe we will not be so lucky on the hunt."

"I doubt that, Slow Wolf says you are a great hunter and warrior." Jedidiah grinned. "Perhaps, if I watch closely, I will learn from you?"

"You will learn, white eye. I will teach you." Again, a grunt came from the warrior. "I will lose face if you do not learn. Now, we sleep."

"The quicker I learn, the quicker you are rid of me."

Walking Horse looked thoughtfully at Jed. "Yes, this is true."

Only the small flame of the hissing and popping fire moved as everything became silent inside the skin lodge, then it too slowly died, turning the shadows of the lodge into darkness.

CHAPTER 3

True to his word, Walking Horse had Jedidiah up and mounted on one of his horses long before the sun came up in the east. Little Antelope handed Walking Horse a small bag of food, then placed her head against his leg.

"How long will my husband be gone?" She looked at the far hills nervously. "Danger lurks when so few ride, I feel it."

"A week, no more." The warrior looked down at her and nodded slightly. He would not admit to himself or anyone, but she was the only thing he cared about in this life. "You will go to the village and stay with your mother until my return."

"Why?" She looked up at him curiously. "The other lodges are near. Do you fear for me?"

"My wife knows it is the raiding season of our enemies." Walking Horse looked around, then down at her. "I feel danger on the air, the same as you. Do as I say, woman."

Bowing her head meekly, she nodded. "It will be as you say."

"Good."

Little Antelope looked to where Jedidiah sat his horse, and whispered up at the warrior. "He is young yet, but he will be a good man someday. Be patient with him and make him a great warrior as you are."

Walking Horse looked over at Jed, and smiled. "Should I be jealous of one so young?"

"He is but a boy in years." The small dark face smiled, her pearly white teeth shining brightly. "I have eyes for only one man, you know that."

"He is not that young." Walking Horse smiled again. "I am a jealous husband, you know that."

"Yes, I know you are jealous." She pressed her head against his knee again. "Hurry back to me, Husband."

Since leaving the village in the early hours, Jed had followed Walking Horse all day at a slow trot without stopping until the sun stood directly overhead. He had ridden all his life, but not for such an extended time and he always had a saddle. The small, wiry Arapaho horses they were astride had no saddles and their backbones with sharp withers had already become uncomfortable to the youth.

Reining in beside a small, swift running stream, Walking Horse slipped silently from his horse and looked to where Jed landed lightly on the deep grass. The stream traversed the middle of a small valley that was heavily covered in oak, sycamore, spruce and stands of willow trees. Jed watched as the warrior scanned the beautiful valley for several minutes before finally settling down on the bank of the stream. Jed stared around in awe, never on his westward trek had he seen any land that compared with this valley's beauty. Every color of flower he could think of covered the small valley. The beauty of the flowers, the aromatic smell, and wonderful fragrance they emitted on the fresh breeze was pure breathtaking, he couldn't get enough into his lungs. The water babbled noisily from the clear mountain stream as it flowed across the round smooth rocks, and flowed clear and pristine across the pebbly bottom. Green grass, belly deep on their horses, covered the valley floor and sloping hills of this untouched paradise.

"Why does no tribe live here in this place?" Jed was wonder struck at the beauty of the valley, the trees, and clear blue sky. "This is the most beautiful place I have ever gazed upon."

Digging in the leather bag, Walking Horse seemed to ignore the question. Tossing Jed a heavy slice of cured buffalo haunch, he looked across the valley. "Once, long ago, when I was very small, the Arapaho did live here, but the Pawnee come to this place and make big fight."

"Big fight?"

"Many warriors died, both Arapaho and Pawnee." Walking Horse nodded. "This is the place where the son of Slow Wolf, the one called Fast Wing, died."

"Fast Wing?"

"One of the greatest Lance Bearers of the people." Walking Horse looked across at Jed and frowned slightly. "His body carried the same mark on his back that you carry."

"He was killed here?" Jed studied the small valley closer. "In this place of beauty?"

"Yes." Walking Horse remembered the many times he had heard the story of how Fast Wing died so bravely saving his village, fighting for his people. "He died staked to the ground, facing his enemies. Many enemy warriors died by his hand, and the Arapaho defeated the Pawnee that day."

"He staked himself to the ground?"

"In doing so, Fast Wing rallied our warriors and gave them courage. He gave them a great victory over our enemy." Walking Horse looked again across the small meadow. "Even though they fought bravely and won over the mighty Pawnee, our warriors could not save him."

"Is that why Slow Wolf spared me?" Jed watched a small leaf absently as it was carried down the stream. "The mark on my back?"

"It is the prophecy. My uncle and the old one believe in omens." Walking Horse walked to where his horse grazed on the abundant grass growing along the stream. "I don't believe in such stories, white eye. I lived with a white trapper for many years. Maybe I listened too closely to his words to believe in any such things.

"This white hunter you lived with, did you like him?"

"He was a great hunter and fighter." Walking Horse knelt and scooped water to his lips. "He was a good husband to my mother, and good father and teacher to me."

"What happened to him?"

"Why don't you ask him, white eye?" Walking Horse uncupped his hand, releasing the water. "You know him. He was with the wagons you were with."

"Who do you speak of?" Jed looked sharply at the warrior.

"The scout and hunter who led your people, the one you call Hatcher."

"Lige Hatcher." Jed nodded, surprised by the name. "Yes, I know him. He is a good man and a good hunter."

Walking Horse changed the subject as his feelings for Hatcher was mixed; both respect and hate filled his emotions. "We are far from our village. Our enemies could lurk anywhere in this land. Now, you will watch our back trail, while I watch our front and hunt for game."

Remounting their horses, the warriors followed a small game trail, leading up and over a small ridge. The trail meandered down into another valley, almost as beautiful as the one they just left. Jed had to keep alert, focused, and not let his mind wander across the beautiful valley. Deer, buffalo, wild horses, and elk slipped silently out of their way as the two men passed across the valley. Cold mountain streams flowed unobstructed through every valley, only slowed by the beaver dams that blocked them. The dams occasionally caused the streams to spread out into small shallow ponds before finding a course around and then flowing freely on down the valley.

Jed was curious, earlier Walking Horse had warned him of the enemy. However, now he was leading them down the center of the valley, appearing not too worried about being seen. White Swan had told him that Walking Horse was a great warrior, but should they be riding out in the open, ignoring any lurking enemies that could be nearby, ready to strike? He had ridden with Lige Hatcher many times in the past, and the wagon train scout would have never ridden out in the open, unconcerned.

Sundown came as the sun slowly dipped in the west, casting a long shadow over the valley. The call of the whippoorwills sounded from the small stream and the many creatures of the night started calling out as darkness engulfed the land. Walking Horse dismounted and tethered his horse in the deep grass alongside the bank of yet another meadow stream. Kicking together a few limbs, he quickly had a fire burning in a small wash that led down to the stream, deep enough to shield the small blaze from an enemy's sight.

"We eat and rest here tonight. Tomorrow, we will hunt this valley." Walking Horse watched as Jed fingered the stout willow bow. "Then we will begin your training."

For two days, the two walked the valley hunting. Under Walking Horse's instructions, Jed began his lessons practicing with the bow. Arrows flew harmlessly past their intended targets, but miraculously on the second day, he finally killed a fat rabbit for their supper. Holding the furry animal up for Walking Horse to see, Jed laughed. He knew it was a lucky shot, but at least they had something fresh to eat. The buffalo meat, Little Antelope had sent with them, was beginning to get a little dried out and rancid.

Walking Horse bit into the steaming rabbit and looked across the fire at Jed. "Tomorrow, we hunt for elk and deer. If our hunt is good, we return to the village, if not, we stay longer."

"Can the bow of the Arapaho kill a bull elk or buffalo?" Jed studied his bow and the thin straight arrow.

Walking Horse nodded. "I have seen a strong bow arm send an arrow all the way through a bull elk, killing him where he stood. Tell me, white eye, do you have a strong arm?"

"Strong enough." Jed tested the pull of the fine bow Walking Horse loaned him. "It feels powerful, but I didn't know they were that strong."

"An Arapaho strong bow in the hands of a powerful warrior is a dangerous weapon." The muscles in the warrior's arms corded as he pulled back the heavy bow. "They can fire quickly, many times, and are silent when they kill."

"I believe it." Jed was impressed. "They may be better than the gun we use."

"Tomorrow we hunt, sleep now." Walking Horse turned to his buffalo robe and spoke over his shoulder. "No, the gun you speak of is better, it shoots farther with more accuracy."

"Why don't the Arapaho have them? I've seen them carried by other tribes farther east."

"One day, we will have the white man gun." Walking Horse seemed to be making a promise to himself.

For three more days, they hunted the valley hard. Walking Horse was working tirelessly, showing Jed the use of every weapon, and how to track deer, elk, and grouse that thrived along the mountain valleys and slopes. Several times each day, when both men were dog tired, he would suddenly spring at Jed throwing him to the ground, trying his best to pin the younger man against the ground. He was amazed at the strength and quickness, Jed exhibited, as he avoided being pinned by the older warrior.

Finally, Walking Horse turned their attention in seriousness to the elk that grazed the valleys in small herds. Jed's first attempt at stalking the elusive and sharp-nosed animals was a complete failure. Walking Horse watched and waited, as Jed stalked a bull with cows. The bull sensed or smelled the hunter, snorted the alarm before trotting quickly out of range of the bow and out of sight, followed by his females. The warrior rose from his observation place and walked to where Jed was waiting with a long face.

"Our brothers the elk are very good warriors." The warrior looked at the disappointed face of Jed and laughed. "Do not give up, white eye. It took Walking Horse several tries before I killed my first elk."

"Was it a bull?"

"No, the truth is, it was a very young calf, very small."

The next morning broke cold and crisp with a heavy dew as the two hunters picketed their horses in a deep ravine, hidden from the eyes of any unwanted enemies. Walking Horse pointed to the rolling slopes to the east, following Jed as he stealthily started forward, his eyes searching out the deep grass where the elk could still be bedded from the night. Not a sound was made as their moccasins slowly padded forward. Walking Horse studied Jed's broad back as the muscles rippled in his powerful arms and his strong legs carried him effortlessly up the rough grade leading out of the ravine. If he didn't know, he would have mistaken the warrior in front of him for a full-blooded Arapaho warrior. The sign of the Lance showed plainly on the bare shoulder of the white as he eased forward and peered cautiously over the rim. Pulling his head back out of sight, Jed motioned to Walking Horse, their quarry was close. The warrior moved forward and peeked over the rim. Not seventy yards in distance on the flat valley before them, stood six cows and a huge bull.

"We must get closer." Walking Horse whispered. "They are too far for the bow."

"This is where the long gun would come in handy." Jed looked down at his bow.

"You only have the bow, my young friend."

"Well now, Walking Horse has called me his friend."

"Only talk, white one. We are not friends." The warrior frowned; embarrassed to let on that he actually liked the young man.

"Well, cross your fingers. Here I go." Jed slipped slowly over the rim, keeping below the grass line.

"Why would I cross my fingers?" Walking Horse looked curiously at his fingers, then at the crawling form of Jed. "Whites are crazy, they say strange things."

Both elk were stalked and killed by Jed using the heavy bow. His first arrow hit low in the bull's rib cage allowing him to turn and try to flee as Walking Horse's arrow finished the elk off. Jed's second arrow killed the cow in her tracks.

Walking Horse stood over the downed animal and nodded at Jed. "You have done well today. You have become a hunter." The warrior studied the arrow's shaft. "Your arrow was true, straight through the heart."

"I was lucky, and you know your arrow killed the bull."

The carcasses of the bull and one cow elk lay skinned and quartered, wrapped and secured in their own hides, ready to be loaded onto the horses. Walking Horse kicked apart the small fire that had been cooking fresh elk liver for their dinner.

"We will start to the village, now." Walking Horse gathered his weapons and stared for several seconds across the valley. "We must return to the village before the meat spoils."

"I spotted it, same as you." Jed saw the same flash that made Walking Horse suddenly stiffen. "Across the valley, in that stand of post oak."

"Your eyes are sharp, white eye." The warrior nodded. "Our enemy is near; they will try to attack us after we go to sleep."

"I was told Indians never attack at night."

"Lige Hatcher never spoke these words."

"No, I heard it from others. Lige never said anything like that."

"Some Indians don't fight at night, but all will steal horses at night." Walking Horse started to load the meat. "These are after our horses and our kill. Come, we must hurry. They will come here looking for us."

After two hard days and nights of walking with the horses loaded down with heavy elk meat, both warriors were tired and happy to see the stream bordering the village. Walking Horse already spotted the Arapaho sentries that patrolled the village and protected its great horse herd, watching closely for any raiders from other tribes. As they neared the village, several voices rang out causing quite a commotion.

Little Antelope also ran from her lodge, racing to greet them with her small curved figure almost flying across the flat ground. Walking Horse's dark eyes warmed, watching the small figure as her lithe form seemed to skim the ground as she ran. Reaching out his great arms, the warrior took her lightly into his arms. Jed stopped behind the lead horse and watched, embarrassed as the two embraced. He finally averted his eyes and looked off toward the village where the people were gathering and walking their way.

Looking at Jed, Little Antelope smiled up at him. "How did your student do?"

Walking Horse nodded politely. "These are his kills, both of them."

"Without your help it wouldn't have been possible."

"Take the elk to the village, white eye. Give them to the women and old people who have no men to hunt for them."

"Save me some of the meat." Little Antelope leaned against Walking Horse. "I will cook you great hunters a fine stew."

Jed smiled, then turned and led the horses into the village where the people waited expectantly. All eyed the packed meat eagerly, but no one pushed forward, everyone waited patiently until he handed the lead ropes to one of the older squaws. "Walking Horse sends this for the ones that need meat."

For several days, Jed walked the encampment, talking with the younger warriors, and enjoying the peace and tranquility of the people. The warm days found him swimming in the cold waters of the nearby stream or lying on the sandy banks enjoying the sun. Several times, he spent his time taking his turn riding patrol around the village.

"The young women walk this way to do their washing." One of the young warriors accompanying Jed laughed as they lay on the banks of the stream. "Perhaps to see you, my friend, without your clothes on."

"I have a breechcloth covering me."

"Then maybe I was wrong, they just come here to do their clothes."

"Bow Legs is wrong." Jed nodded his head embarrassed. "As usual."

"True, sometimes I am as you say, wrong." The younger warrior laughed. "I am young, it is the way of the young to be wrong at times. Tell me, my friend, why do they come this far from the village with heavy baskets of clothes, when before they always stayed near the lodges?"

Disgusted, Jed rolled to his feet, and grabbed his breechings and leather shirt. He couldn't help hear the giggles coming from the young girls as they passed, casting sideways glances at his heavily muscled chest and arms. Motioning that he was leaving, Jed took a final embarrassed look at the young women, then with Bow Legs and the others following, walked back to his lodge.

While they had been away, Little Antelope and several of the younger women had put a smaller lodge together so Jed could be alone and have his own place. He was pleasantly surprised and thanked each one, causing the young women to beam with pride and smile.

Another warrior grinned. "Perhaps, it is me they look at."

Bow Legs laughed out loud. "You, Elk Runner, are too ugly even for your own mother to look at."

The young women studied the group of young warriors as the laughter broke out, wondering what was being said about them. Yes, they had walked this way to see the newcomer with the scar down his cheek. Each young maiden had already fallen madly in love with the young warrior, and thought he was strong and handsome. The warrior each one dreamed would bring horses to their father's lodge and ask her to be his woman. They knew they only dreamed, as he was too young for marriage, and he has yet to prove himself in battle and prove himself as a warrior, worthy of marriage. However, they sensed this one was unlike the other young warriors accompanying him. He cared nothing about teasing the young women, nor did he watch for their glances and smiles. This one was different from the others, as he was more serious, much older than his young years. Perhaps, they wondered, has his heart already found someone?

Jed hardly said good-bye to Bow Legs and entered his lodge when he heard the unmistakable sound of soft footsteps approaching. Stepping outside, he found Little Antelope standing before the lodge. Her attention centered on the young women as they passed back down to the riverbank, talking and laughing.

"The young women seem to be taken with you."

"It is not me. It is the others they look at." Jedidiah could feel the sharpness in her voice.

"Oh, really?" She studied the bulging muscles of his bare chest. "I don't see them walking toward the other lodges."

"They are just being silly." Jed sputtered embarrassed. "Young girls can be that way."

"Are they? I too was once unmarried and young." She laughed. "I remember Walking Horse being done the same way by the young women back then."

"I wasn't alone by the river, there were others there also."

"No, Jed. In their eyes, there was only you." Her eyes narrowed as they followed the laughing girls. "Only you."

"Why are you here, Little Antelope?" Jed was a little exasperated by her words.

"Walking Horse wishes for you to come to his lodge tonight to eat."

"I am sorry for my sharp tongue." Jedidiah dropped his eyes. "Thank him for me. Tell him I would be honored, and it will be a joy to eat your good cooking again."

Little Antelope laughed softly again. "Perhaps, one of the maidens would cook for you if you asked.

"Little Antelope!" Jed raised his voice again as she skipped away laughing.

"Hurry, Jed. Walking Horse waits."

Jed watched as she walked away, his eyes taking in her small frame and her long black hair. Embarrassed at his thoughts of the young woman, Jed looked away. Shaking his head, he knew he had to remember she was the wife of Walking Horse, a warrior he has much respect for.

Walking Horse leaned against his backrest and studied his guest as they ate the food Little Antelope had prepared. "Our Chief Slow Wolf has had reports from our hunting parties that enemy warriors have encroached into our hunting grounds and killed our game."

Jed nodded thoughtfully, remembering the game animals he had seen on their recent hunt. "Is there not enough elk, deer, and buffalo for all?"

"You do not understand, this is Arapaho hunting grounds, all others are forbidden to hunt here." Walking Horse waved his hand. "If one tribe gets away with killing our deer and elk, then others will come and there will be no meat for our bellies, no hides for our clothes and lodges."

"What will Walking Horse do?"

"With the new day, we will ride out and see if this is true." Walking Horse looked out through the open doorway of the lodge. "If we find nothing, then we will hunt again and bring meat back to our lodges."

"And if we find others hunting Arapaho lands?"

"Then young one, we will begin your other training."

"You mean fighting?"

"No, I mean killing and counting coup on our enemies."

Daylight broke in the eastern sky, a beautiful dawn with low fog covering the higher valleys. Jed felt himself shiver slightly, this high in the mountains, even the summer mornings were almost frosty. For two weeks, they had ridden the mountains, searching the hunting grounds of the Arapaho people. No sign of the enemy was found in the high meadows, no unexplained horse prints, no dead carcasses, nothing suspicious. Walking Horse decided the reports were false since nothing was amiss. Satisfied no enemy had entered Arapaho lands, the two gave up their scouting and became hunters once again. Their attention focused on the grassy meadows and timberland that were filled with abundant game animals; meat that would feed the village. Bow Legs and another warrior who had been out scouting with them went back to the village to inform Slow Wolf of their findings. Now, Walking Horse turned his full attention on hunting another kind of game, the four-legged kind.

Late in the afternoon, they had left the horses hidden in a grove of trees behind them. Now, they silently stalked a small band of elk that were still bedded down higher up in another beautiful valley where they had spent the night. Today, Walking Horse took the lead, he wanted to quickly kill enough meat to pack the horses, and return fast to the village to report to Slow Wolf. There was no time to teach Jed to track or move quietly through the deep grass. Today was serious, a day only for hunting.

Suddenly, Walking Horse stopped in his tracks and dropped to his knees motioning Jed forward beside him. Nodding his head, he looked toward a small stand of mountain spruce intermingled with a few oak trees. "Is your white blood strong, white eye?"

"What?" Jed was curious, as he didn't understand the question.

"There, under the taller trees." Walking Horse watched the expression of the younger man. "The ones we have been seeking."

"Yes, now I see them, five riders."

"Crows." Walking Horse studied the riders carefully. "They are young men, not seasoned warriors."

"How can you tell from this distance?"

"The markings on their horses, they are not painted as a seasoned warrior would paint his war pony." Walking Horse nodded. "Only one is painted, the others have not earned the right. That means they are young men out to count coup or cause mischief."

"What will we do?"

"They trespass here in our lands." Walking Horse questioned Jed. "What do think we should do, white eye?"

"I've got a name, Walking Horse, and white eye is not it." Jed frowned. "I follow you. This is your hunt."

"A warrior earns his name by his deeds." The warrior looked over at Jed, then back at the Crows. "Perhaps if your medicine is strong today, you will earn yours."

"I will not shame you or the Arapaho people."

"Maybe you speak the truth, but first let us see." In a fast trot the two quickly retreated to their horses and mounted. "Yes, white eye, soon we will see if you are brave enough to carry the mark."

Topping out over a slight rim, the two rode into plain sight and pulled in their horses. Jed and Walking Horse sat motionless, watching as the five riders left the shelter of the trees and spread out in a line, riding slowly and deliberately toward them. Jed looked over at Walking Horse and then back at the advancing line of warriors.

"I hope your medicine is strong, young one."

"What does Walking Horse mean?"

"Our enemies, the Crows, have been given to us this day."

"There are five of them. Perhaps, we have been given to them." Jed shrugged his shoulders. "Are we gonna run or fight?"

"Two Arapahos running from five Crows?" Walking Horse scoffed. "The ancient ones would look down and laugh in shame."

"Do they think I am Arapaho?"

Walking Horse nodded slightly. "You are dressed like an Arapaho. Your horse is Arapaho. What should they think?"

Jed smiled. "Well, at least you ain't calling me a white eye any longer."

"I called you nothing." Walking Horse watched the approaching warriors intently. "Be ready when they ride closer; do as I do."

"What will they do?" Jed studied the scowling faces, the single loose eagle feather hanging from each warrior's topknot.

"We will wait and see what they do; be ready."

Jed looked at Walking Horse, taking in the calm expression on the dark face as he stared at the oncoming youthful warriors. "You were right, these are young men looking for a fight; I can see it in their faces."

"They are foolish, too young to die. The Crow are a great warrior race and they want to count coup on us. They will not shame themselves by turning away." Walking Horse hung the bow across his back, then pulled his war axe. "But, they are the enemy and they are in our land. Today, they will be punished for hunting here."

Jed followed the warrior's lead and looped the leather thong that held his war club around his wrist. "I am ready."

"Is your white blood strong?"

"We shall see soon enough." Jed couldn't figure whether Walking Horse was serious or just joking about him being scared. One thing was certain though, the approaching warriors were getting closer all the time and they were definitely not turning away.

Both of their horses sidestepped, they could feel the excitement of their riders as the strange horses approached. Walking Horse kicked his sorrel, jerking him hard to stop fidgeting and prancing, until he was ready to charge. The Crow were close, close enough for Jed to make out the outlines of their faces; the dark eyes, long black hair, and even the ermine skin braided into their hair, holding the lone eagle feather in place.

Walking Horse rode his horse a few feet forward and raised his hand, causing the Crows to rein in their horses and stop. Jed looked at the warrior beside him as if he had never seen him before. No sign of fear on the handsome face, only a frown of arrogance and contempt. His facial features changed as he glared across at his enemies. Powerful muscles bunched in his forearms as he gripped the horse's mane tightly. Suddenly, in less than an eye flick, the heavy war club was raised in his huge hand, as he let out with a war whoop, and charged the young Crow warriors. Jed kicked his horse to catch up, not knowing what he would do or what was expected when he reached the line of warriors. He had never heard such a horrendous and scary yell as Walking Horse put forth as he charged forward, waving his war club crazily. In his short life, Jed had been in many a rough-and-tumble fistfight, but never in his life had he been in this kind of a deadly confrontation. He knew this would be a life-and-death struggle. A bare-knuckle fistfight was one thing but a fight like this was deadly serious, and he could feel it. The heavy war axe he was holding was a dangerous and deadly weapon, and held in the hands of a strong warrior, it was capable of killing anything.

Walking Horse pulled his gelding to a sliding stop, less than twenty feet from where the young Crow warriors had stopped and were waiting silently, unafraid. Jed pulled up alongside the warrior and studied the five young warriors as one of the Crow stepped his horse forward and screamed across at Walking Horse, waving his hands crazily.

Walking Horse waited until the Crow quieted, then pointed at the rider. "You are in Arapaho lands, being so young, perhaps you did not know this."

"We are Crow; we ride and hunt wherever we wish." The young warrior laughed when the others started taunting the Arapaho. "Yes, Arapaho we are young, but he is not so old either."

"You do not have permission to hunt in Arapaho lands; leave this place."

"And if we don't, Arapaho?" The Crow thumped his chest. "I, Wild Wind, will hunt wherever it pleases me."

"Then, Wild Wind, you will die! I, Walking Horse, will carry your scalp on my scalp pole." Walking Horse gave the slit throat sign. "Then your people can mourn for a young fool."

Turning his dark eyes on Jed, the Crow laughed and pointed his finger. Whirling his grey horse several times, he tossed down his bow and quiver of arrows. "Yieee yah!"

"What does he want?" Jed was curious at the warrior's actions. He knew he was being spoken of by the way the warrior kept pointing at him.

"He says it would shame the mighty Crow Nation if five attacked two poor pitiful Arapaho." Walking Horse watched the movement of the Crow's hands. "Also, he says it would not be honorable, no test of a warrior."

The Crow finally quieted and waited as the two Arapaho spoke. "What does he want then?"

"He has made a challenge to fight, one of them against one of us."

"Now, why would they do that?" Jed was curious. "They may be young, but they do have us outnumbered."

"Yes, they are young, but they have watched their elders in battle. Crows have much pride and a funny sense of humor. To them this is sport; just a game." Walking Horse nodded solemnly. "When you are dead, then they will challenge me."

"Me?"

"The Crow warriors are great fighters. Ones like these may be young in years, but they are very proud, very arrogant, and they listen and learn from their elders." Walking Horse shook his head sadly. "Most like these dream of being mighty warriors. They are young, it is a bad fault of the young to be conceited, it can get them killed."

"Reckon it could at that." Jed studied the warrior before them. Though young, the Crow was an exceptional physical specimen, heavily muscled, with a straightness of his back that spoke of his confidence and strength. The Crow had a broad face with heavy nose and coal black eyes that stared straight through him, as if mocking him.

"He has challenged you, white eye." Walking Horse replied. "But, he says if you are a coward and do not wish to fight, you can give him your horse. He will let you return to your village with the other squaws."

The Crow, who had been speaking slapped his horse and advanced a few steps, then pointed across at Jed again. Waving his war axe, the Crow warrior swiped the air challenging the younger looking of the Arapaho, figuring him for the easier opponent.

"I reckon he wants to fight, alright." Jed studied the warrior's belligerent actions. "He sure ain't getting your horse, so let's get to it."

"Remember, to them this is but a game. Killing is but a game, and there is no doubt he intends to kill you." Walking Horse looked at Jed's calm face. "Be careful, white eye, this one may be young but he is strong. He seeks honor and a scalp for his lodge."

"I will not be so easy to kill." Jed gripped his own war axe tightly, then grinned over at the warrior. "Look at it this way, if he kills me, you won't have to teach me anything else."

"This is not funny. He is a Crow warrior; young, perhaps as young as you, but he has killed before and he is skilled. You see the markings on his war shield? He has taken coup two times on his enemy, maybe killed them." Walking Horse studied the Crow. "My Uncle Slow Wolf would not be happy with me if you did not return to our village. I think he would be very upset with me."

"We wouldn't want you in trouble again, would we?' Jed dropped his bow and quiver of arrows to the ground, then turned to meet the young Crow. "One thing; if I survive this, you will call me by my given name, not white eye."

"All right, white eye, it will be as you ask. You have my word." Walking Horse nodded. "But first, you must win."

The clash of the two war clubs slamming together sounded like the heavy, dull thuds of two mountain rams butting heads, and the blows sent reverberating sounds along the valley floor. Both young men swung the heavy clubs with all their strength as the two horses pushed hard, shouldering up against each other. The Crow was slightly older than Jed, but he was still young, and he was an expert in the use of the war axe he wielded. Still, with speed and dexterity, Jed was able to parry every blow and avoid every move the warrior tried. Walking Horse was surprised at the white's reflexes and speed, faster than he has ever seen, much quicker than the young Crow, and much quicker than himself. The white was strong for his age, and along with his agility, speed, and fighting spirit, he would be a match for any warrior. At last a relieved sigh came from Walking Horse's mouth, as he was trying to figure out how to tell Slow Wolf the white was killed while in his care. This white was in no danger and he even seemed to be enjoying the fight with the Crow. Maybe, he was wrong in his judgment, and perhaps the prophecy White Swan and Slow Wolf spoke of was true.

The battle waged back and forth. The horses were straining with all their might, as they shoved into each other and began to tire. Both war shields of the combatants had been beaten and scarred from all the blows they had taken. Jed was tired, exhausted, even wielding a chopping axe all day had never exerted him so much. Once light, the war axe now felt heavy as a log on his arm, weighing him down. Staggering with exhaustion, the bay horse of the Crow crumbled suddenly to his knees, throwing the young Crow warrior forward right into the path of Jed's heavy war axe as it descended. The dark head of the Crow crushed like a melon from the blow, causing blood to flow freely across the carpeted valley floor. Jed pulled his war axe back in shock as he watched the once-proud face shatter under the heavy blow, causing the warrior to tumble onto the deep grass. He was trying to thwart the young warrior's blows and didn't intend to kill the Crow outright, only disable him. The killing blow caused by the horse's fall was partly accident, but Jed's adrenaline rush and lust for battle strengthened his arm, causing the young Crow's death.

The others didn't realize what had happened. All they saw was the mighty blow that practically beheaded their leader and they were temporarily paralyzed by the abrupt end to the fight. Blood from the Crow's crushed head flowed out onto the grassy meadow, and the limp form of the dead warrior was all they could focus on. Turning his tired horse to face the shocked friends of his adversary, Jed could see the look of disbelief on their faces. Raising the bloody axe, he screamed his own challenge and charged toward the line of warriors. Walking Horse sat his horse watching in disbelief. Here was one he thought was weak, but before him the white fought like a grizzly bear, with the heart of an enraged buffalo bull. Walking Horse could only sit and watch without moving. The fight was over. The Crow warriors lost courage before the oncoming crazed Arapaho, and retreated as fast as their horses could carry them.

Reining in his blowing gelding, Jed slowly lowered the war axe and exhaled deeply. In the heat of battle, he had wanted to fight, to kill. Now, he sat motionless on his blowing gelding as the adrenaline slowly ebbed from his body. The Crow warriors rode off in terror without trying to confront the crazed warrior that rode toward them, even leaving behind their dead warrior laying alone, lifeless in the tall grass of the meadow. Jed rode to where the dead warrior lay crumpled in death, his vacant eyes staring, unseeing into the blue sky.

"You said they were brave warriors, these Crow people." Jed looked to where Walking Horse sat his horse staring curiously at him. "Why did they flee so quickly?"

Walking Horse shook his head as he had seen the same thing the Crow had seen; the mask of death emanating from the charging Arapaho's face. Slow Wolf sensed something in the young white. Now, Walking Horse saw it with his own eyes. This one did possess the power of the prophecy. He knew someday this one would be a great warrior of the Arapaho.

"They were not afraid, but they are superstitious. They believed their medicine went bad when their leader was killed."

"Will they come back for him?" Jed looked over at the dead Crow.

"No." Walking Horse shook his head. "This place holds dark and evil spirits for them now. They have seen your power, the horse stumble and throw its rider in the path of your war axe. They think this is bad medicine and perhaps you are the devil."

"What power, it was just luck for me." Jed shook his head. "Bad luck for him; his horse stumbled and threw him forward into my club."

"It does not matter how it happened, they will never return to this place. Perhaps, the young one's father will come alone to get his son's body." Walking Horse dismounted and handed Jed the Crow's war axe. "You have earned your first coup in battle.

"And if no one comes for him?"

"Then he will be food for the wolves and buzzards." Walking Horse remounted. "Here in our mountains, sometimes life is short, young one. The wild things like us have to eat."

"He deserves more. He was brave." Jed looked over at the unseeing body, a warrior who only seconds before was alive, full of life and vitality.

"You honor your enemy, will you take his scalp?"

"No!" Jed looked away from the dead Crow. "That part of me is still white."

Nodding quietly, Walking Horse turned his horse back down the valley.

CHAPTER 4

After the fight, the two Arapaho stayed five days in the lower meadows, hunting and dressing out the deer and elk they had killed. Each animal was prepared for the journey home by quartering and rolling them in their hides. Earlier in the day, they had heard the far-off chanting of the death song of the Crow; someone was near the place where the warrior had died. Slipping to a high ridge, they watched as a lone rider, dragging a travois, made his way slowly to the north as his song of sorrow echoed from the valley's depth. The sad words of the chant, along the steep ridges, were almost eerie as the shrill voice slowly faded with the rider passing over the ridge, out of hearing range.

"The Crow father grieves for his son." Walking Horse stood up and watched as the warrior led the travois slowly away. "Now, he takes him home to the Crow burial grounds to be with his ancestors."

"You seem sad?"

"No, I am not sad." Walking Horse turned back down into the valley. "He was an enemy, a very foolish enemy. Now, he is dead."

"You will not challenge the lone Crow, who is in Arapaho land?"

"He has come for the body of his son. It would not be honorable to kill this one who has enough sorrow already. We will meet another day."

"How far is it to the Crow Village?"

"From here, two, maybe three days if one rides hard."

Jed wondered at the words. He knew Walking Horse was serious as his solemn voice spoke with deep respect for his enemy. Perhaps, this warrior wasn't as cold hearted as he wanted Jed to believe.

Again, no pack animals had been brought as Jed and Walking Horse had been sent forth to look for interlopers in Arapaho lands. Only the extra horse of the dead Crow permitted them to carry the immense amount of meat they had acquired in the last few days. Leading the burdened horses, Jed followed Walking Horse as they made their way home afoot without stopping. Even though the weather was cool in the valley, speed was essential as the meat had to be preserved so there was no time to stop or rest on their return trip. Walking Horse was in a hurry; perhaps on account of the meat, perhaps to speak with Slow Wolf, or maybe to see Little Antelope. Anyway, very few words passed between them as the miles fell away and the village neared. Occasionally, Jed noticed the warrior watching him intently as they traversed the vast, beautiful valleys, but nothing more was said about the fight.

"You will take the meat into the village and let the squaws divide it up among the people." Walking Horse took a back strap of venison from one of the horses. "Hurry back, Little Antelope will make us a welcome home feast."

Taking the reins of the horses, Jed nodded at the warrior as he turned. "I thank Walking Horse for the knowledge he has given me on this hunt."

Stopping, the warrior turned. "What is your name?"

"Jed."

"A white name. You will need an Arapaho name now." Walking Horse nodded thoughtfully. "And you shall have one."

"Why now?" Jed was curious.

"You have counted coup on your enemy. You have killed an enemy. Now, you are a warrior." Walking Horse smiled only slightly. "What kind of name is Jed for a Lance Bearer of the people?"

Warriors, women, children, and the old ones, all watched as Jed passed with the three heavy laden horses. Stopping in front of White Swan's lodge, Jed handed the horse's reins to one of the older squaws. He turned to where the old medicine man sat in the shade of his lodge.

"Again, you have brought meat to the people, this is good." The medicine man smiled as he looked at the covered meat. "You have done well, my son."

"Walking Horse sent it, Grandfather."

"You had a good hunt, tell me of it." The old one nodded, looking closely at the sorrel horse Jed had ridden from the village. "Did you learn much? What else did you kill?'

"We killed elk and deer this time." Jed smiled as an older woman passed, touching his arm, thanking him.

"Is that all?" The old eyes seemed to penetrate his thoughts, questioning him curiously.

"No."

"We will speak of the Crow later." Quietly, White Swan stood, then ducked back inside his lodge. "Now, these old bones are tired."

Jed was curious; did he really possess the ability to foretell the future as the people said? There was no doubt, he knew about the death of the Crow. Jed could feel the way he looked at him and the way he asked, it was more of a statement than a question. Without being told, the old one already knew about the fight, but how could this be?

Returning to Walking Horse's lodge, Jed found himself a soft spot under an oak tree and leaned back, relaxing his tired muscles. Walking Horse was inside the lodge with Little Antelope. Until their time together passed, it would not be polite to enter. His mind wandered back to the hunt and the fight with the Crow. He could remember the low keening cry of sadness from the old warrior as he took his son back to their village. If the Crow had been the victor, would there have been anyone to cry out for him? Somewhere in his future, Jed knew the life he chose with the Arapaho could cause him to end up the same way as the young Crow, and possibly without mourners.

Walking Horse exited the lodge and walked away toward the village without a word, not even a glance over to where Jed sat idly whittling on a stick. As usual, the countenance on the warrior's face was unreadable, a mask drawn shut against everyone.

"Have I done something to upset him again?" Jed looked to where Little Antelope came out from the lodge holding a bowl of deer meat in her hand.

Smiling, she handed him the bowl. "No, Jed, you have made him proud. You have made the people proud, your people."

"Why, because I have killed?"

"The whites do not kill their enemies?"

"Yes, I'm afraid they do."

"Are they not proud of defeating their enemies?"

"Some are, I reckon." Jed remembered the men on the train laughing and bragging about shooting two Cheyenne warriors who were trying to steal horses. "Yeah, some are."

"It is the way of the Arapaho and the way of all the tribes; to kill their enemies." The small woman shrugged. "If we did not kill our enemies; we would be defeated and chased from our lands."

"I reckon that's so."

"You are Arapaho now, Jed. Walking Horse is proud and the people are proud. Now, it is your turn to be proud." Little Antelope smiled. "Walk proud with your head up and your shoulders straight, you may even swagger some. The young women will take notice and look at you."

Jed looked over to where the small woman sat and stared at her. She was beautiful, small, and trim with the longest jet-black hair he has ever seen. Her smooth dark complexion and oval face encased dark almond eyes and full lips. Yes, he couldn't help notice, she was beautiful. When she walked, she seemed to glide across the ground silently with the grace of a stalking cat. Yes, she knew about pride as she was the wife of a Lance Bearer and was as proud as any warrior. Embarrassed for his thoughts of her, he averted his eyes quickly as she looked up at him.

"Tell me, how did White Swan know of the killing of the Crow warrior?" Jed looked back at her. "Can he see the future?"

She smiled. "Is this what turns your face red, you think he knows?"

"He knows." Jed ignored the question. He knew his face turned red and she read his thoughts. "How?"

"White Swan knows many things and he sees things others do not. It is said he can read a person's thoughts."

"Do you believe this?"

"Sometimes a person can read another one's mind." Little Antelope looked straight into Jed's eyes and smiled, causing him to blush redder. "But, I would guess, it was the red hand of death Walking Horse put on your horse that gave you away to the old one."

"What!" Jed looked over to where the sorrel horse stood grazing.

Sure enough, there was a handprint of blood on the front shoulder. "So, he can't read minds after all."

"Don't be so sure." Little Antelope laughed. "We all can read some minds if we look hard enough, and that sorrel horse has Crow blood on him."

Rising quickly, he mumbled something about checking the horses and strode away without a backward glance. He could hear her laughing, even after the lodge disappeared far behind him. The horse herd was forgotten as he walked quickly to the river's edge, and looked about for prying eyes. He needed a bath; the trail dirt, the blood from the Crow warrior and the elk they butchered, stained his hands and splattered on his face. Seeing no one around, Jed quickly peeled his leather shirt and leggings off, and slipped quietly into the water. The water was cold from the mountains, but even with the chill, it felt good to clean himself using the sand from the bottom. Emerging from the water, he sat on a rock letting his body drip dry before donning his clothes. He thought back on Little Antelope as they have grown close; thrown together while he was recuperating and while she was teaching him the Arapaho language. He has never been around many girls or women in his life, but he has grown fond of her, missing her when she was absent from his view. Cussing himself silently, he quickly dressed. She was Walking Horse's wife, nothing more. She was his friend and nothing more. He knew his feelings were strong for her, but from now on he would keep his mind from her, stay away and forget her.

As the sun fell, he emerged from the riverbank, and the drums of the village started to beat a steady rhythm, calling out to the villagers. He could hear the drums clearly as he made his way past the horse herd and walked toward the lodges. A lone rider's voice rang out, as he walked his horse through the excited village, inviting everyone to White Swan's lodge for a feast. Jed knew it was the way of the Arapaho, to have a feast after a good hunt or good raid on their enemies, and to give thanks for their good fortune. Despite trying to avoid them, Walking Horse and Little Antelope intercepted him near his own lodge. They slowly walked with him, the rest of the way, to the huge fire that was roasting the elk and deer meat they had brought in.

"The feast is in your honor." Walking Horse grinned widely. He was in a good mood, a side of him Jed has never seen before. "The people will have much food and a dance tonight, thanks to you."

"It should be in your honor, Walking Horse. If it weren't for you, I never could have brought in the elk, maybe the deer."

"The dance is in honor of your victory over the Crow." Walking Horse nodded. "I did not do that."

"Remember what I told you; walk proud, Jed. You have earned it." Little Antelope whispered. "Hold your head high and stand straight as an arrow. You are now a warrior of the Arapaho Nation."

Jed had lived among the Arapaho for over two years, and this was the first time he had ever seen the elders of the village decked out. The elders were attired in their feathered headdresses and finest beaded war shirts, adorned by the squaws with porcupine quills and pieces of their enemy's hair, showing the many coups they had earned. Many warriors already danced and gyrated around the large bonfire that was roaring, throwing out sparks and embers, lighting up the early evening. He was shocked; people were touching him as he walked, smiling at him as he passed, and all trying to get closer to him. Jed couldn't understand all the fuss they were making over him. Suddenly, several warriors picked him up, despite his protesting, and carried him to the center of the circle where the elders sat.

Slow Wolf smiled as he stepped in front of the embarrassed youngster, waving a large eagle feather across his head and chest. The Chief turned to where Walking Horse stood with the other warriors. "Tell us, my Nephew, why should this one be given a Brave Heart name?"

Jed didn't notice before, Walking Horse was attired in the fanciest deerskins and beads he has ever seen on the warrior. A breastplate of the finest bones and workmanship adorned his chest. The warrior stepped into the firelight where all could see him, raising his great arms. Slowly in a calm voice, almost sad voice, Walking Horse began to speak in a way Jed has never heard him talk before. The tall warrior started singing a song, telling about the bravery of Jed; the battle where he was challenged, and how Jed killed a very strong and dangerous enemy. Jed stared as the warrior started to dance and shuffle slowly. His voice was rising and falling as he made the Crow warrior, a man of gigantic size and strength. He couldn't believe his ears as Walking Horse was talking about him this way; bragging about his bravery in facing five enemy Crows alone, killing one and chasing the others from their hunting grounds. Sweat glistened from the warrior's heavily muscled body as he danced around the fire, flourishing his war axe.

The song seemed to go on forever with Walking Horse repeating the same words, making Jed appear like a Herculean figure to the villagers. The voice lowered, then rose to a crescendo before finally ceasing and growing quiet. All eyes stared in awe of the tall young warrior standing before the elders; young maidens screeched in admiration, and young children drew back into the safety of their mother's arms afraid he would take them. Walking Horse made the young man into a super warrior with his song, bragging of his ferocity and bravery in battle.

Slow Wolf motioned to where White Swan waited in the shadows, then stepped back. The old medicine man started to chant and sprinkle powdery dust across the ground and around Jed as he approached. Fire flew from his hands as he flung a magic potion into the fire, then whirled three times around the straight form before him. Jed straightened his shoulders more as he found the enraptured face of Little Antelope staring at him from across the circle. He could still hear her last words ringing in his ears. "Stand tall and proud. You are Arapaho."

"The warrior before us has come from the east as the prophecy has spoken." White Swan stared into Jed's face. "He has counted coup on our enemy as the prophecy has spoken. He will now become an Arapaho Lance Bearer; one who will always defend and protect the people. Who here says otherwise?"

No one spoke as the old medicine man studied the crowd and waited. It was the custom of the Arapaho; if only one person objected, a warrior could not become a Lance Bearer. To object would be taboo, and the strong medicine of the Lance would be gone for all if this prophecy was broken.

The old one continued. "His name will no longer be Jedidiah, a new name has been sent by the ancient ones for this warrior."

"Yiee, yiee!" The voices hollered out in expectancy, waiting for the name. "Tell us."

"Yes, tell us, Uncle." The usual calm Slow Wolf was impatient. "Speak!"

Once again, the yellow powder was thrown into the fire, causing a large puff of smoke to bellow up. "His name!" White Swan pulled back the bloody hunting shirt and showed everyone the mark of the Lance on Jed's shoulder. "For his greatness and bravery in battle, he shall be called, Crow Killer!"

An insane amount of screaming and yelling engulfed the village, making dogs and horses retreat from the loud uproar that resounded all across the lodges.

Walking Horse was the first to congratulate Jed as he handed him a lance bearing the markings of an eagle and trimmed with four eagle feathers. "This Crow Killer is your lance, you have earned it."

"Thank you, it is beautiful." Jed looked at the lance. "I will honor it."

All kinds of gifts were placed at Jed's feet as, one by one, the villagers passed before him, smiling happily. His face was beet red as he has never been treated with so much adoration, and it was embarrassing for him.

Waiting her turn, Little Antelope was the last to approach Jed. She presented him with a beautiful hunting shirt and a pair of quilled elk-hide moccasins. The small woman smiled up at him shyly. "I am proud of you, Crow Killer, but somehow I prefer the name of Jed more."

"Then call me Jed." Smiling down at her, he accepted the presents. "Thank you."

Bow Legs approached, laughing as Little Antelope walked off with Walking Horse. "Now, my friend, you have your pick of the young women to dance with tonight."

"Are women all Bow Legs thinks about?"

"No, sometimes I think about eating."

Jed didn't know where the people got the energy. For hours, they danced and gyrated around the blazing fire, stopping at times to catch their breath, then falling back into the festivities again. Several young women came forward, pulling him into the ring to dance. A huge cry always went up as he entered the ring and then Walking Horse would sing out his praises. Embarrassed by all the attention, he tried to fade back into the crowd and disappear, only to have someone pull him back into the firelight. Finally exhausted, he excused himself for the last time and slipped silently back to his lodge. As he pulled the lodge flap shut behind him, he could still hear the drums beating out their rhythm and the dancers yelling as they gyrated around the fire. Once almost vacant, the lodge was now filled with presents the villagers had presented him. While he was dancing, someone brought them to his lodge, aligning them around the interior.

Walking Horse sat cross-legged across from him as he blinked his eyes open to the new day and the rising sun. Sleepily his eyes focused on the smoke from the warrior's pipe as it drifted slowly upward through the smoke hole of the lodge. Neither spoke as Jed slowly rose to a sitting position.

"If I had been the enemy, you would have been without your hair."

Stretching, he rubbed his face and nodded. "I was so tired it wouldn't have mattered."

"You came to your lodge early?" Walking Horse looked curiously at Jed. "The people missed you at the dance."

"A lodge is for sleeping, and I was weary." Jed shrugged. "Very tired."

"Maybe you found a woman at the dance last night?"

"No, I found none." Jed shook his head. "You, Bow Legs, and your women."

"Perhaps, I will ask Little Antelope to find you a woman while we are away." Walking Horse nodded. "A fat one who will keep you warm when the cold winds blow."

"We are going out again?" Jed ignored the last comment. He knew Walking Horse was just teasing him to watch him squirm.

"Slow Wolf wishes Crow Killer to continue his training, but he really wants us to seek out the Crow." Walking Horse looked around the lodge. "Our chief wants to know what our enemies are doing. He predicts they will come seeking to avenge the one killed."

"Slow Wolf thinks the Crow will come here on a raid?"

"Yes, so now it is time for you to learn the lessons of war, the trails, and hunting grounds of other tribes. There is still much for you to learn about our enemies."

"Don't you people ever have fun?"

"What is this fun?"

"You know swimming, fishing, horse racing."

Walking Horse grinned over at Jed. "You do not think fighting our enemies, is this thing you call fun?"

Jed remembered his fight with the Crow. "No, can't say I do, fighting could get you killed."

"You Crow Killer are a Lance Bearer; it is your duty to get killed."

"Now that sounds like real fun to me." Jed shook his head. "Yes sir, a real ripsnorter. Do you mind if I put dying off awhile?"

"You still speak like a white, sometimes." Walking Horse tapped out his pipe. "All times."

For three weeks, Jed had followed Walking Horse along the narrow mountain trails through the lush valleys and over the mountain passes that divided the hunting grounds of the different tribes. Pointing out the buffalo skulls with the red and yellow markings; Walking Horse explained they were boundary signs, marking the tribe's boundaries, telling them they were entering hostile grounds, and warning them to go no further. Here in the deep mountains, they had to ride carefully as any turn in the trail could find them confronting another tribe face-to-face.

"Don't the Arapaho have any allies, friends?" Jed was curious, as Walking Horse always spoke of caution; not to talk, ride in the shadows, be careful with fire and smoke, and leave as few tracks as possible, which on the sandy mountain trails was mostly impossible. Lastly, he cautioned, never use the same trail twice.

"We have strong friends, the Cheyenne and Sioux." Walking Horse nodded. "But, they are far to the northeast. There are no allies of the Arapaho to the north or west."

"Would these people come here to help fight for the Arapaho if they were needed?"

"Maybe, but our allies will only help if they decide we deserve help." Walking Horse shrugged. "The tribes decide these things on a whim, it can go either way."

"I understand now, we are a small tribe compared to the many villages of the Crow, Pawnee, and others." Jed nodded. "And all on our own."

"This is why Slow Wolf has sent us here for you to learn, and why our Lance Bearers and warriors need to be strong, fierce, and unafraid."

"I will learn with your help."

"We are not friends, Crow Killer, not yet, but I will teach you all I know for the benefit of all." Walking Horse looked closely into Jed's eyes. "I think like Slow Wolf, the days ahead could be very dangerous. We must ride like ghosts while we are in these lands."

"That's fine with me, but I wish we could be friends. I understand your feelings for the whites." Jed stared back hard into the dark eyes. "I have chosen to be Arapaho. I ride with you as an Arapaho. Did you not say yourself I am now a full-fledged Lance Bearer?"

"Yes, I did, the same as Slow Wolf and White Swan did. We need brave warriors, Crow Killer." Walking Horse studied the valley below. "But, we have yet to become friends."

"I will learn." Jed nodded as he already learned many things from the tall warrior. He also learned to listen and freeze if Walking Horse raised his hand in warning. He knew he had many things to learn in just a short time. Arapaho warriors have a lifetime from childhood until they became warriors, but he only has the days ahead.

Several times riding through the valley, the two Arapahos blended into the heavy tree lines, watching as warriors passed by unknowingly along the trail below them. High on a tree lined ridge, one of the enemy's horses nickered when he smelled the strange horses, only to have his rider kick him hard without investigating what their horses sensed.

"There is a young and very foolish warrior." Walking Horse shook his head. "Always listen and pay attention to what your pony tells you, Crow Killer. His sense of hearing, smell, and his ability to seek out hidden warriors is much better than ours, much better."

"What should he have done?"

"Always watch your horse's ears and nostrils as he will point out your enemy or another horse or deer, and then you can locate him even in the deep trees." Walking Horse dismounted and clamped his horse's nose. "Dismount quickly and clamp your pony's nose tightly so he cannot call back."

"They could have found us."

"Perhaps, if the warrior had listened to his pony, but he was listening to his friends talk of the war trail or girls. The Arapaho are not that careless."

"Even in their own hunting grounds?" Jed thought of Bow Legs and his constant talk of girls.

"Especially in our own lands, there is where one should be more careful." Walking Horse remounted and motioned forward. "Here in this land one must be cautious. If you want to live, always be alert, the enemy can be lurking anywhere."

Walking Horse intentionally led Jed deep into enemy Crow lands. Now, they lay concealed in the deep stands of mountain cedar and spruce trees, staring down into the valley at the immense village of lodges and large herd of horses roaming the valley floor. Here in these mountains, the two men were in grave danger of being discovered by roving hunting parties or even young boys riding the mountains having fun. Crow Killer would have to learn, in this dangerous ground, he must be alert and steady to survive. The warrior knew the young white had courage as he had killed the Crow without flinching or showing fear. This was different as he has time to think, and he would have to use all his cunning and courage to stay calm and follow Walking Horse without question. Walking Horse could watch and observe his student, also teach the young warrior in the midst of many enemies. Walking Horse knew all the Arapaho warriors in his village as he has known and ridden with them all their lives, and they were trustworthy and dependable on the war trail. As he looked back at Jed, he felt this warrior was also trustworthy, one of the brave hearts. The reason he brought Jed into enemy territory was to give him a lesson in stealth, one more chance to prove himself as a warrior, and to have fun, as Crow Killer had said.

"We will wait until the moon rises, and then we will enter the village."

"Enter the village!" Jed couldn't believe his ears. "For what?"

Walking Horse looked to where Jed lay under a heavy limbed spruce. "We cannot come all this way without proving we were here."

"Prove we were here?" Jed sputtered. "Why, what for?"

"Soon you will see."

Walking Horse didn't lie, the sun hardly set when he had them moving down the slope, leading their horses onto the gravel bank of the clear stream the village was encamped along. Fires burned throughout the encampment, silhouetting figures as people moved about the village preparing to sleep. Jed studied the village with its hundreds of lodges and roving mongrel dogs. What could Walking Horse be up to?

"You're going in there?"

"Not me, my young friend, you are." The warrior whispered.

"What for?" Jed couldn't believe his ears. Was Walking Horse trying to get him killed or was he just joking?

"We are here. It would be a great thing for you to bring back a trophy from the village." Walking Horse was serious. "If this thing is done, it will make the Arapaho proud, and it will give Crow Killer big medicine."

"What do you want me to bring back?"

"Anything, anything but a woman." Walking Horse looked about the village. "Just like our village, the largest lodge will contain the greatest trophies to take back to our people."

"You really are serious."

"This is fun, is it not?"

"Fun?" Handing over the reins of his horse, Jed laid his bow and quiver of arrows on the ground. "I go."

"You must hurry. We must leave this place long before the new sun rises." In the lingering light, Walking Horse motioned to a large lodge in the middle of the camp. "A very important warrior is there."

Walking Horse watched as Jed waded quietly across the stream and disappeared among the horse herd. He nodded, as the young white went forward without hesitating or questioning. The warrior remembered years before when Slow Wolf had sent him into a Shoshone Village just as he was doing tonight. He also remembered his heart racing. He wasn't afraid for himself, but of failing his uncle. He also remembered almost being caught that night when a squaw had tripped over him in the dark. His knife had done its work quickly as he had to cut off any shrieks before she could call out.

No, he did not want the white hurt, but he had to know, did this young man really possess the great medicine or power the prophecy predicted? Would he return with a prize from the Crow Village? He was the young one's teacher and it was his job to find out his worth by placing the young man in a dangerous situation. Yes, it was very dangerous, but in the lodges of the Arapaho it had always been so where young men had to prove their manhood before they were accepted as warriors, even if it meant placing them in harm's way.

The cooking fires of the Crow Village burned down to red embers, dousing the lodges in semi darkness. The shadowy forms of the lodges and the shuffling dark shapes of the tethered horses as they shifted positions were plain to see, and all else was gloomy. Jed quickly wrapped himself in a green deer hide he found as he entered the village and passed the first lodge. Walking Horse said it would disguise his smell from the village dogs who roamed throughout the camp. So far, the warrior had been right, several curs had smelled of him as he passed where they lay curled up, and none had given an alarm by barking. He still didn't know what Walking Horse wanted him to return with, only something to prove he had been in the village. Nearing the middle of the camp, he spotted the lodge that Walking Horse had pointed out. The lodge was much larger than the others and Jed knew now what he was looking for. In the Arapaho Village, one of the most admired possessions of Slow Wolf was his headdress and another was his pipe encased in a doe skin case; either of these trophies would do.

Lying flat, Jed crawled silently across the ground, worming his way to the entrance of the lodge where he could peer into the opening. He could hear the soft breathing of the squaws and the heavy snoring of a warrior in the back of the lodge. Slowly, he worked himself inside, feeling along the edges of the hide tepee as he moved soundlessly forward. Jed knew this was dangerous as one of the occupants might sense him and yell out a warning, then there would be no way to escape from the village. Nevertheless, to prove his courage to Walking Horse it was worth the risk, providing he could locate this warrior's most prized possession in the dark lodge and make off with it. Still, the thought of the Crow women getting their hands on him, gave him pause as he had heard of their cruelty to prisoners.

His hand stopped, frozen in place as he touched the tips of feathers. It had to be what he sought, the headdress of the sleeping warrior. It was hanging down from the side of the lodge as Jed felt around in the dark. Standing straight, Jed untied it from its leather thong and let it settle silently to the ground beside him. Rolling the feathers in a tight bundle, he tied the thong securely around the feathers, then started easing back out of the lodge. From deep within the lodge, movement caused him to freeze in place, and roll closer against the lodge wall. A figure stepped quietly past where he lay, then ducked through the opening outside. Sweat poured from his forehead as he listened for any further sound of movement. His hand grasped the long hunting knife tightly, prepared to use it if he was discovered when the warrior re-entered the lodge.

Walking Horse looked up at the rising moon, worried as Jed had been gone a long time, too long. The warrior knew if the youngster had been discovered, the village would have been awakened and would have set up a clamor, whether he was caught or not. He wanted to go into the village after Crow Killer, but where would he look. No, it was better he remained here, waiting for his return. He paced nervously back and forth, worrying what Crow Killer was doing. What was taking him so long?

Jed strained his eyes and ears listening for the return of whoever went outside. Finally, after what seemed an eternity, the warrior returned to his bed and settled down. Waiting for the snoring to resume, he quickly exited from the close confines of the lodge. Breathing a sigh of relief in the fresh air, Jed straightened slowly, but whirled when a horse stamped a foot as it smelled the strange warrior. Moving stealthily to where the horse stood tethered by his master's lodge, Jed spoke softly to the animal. Feeling along the picket line as he petted the horse, he grinned; he might as well be a hog and take the horse too. Looking around, he found the village was shrouded in darkness, not a person or sentry questioned him as he led the large horse away, walking straight back through the village as he had come. Stopping as he passed the last lodge, Jed rolled the headdress in the deer hide he was wearing, tying it securely again with the thong. He didn't try to mount the horse as he sensed it was nervous of him and the last thing he needed was for it to snort or spook backwards at his strange smell. Well trained war horses were like camp dogs; some were even better than dogs at detecting the enemy.

Quickly making his way back to where Walking Horse waited, Jed sighed in relief as he never thought what he had just done could be accomplished so easily. Could it have been beginners luck? He felt of his bare skin where sweat still beaded, as it felt clammy to the touch. Had he been scared he wondered, or nervous when the warrior suddenly exited the lodge? He grinned again as he knew he had been scared and with good reason. Whistling softly, he waded into the stream and crossed to where Walking Horse waited.

Grasping the younger man's arm the warrior nodded in relief. "I was beginning to think you got lost, or the Crow squaws had you."

"Only held up." Jed nodded in the darkness.

"For what?"

"I had to wait while a warrior made water."

"What?" Walking Horse asked curiously. "Made water?"

"Yep, that's a fact." Jed laughed lightly. "A huge warrior stepped right over me, leaving his lodge to go outside."

Walking Horse rubbed his hand over the horse Jed had taken from the village, and then motioned to the southeast. "Come, we go."

"I'm ready." Jed looked back at the village. "Very ready."

"What is in the hide?" Walking Horse noticed right off the dark bundle Jed held across the withers of his horse.

Holding the bundle up, Jed smiled. "It is a present for our Chief Slow Wolf."

"What is it?"

"When we get out of here and return to our village, you will see."

Nodding his head, Walking Horse kicked his horse and headed back to the south in a slow dog trot. "I will wait then."

While Jed was in the village, Walking Horse had watered the horses and turned them loose to graze. Now, rested and full of the luscious green grass growing alongside the stream, the horses were ready and able to travel back to the village at a fast pace. Daylight found the two warriors pushing the horses hard, riding fast to the south, many miles from the Crow Village. No sound of pursuit or sighting of the enemy came forth yet so Walking Horse figured they have several hours lead on the Crow warriors but he knew they would follow. Also with the coming of daylight and the new sun, Walking Horse immediately recognized the horse Jed had stolen from the village. Now, there was no doubt as he knew for certain the Crow would be following fast, trying to recover the horse. Grinning from ear to ear, he smiled over at Jed.

"Does Crow Killer know who this magnificent animal belongs to?" Walking Horse stroked the arched neck of the stallion Jed was leading.

"No, I do not know this horse."

Walking Horse looked at Jed and laughed. "You have taken the most prized horse in the Crow Nation. This is the war horse of the mighty Crow Warrior Red Hawk, son of Chief Plenty Coups. This horse is a prize worth many coup, even more valuable than scalps."

"And that means we'll be followed hard, doesn't it?"

"Yes, Red Hawk will run his horses to death trying to catch us before we reach our hunting grounds." Walking Horse was truly in shock at seeing the great animal. "How did you know to take this animal, the spotted stallion of Red Hawk?"

"He was tethered outside the lodge where I stole this, so I grabbed him." Jed held up the bundle. "Purely an accident, I assure you. I wasn't looking for him."

"Red Hawk will follow quickly after his horse. We must ride fast for our lands." Walking Horse turned and studied their back trail. "Aiyee, young one. You have done well this day, but you have made a lifelong enemy as well."

"Lifelong enemy? I don't understand."

"There is no time to explain."

"If he is so valuable to this Red Hawk, maybe we should release him?" Jed watched Walking Horse's reaction.

"Every warrior in these mountains knows who rides this stallion, and it will make the Arapaho people strong. Other tribes will know our medicine is strong and our warriors are strong." Walking Horse laughed deeply. "Release him, never. Come, we go."

"Yep, real fun." Jed mumbled.

The mountain stream marking the beginning of Arapaho Country ran fast and cold as the three horses and two men splashed across. Walking Horse looked behind them where several horses pulled up and were watching them from a distant low range of hills.

"Will the Crow stop, or will they follow?"

"Red Hawk will be forced to stop. To come into Arapaho lands in the light with so few warriors would be foolhardy." Walking Horse raised his arm, taunting the watching warriors on the hill. "The great Crow warrior Red Hawk is no fool, very brave, but no fool. He will not put his warriors in danger."

"Like you did me?"

Walking Horse looked calmly at Jed. "You were in no danger; you bear the mark."

"What about his horse and this?" Jed raised the bundle. "Won't he come for them, if the horse is so valuable to him?"

"I do not know what Crow Killer has wrapped up hidden from my eyes." Walking Horse looked at the bundle. "Red Hawk knows who we are now, who has stolen his great stallion. Yes, he will come for the horse. He will come when we do not expect him."

"They know who we are, how?"

"Red Hawk has sharp eyes, the eyes of the hawk. We have fought many times before, he knows me. Now, he will remember your face."

"From this distance?" Jed scoffed. "No one can tell who a man is, this far away."

"He will recognize you by the way you ride, sit a horse, your size. Yes, he will know you when you meet."

"This may be more valuable to the Crow." Jed patted the bundle resting across his horse's withers.

"You will not tell me what is hidden under the deer hide, but I do not think Red Hawk would value it more than the stallion." Walking Horse waved again at the Crow warriors watching, then turned his horse toward home.

Jed looked over at the heavily muscled Appaloosa horse he was leading. He was indeed a thing of beauty and power. "Where would the Crow get such an animal as this?"

"It is said that Red Hawk rode to the west and north for many moons and stole him from the great Nez Perce people."

"This Red Hawk must be a great warrior." Jed looked again at the horse thoughtfully. "That is a long way off. Lige Hatcher spoke of these Nez Perce, a tribe that lives where the wagon train was headed."

"He is the greatest of the Crow warriors." Walking Horse nodded. "Yes, it is many days away. To gain an animal like this, danger and a long ride is nothing."

"He went alone?"

"That is what was told. Red Hawk may be a Crow, but he is still a great and brave warrior, same as his father Plenty Coups." Walking Horse heeled his horse. "If you ever meet him in battle remember this, he is strong, quick as a cat, and has counted coup many times."

"More than you, Walking Horse?"

"Yes, many more times than me." The warrior nodded. "Red Hawk is an honorable man, and all who died by his hand had a chance for their lives."

"You sound like you admire this Crow."

Walking Horse pulled his horse in, turning one last time before disappearing from the watching Crow's view. Raising his powerful arm, he waved toward the warriors, who had advanced to the river's edge. "I do. One should always admire a great enemy; it makes you a stronger warrior."

Jed was amazed when a loud shout went up from the Crow as they raised their voices in respect. "They seem to be cheering for you."

"They are." Walking Horse nodded. "The Crow admire a strong enemy same as we do."

CHAPTER 5

The stream leading into the Arapaho Village was reached just before sunup as the village fires were being lit and the villagers were waking up.

As they sat watering their tired horses, Jed slid from his animal and approached Walking Horse. "The spotted stallion is for you, Walking Horse, for your help in teaching me the war trail and to become a Lance Bearer.

The warrior was shocked as Jed handed him the lead rope of the stallion. "Are you sure, Crow Killer? This is a great and valuable gift."

"He is yours, ride him into the village. Little Antelope will swell with pride. She will be even more proud of you than she already is."

"But, you captured him; the honor should be all yours."

"I couldn't have taken him without your help, my friend." Jed shook his head. "The spotted one is yours."

"Perhaps, young one." The warrior looked at Jed as if he was seeing him for the first time. "Perhaps, I have been wrong. Thank you for such a gift."

The spotted stallion pranced with his neck arched as he entered the village to the keening and cheering of the women. Little Antelope emerged from her mother's lodge, when the uproar started, in time to see her husband proudly riding the beautiful spotted stallion through the village toward the lodge where she stood. Her chest swelled with pride as she watched the horse approaching. With his powerful arm, Walking Horse reached down, swung her up behind him, and turned toward their lodge.

Jed watched as the two disappeared behind several lodges as they went on to their lodge. Dismounting, he looked down at the bundle he had taken from the Crow Village, and walked to where Slow Wolf and White Swan stood waiting. Greeting the chief and old medicine man, he held out the bundle to Slow Wolf, and smiled.

"This is for you, my Chief." Jed passed the bundle to Slow Wolf. "A gift from me and Walking Horse."

Looking about at the many curious faces watching them, Slow Wolf motioned Jed into his lodge. "You have brought this from the Crow lands?"

"Yes, I took it when I took the stallion." Jed nodded. "I only went after this bundle, but the horse was just standing there asking to be taken."

"You are modest, my son; this is good." The chief motioned for Jed to sit. "Most young warriors with their great egos would be bragging for all in the village to hear."

"I was lucky, that's all." Jed sat down on a pile of buffalo robes. "There is nothing to brag about."

Untying the thong, Slow Wolf carefully unwrapped the bundle and spread the great eagle headdress of a Crow Chief on the lodge floor before him. The old eyes lit up in disbelief as he studied the headdress. He had seen this eagle bonnet before on the head of his age-old enemy, Plenty Coups.

"You must tell me of this great miracle, my son. How did you come by the headdress of my enemy, Plenty Coups?" The chief was in awe of the beautiful plumage. "There is no other like it in the Crow Nation, or in any nation."

Jed smiled as the chief eyed the headdress. "Like I said it was pure luck, my Chief. I slipped into a lodge of the Crows, and stole it while they slept."

"Luck?" Slow Wolf shook his head in disbelief. "It was more than luck, my son. It is the prophecy."

"I had no idea whose lodge I was in, and I sure didn't know what I was stealing when I took it in the dark." Jed lied.

"And the great spotted stallion?" Slow Wolf looked across at Jed. "You say that was luck also?"

"The same; he stood in the shadows of the lodge as I was leaving the village." Jed nodded. "I took him for a gift to Walking Horse for all his help. When I took the horse and headdress, I didn't know who Plenty Coups and Red Hawk were, or anything about the spotted horse. I tell you, my Chief, it was pure blind luck that I managed to steal either trophy."

Slow Wolf shook his head in amazement. "To take such a thing as this in the dark of night was not luck; it is the prophecy. The ancient ones guided your hand to these things. Your destiny is to lead our people to greatness, as the prophecy now comes true."

"Will not the taking of these things cause the Crows to attack our village in revenge?"

"This is true." Slow Wolf nodded slowly. "Red Hawk's pride and arrogance will make him come for the horse and headdress. We must watch, always be on the alert, and be ready for them."

"Their village I entered was much larger than ours." Jed remembered the immense village and the many fires that dotted it. "The Crow must greatly outnumber the Arapaho."

"Perhaps, what you say is true." Slow Wolf nodded. "But, we have the greatest of all warriors and they will defend our people, the village, and our hunting grounds."

The chief stopped speaking as the old Medicine Man, White Swan, entered and stepped near the small fire in the center of the lodge. His eyes seemed to light up like flames of fire as they settled on the headdress of the Crow. Chanting softly and beating his gourd rattle, the old one raised his hands toward the top of the lodge, and with a final burst of his voice, ceased to speak.

"Crow Killer has brought us a great gift today." Slow Wolf beamed as he showed White Swan the headdress. "It is time. I wish White Swan to prepare a secret charm or magic ritual that will keep this one from harm in the coming days ahead."

White Swan ran his hands lightly over the war bonnet and smiled. "This I will do, but the young one must go through the purification rites first."

Slow Wolf nodded in agreement as he knew the warrior's body must be cleansed; purified of the old smell on his body and in his nose before any magic charms could ward off an enemy's weapons to keep him from harm. "It will be as you say; there will be no raiding of any kind until the cleansing and purification rites are held for all."

"In three days, we will have a Sun Dance." White Swan looked once more at the headdress and then abruptly exited the lodge.

"Go, Crow Killer and send Walking Horse to me."

The village was in bedlam as everyone, young and old, was in a frenzy scurrying about the camp, making ready for the coming ceremony. Wood had to be gathered, food prepared, and the best hunters were sent out to kill enough meat to feed the village for three days of feasting. Forever vigilant against attack, Walking Horse heeded Slow Wolf's words and ordered the young warriors to ride the boundaries of all Arapaho Lands. The warriors made sure the village was not surprised or attacked while the people focused their attention on the Sun Dance. Small hovels for the sweat lodges were prepared and round rocks from the river were brought in by the younger children. Jed has never seen so much activity in the Arapaho Lodges since he had first arrived. Walking Horse tried to explain the enormity of the event, but still Jed could not comprehend how much stock the people put in the ceremony. Even Little Antelope suddenly disappeared and Jed didn't see her throughout the day.

"What do you wish for me to do?" Jed walked to where Walking Horse was bridling his horse.

"Crow Killer must stay here, inside the village, until the purification rites are finished." The warrior raised his hand to Jed's objections. "This is White Swan's wishes, and it is Chief Slow Wolf's orders."

"I can hunt. I can guard the village." Jed was frustrated, worse yet, he was bored having to stay confined to the village like a woman.

"A warrior's medicine is weak during the days of the ceremony. When the purification rites are finished, you will be protected. Our medicine man sees much danger for you, and fears for you to leave the safety of the village."

Jed shook his head in disgust. "It sure ain't right, the rest of you doing all the work, just so I won't get hurt."

"It is our chief's wishes." Walking Horse smiled. "If I were you, I would obey him."

"I need to be helping."

"Listen to me, Crow Killer, soon you will have all the fighting and hunting you want." Walking Horse swung easily on the spotted stallion. "The meat taking time is near. We will hunt the shaggy ones together, and don't forget Red Hawk will be waiting."

"Red Hawk, bah."

"Young one, Red Hawk is a great warrior, remember that, if you should meet him in battle." Walking Horse was stern as he warned Jed. "He has learned the way of war from the best fighter of the Crows, possibly of any nation."

"What warrior is this?"

"The mighty Crow, Plenty Coups." The warrior laughed. "The huge warrior who stepped over you to relieve himself; the very one the eagle headdress was stolen from."

"Plenty Coups?"

"The father of Red Hawk."

Jed remembered the huge warrior who had passed by him in the Crow lodge. "Well, he is a big man, that part is certain."

Turning for his lodge as Walking Horse loped the stallion away from the village with Bow Legs and several others following, Jed kicked at every stone he passed strolling along the flat ground. In his disgust at having to stay in the village like a child, he didn't see Little Antelope step from her lodge and come up behind him.

"Is Crow Killer mad at those little rocks or is he trying to wear out his moccasins?" She laughed easily.

"You surprised me, little one." Embarrassed as he turned, he could only frown down at her. "They treat me like a child."

"In three days you will be a full-fledged Arapaho warrior and Lance Bearer, then no one will be able to tell you what to do, not even Slow Wolf." Little Antelope smiled up at him. "Now, forget the rocks and come with me to my lodge."

"To your lodge?" Jed looked to where Walking Horse had disappeared across the river.

"I will not bite, but if you are afraid?" She pursed her mouth like she was pouting.

Following the small woman to the larger lodge, Jed looked around wondering if anyone was watching. Hesitating at the entrance, he felt her grab hold of his hunting shirt and pull him forward.

"What are you doing?" Jed's eyes had trouble adjusting to the gloomy interior of the lodge. When he could finally see, he could make out the shapes of three other women in the lodge.

"Remove your shirt."

"What?" Jed gulped, looking down at the smiling faces of three young women.

"Take off your hunting shirt, Crow Killer." Little Antelope laughed. "We only want to fit this shirt to you. We will not attack you."

Jed could see the newly stitched deer-hide hunting shirt that one of the girls held in her hands. Bashfully, he pulled his worn and bloody hunting shirt over his head. He could feel his face turning hot and beet red as the girls giggled as they looked up at him.

Laying the new shirt against his broad shoulders, Little Antelope let her fingers glide slowly down his hard, heavily muscled chest and flat stomach. The other girl's hands were all over him as they surrounded him affixing the wooden pins, holding the shirt firmly in place.

"There, that was not hard for the great Crow Killer, was it?" Little Antelope laughed. "Now, let's take it off slowly so the pins will stay in place."

"What is this for?" Jed felt the softness of the beautiful shirt as she pulled it over his head. "It is beautiful."

"It is your new courting shirt." One of the girls giggled as her hand slowly ran down the shirt smoothing it. "Walking Horse instructed us to make it for you."

"For me!" Jed blushed. "I don't need a courting shirt. No, sir."

One of the young women giggled again. "Soon you might."

"Yes, silly, for you." Little Antelope pushed him toward the lodge flap. "Now, out with you, we have work to do."

"He could stay." One of the young women spoke up from the gloom. "We wouldn't mind if he helped."

Watching his face turn red again, Little Antelope grinned, then tossed him his old shirt. "Go Crow Killer, before your face catches fire."

Jed stood beside his lodge as several warriors rode past, oblivious to the people watching and yelling at them. He has never seen such a proud, yet stern, look on any warriors as was manifested on these riders. All were tall, powerfully built men, unknown warriors, whom he has never seen in the village before. He knew they were not Arapaho, maybe Sioux or Cheyenne.

"They are our Cheyenne brothers from the far north." White Swan appeared silently at his side.

"They are something to behold." Jed nodded. "What are they here for?"

"They have heard of the prophecy and of the great Crow Killer. Now, they come for the Sun Dance." White Swan followed the warriors with his eyes as they rode toward Slow Wolf's lodge. "Soon, others will come."

"That is why Walking Horse hunts for so much game?"

"Yes, we must feed our guests." The old one smiled a toothless grin. "These warriors, they eat a lot."

"I'll bet."

"Come, I will introduce you to Yellow Dog. He is a blood brother to Walking Horse."

"Blood brother?" Jed was curious.

"Once, many moons ago, Walking Horse saved Yellow Dog from the skinning knives of the Crow squaws, who were about to cut him into little pieces."

"How did he do that?" Jed watched as the Cheyenne warriors dropped nimbly to the ground in front of Slow Wolf.

"It is a long story, one for a winter night when the snow is falling and it is too cold to hunt or venture from the lodge." White Swan motioned Jed forward. "When that time comes, I will tell the story."

"When that cold night comes, I will be sure to remind you, Grandfather." Jed just had to hear this story. "I will not forget."

A tall, slender warrior stood off to the side of the others as they greeted the Arapaho Chief with respect. Long black hair, hanging halfway down his back, held two eagle feathers that were tied to his topknot. A splendid specimen of a warrior, the Cheyenne stood over six feet tall with long well-proportioned arms and legs. Jed knew he was near

the same age as Walking Horse, and although he has the same look of
pride as the others, this warrior was different, prouder and even more
arrogant.

Pulling Jed with him as he stopped beside the Cheyenne, White
Swan smiled up at the young warrior. "My son, Yellow Dog."

"White Swan, Grandfather." The Cheyenne called to the old one
with respect and honor. "It has been too many moons since we have
greeted each other."

"Yes, far too many, my son." White Swan agreed. "It is good you
have come for the Sun Dance. Our friends the Cheyenne honor the
Arapaho with their presence."

"Our curiosity makes us come. We could not stay away." Yellow
Dog looked at Jed. "We have heard much of a great Arapaho warrior; a
Lance Bearer, a killer of enemies, a warrior called Crow Killer."

"What has Yellow Dog heard?"

"That he is invincible to the Crows. He steals their best horses from
under their eyes, kills their warriors, and the great Plenty Coups trem-
bles before him as he gives him his own war bonnet to wear."

"Where did you hear all this?" White Swan looked at the warrior
curiously. "There have been no Arapaho warriors that have traveled to
the north in the last three moons."

"It is on the air for all to hear, Grandfather." The tall Cheyenne
laughed. "The wind blows through the mountains and tells his people,
the Cheyenne, everything."

"Perhaps it was a bird, maybe." White Swan turned sideways and
nodded at Jed. "To cure your curiosity, Yellow dog, this is that warrior,
the one known as Crow Killer."

Yellow Dog studied the younger man's features several seconds.
They were almost the same height, but the Cheyenne was heavier and a
little older, with the maturity of age. "I do not know this one. I have
never seen him in the Arapaho Villages."

"We have not met." Jed stared straight into the dark eyes of the
Cheyenne.

"You are not from this village?" Yellow Dog repeated himself.

"No." Jed shook his head. "I am honored to meet Yellow Dog."

"I am glad to meet such a warrior as Crow Killer." Yellow Dog nodded proudly. "Is what the wind says about you true? Did Plenty Coups give you his war bonnet?"

"This I do not know. The wind does not speak to a lowly Arapaho." Jed shrugged his shoulders. "But the war bonnet of Plenty Coups is now in the lodge of Slow Wolf."

"So it is true?" The warrior nodded. "The wind tells the truth."

"Well, I don't know what else it said, but that part is true enough."

All the gathered Cheyenne warriors cheered loudly as Jed was introduced, extending their greetings to the great Crow Killer, making him feel as if he had known them forever. His chest swelled with pride as the tall warriors before him, the pride of the Cheyenne Nation, were paying honor to him. To be greeted by such warriors as these in such a way, was the highest of honors. Only the warrior Yellow Dog and another Cheyenne, Crazy Cat, were reserved. Their dark eyes studied him, as if he was an enemy warrior and they did not accept him as the others did.

Looking around the gathered villagers, Yellow Dog looked back at White Swan. "I do not see my brother, Walking Horse."

"He rides with the hunters after meat so we can feed our guests, the Cheyenne." Slow Wolf stepped from his lodge and spoke up. "Come sit, my brothers, we will smoke the pipe of friendship that binds the Arapaho and Cheyenne Nations as one."

Jed noticed no women or children came with the warriors, and knew this was more than a few Cheyenne visiting the Arapaho for the Sun Dance. Something was in the air; a raid perhaps, after the ceremonies. Warriors always carried their weapons for war and hunting with them at all times, but these warriors have an abundance of arrows in their quivers, hanging from their horses. No, he knew this was more than a visit. The Cheyenne came prepared, and they were here to fight or raid with their Arapaho brothers if needed.

"Yellow Dog!" An excited yell came from Little Antelope as she appeared out of the crowd, running toward the warriors as they were about to turn to the council fire before Slow Wolf's lodge. "It is you."

"Little One." The warrior picked up the small frame as if she was light as a feather, holding her above his head, then lowering her slowly until their eyes were level with each other. "It has been so long."

No one watching saw the dark blush that came over Jed's face as he watched the two hugging. As Yellow Dog set the small woman down, she turned and noticed the cold hard look coming from Jed's eyes and how dark his face turned. Laughing, she pulled the warrior closer to Jed.

"Perhaps, Crow Killer wishes to meet my brother, Yellow Dog of the Cheyenne people." She was amused, as the jealousy emitting from Jed's face was plain to see.

"Your brother, I thought you were Arapaho?"

"I am Arapaho now, but before I married Walking Horse, I was Cheyenne." Little Antelope laughed. "Walking Horse does not mind that his woman is Cheyenne, would you?"

"No." Slightly embarrassed, Jed congratulated Yellow Dog for having such a sister, excused himself, and then quickly walked away toward his lodge. He knew she saw the jealousy in his face and actions, and hoped her brother didn't notice.

"He is a strange young man." Yellow Dog muttered quietly to her. "Strange."

"Strange?" Little Antelope looked at the tall straight figure walking away. "He is not strange, Brother, he will be a great Lance Bearer of the people."

"He seems to care for you, Sister. His jealousy showed, even I could see." Yellow Dog looked down at her affectionately. "Does Walking Horse know this?"

"We are just friends, nothing more." Little Antelope reassured him. "Go, smoke the pipe with Slow Wolf while I fix you a good meal."

"I hope you have learned to cook better than you did as a little girl." Yellow Dog laughed, remembering her cooking. "I will smoke with Slow Wolf, then I will come to your lodge."

"Walking Horse is still alive. He has not been poisoned yet."

Yellow Dog laughed. "You say this, but I have not seen my friend anywhere yet."

"He will be here soon." She took his hand. "He rides with the warriors."

"Tell your brother the truth, Sister. Does Walking Horse know of Crow Killer's feelings for you?"

"Crow Killer has become a close friend. Walking Horse trains him in the art of war and hunting." She looked over at him. "There is nothing more than friendship between us."

"If you say so, Little Antelope."

"I say so, Brother." Little Antelope frowned. "I love my husband."

"I said, if you say so." Yellow Dog smiled playfully at his little sister. "But then, you always were a good liar."

Fire flashed from her dark eyes as she looked up at her older brother. "Enough, go smoke your pipe and blow smoke to the air, not me."

Walking Horse and the other Arapaho warriors brought in an abundance of deer, buffalo, and smaller game for the feasting that was to come. The celebration, feasting, dancing, and the painful ordeal of those who suffered the passage and hardship of the Sun Dance filled the next three days for the entire village. The whole village was in a frenzy, almost as if in a trance. Their every thought, from oldest to youngest, was on the Sun Dance and the warriors who strolled about the village with their shoulders back and heads up. The warriors were proud men; proud to be Arapaho. The old Medicine Man of the Arapaho, White Swan, was true to his word; Jed was anointed with special herbs and a solid nugget of gold was hung around his neck. The entire Arapaho Nation was alive, exuberant, and full of extreme joy. Even with the threat of the Crow's retaliation on them, they spent the next three days and nights in a state of revelry. During all the celebrations, Slow Wolf never let his guard down. Arapaho warriors, including the Cheyenne visitors, patrolled the lands of the Arapaho, day and night.

"Crow Killer will never go into battle without this piece of rock, never." White Swan spoke solemnly. "Its power will protect you from the enemy, wherever you ride."

"Yes, Grandfather." Jed fingered the solid nugget. He knew exactly what the gold was as the men from the wagon train had searched and dug in the river and gulches every time the wagons stopped for the night.

White Swan presented Jed to the people of the Arapaho. "Here is a son of the Arapaho. Honor him tonight as he will defend and honor you, his people, as a Lance Bearer."

Hysteria rose higher in the village as the words were spoken, and a crescendo of noise erupted from the villagers as Crow Killer was pushed forward by the older warriors for all to see. A huge circle of dancers, including the Cheyenne, encircled Jed, each one touching him with a weapon, paying him homage as a gesture of respect.

Yellow Dog stepped into the open space before Slow Wolf's lodge and raised his huge arm. "With all your food, my warriors grow fat and lazy. They need exercise."

"What does my brother wish?" Walking Horse asked the Cheyenne. "What exercise do you wish for your warriors?"

"Perhaps, we could have a contest between one of my warriors and the great Crow Killer of the Arapaho."

"This will only help one of your warriors exercise, Brother."

"One is better than none." Yellow Dog grinned.

Walking Horse looked over at the warrior, Yellow Dog summoned, as the man stepped into the clear space near the ceremonial sun pole. A ring of warriors surrounded the pole, making a large circle where the two warriors would have room to compete. The warrior was young, but still a couple years older than Jed, and fully matured. Shorter than his opponent, the Cheyenne was powerfully built with long arms that were corded with muscle. For some reason, Walking Horse did not understand why, the warrior stared across at Jed with a coldness coming from his dark eyes.

"What kind of contest, my brother?" Something was amiss here. Walking Horse still did not understand what was going on. "And for what reason?"

A warrior led a jet-black horse into the circle. The horse was so black that he would remain dark as night, year round, not bleaching out to a dark dun color during the strong summer sun. "I, Yellow Dog, will present this buffalo runner to the winner of the contest."

Walking Horse ran his hands over the animal. He was indeed a real beauty; sleek necked with a short back and broad, powerful rear quarters, built for speed. Smooth unblemished legs and dark hard hooves that would carry his rider clear-footed over the roughest terrain. The small head had the brightest dark eyes, gentle, but full of fire if needed.

"He is a beauty."

"There is none faster or surer of foot in our village." Yellow Dog bragged.

"What do you wish us to gamble with?" Walking Horse was curious, not knowing what this was about. "And what is the contest?"

"You will bet nothing." Yellow Dog preened as he walked before the villagers, who upon hearing of the up-coming contest between the Cheyenne and Crow Killer had gathered, eager to watch the match, whatever it would be. Wagers were already being made as they waited for the Cheyenne to finish speaking. "The contest is a show of strength, a wrestling match, but no blood will be spilled."

"Is not Crazy Cat the best wrestler in the Cheyenne Nation?" Slow Wolf raised his voice so all could hear. "We have heard much of him."

"It is just a wrestling match. No one will be hurt." Yellow Dog looked across at the frowning face of his sister, Little Antelope. "But if the great Crow Killer does not wish to take the challenge."

Jed looked over to where Walking Horse stood staring at him, waiting. "I will wrestle him. A no-holds-barred match, catch as catch can."

"What does that mean, no-holds-barred, catch as catch can?" Yellow Dog hesitated. "Is this some kind of trick?"

"It means, Yellow Dog, that me and this warrior will fight anyway we want." Jed pulled his new hunting shirt off, exposing his well-muscled torso. "That is if you're sure you want to lose that black horse."

"We will see, Arapaho, who loses." Yellow Dog grinned and whispered to Crazy Cat. "My sister thinks much of this one. It will shame him in her eyes if you defeat him and make him out as weak and small."

Years before Little Antelope married Walking Horse, Crazy Cat had wanted her for his squaw. He had courted her playing his flute, and many times he stood beneath his courting blanket with her until her mother separated them. Several times, he had offered her father many horses for her, but she had always refused him. Now, jealousy, caused by Yellow Dog's words, raced through his body, making the adrenaline flow as he looked across at Jed. He was anxious to wrestle this warrior and beat him, as his muscles trembled in anticipation.

"Why do you do this, Brother?" Little Antelope slipped quietly beside Yellow Dog. "Why?"

"Don't worry, he won't get hurt." Yellow Dog smiled down at her. "You said he was just a friend."

"He has done nothing."

"Let him prove he is a man, worthy of being called an Arapaho Lance Bearer." Yellow Dog blustered. "All I have heard so far is talk."

"This is not your village, my Brother. You have no right."

"I am a blood brother to Walking Horse, I have every right." Yellow Dog looked across at his warriors. "It is our way to test the young ones, you know this."

"If he is hurt, I will hate you forever."

Yellow Dog feigned shock. "Why, Sister, you said he means nothing to you."

Walking Horse looked deep into Jed's eyes, almost as if he were apologizing for Yellow Dog's actions. The way of the Warrior Society of the Cheyenne and the Arapaho was one of proving their bravery and strength. At any time, a warrior could be called on to prove he was worthy to be called a man. Tonight, for some reason, unknown to Walking Horse, Jed had been called out and challenged to meet the warrior Crazy Cat in combat.

Both contestants stood in the huge circle stripped to their bare torsos facing each other, waiting for Slow Wolf to give the word for them to begin. The women yelled their shrill yells, as their voices rose in anticipation, looking with admiration at the well-proportioned bodies of the young warriors before them. Little Antelope looked across at Jed, catching his eye, she smiled slightly, confidently.

"He will be fast and strong, Crow Killer." Walking Horse was concerned. "You be stronger."

"Would you wager your good sorrel horse with the blaze face?" Jed grinned.

"I wager nothing. I am ashamed this has happened." Walking Horse ignored the question. "Fight hard, I know this warrior, he is dangerous."

"I intend to." Jed laughed. "Now, my friend, this is fun."

Walking Horse only shook his head. "Win first, then it will be fun."

Slow Wolf looked at both warriors, then dropped his hand for the match to begin. Crazy Cat lunged forward, trying to catch Jed off balance, wanting to wrestle him to the ground hard where his experience would gain him the advantage. Only the feet of his opponent met his hard rush, catching him full in the stomach and face as Jed kicked out powerfully at the Cheyenne. Surprised at the way Jed had struck out in midair with his feet, knocking him to the ground, Crazy Cat took a deep breath and rolled quickly to his feet. With blinding speed, Jed moved straight toward the shaken warrior and struck out with both fists, knocking Crazy Cat down again. Springing forward, Jed lunged sideways, twisting his legs into a scissor hold, clasping the warrior's legs as he grabbed one arm in a painful arm bar. Only Crazy Cat's great strength and quickness saved him from having to give up and lose the match. The Cheyenne has never met any warrior who wrestled as this one did; his feet, hands, and even his head was a weapon. Slipping under Jed's arms, Crazy Cat got behind him catching Jed in a choke hold from the rear. Brute strength bore down on Jed as the massive arms of Crazy Cat poured all their strength into the hold.

Twisting and turning, his face beet red from being choked, Jed elbowed the Cheyenne powerfully to his rib cage, then head butted the warrior, knocking the deadly grasp of his powerful arms loose. Stepping back, retreating from the oncoming warrior, Jed gasped for breath as he tried to shake the ringing from his ears. The villagers turned quiet as they knew this was not just a simple contest between two warriors. The match was turning out as an all-out battle, maybe to the death. Retreating around the circle, trying to regain his breath as Crazy Cat stalked him, Jed steadied himself and waited for the assault he knew was coming from the Cheyenne. Suddenly, with the speed his name spoke of, Crazy Cat launched himself once more across the flat ground, bent on bringing Jed down. As fast as the warrior was, Jed was faster, throwing the rushing Cheyenne over his shoulder, slamming him hard against the ground. With the speed of youth, Jed fell beside the warrior and held his wrist in a viselike grip with his foot against the warrior's neck. Extreme pain showed in the warrior's face as Jed poured all his strength into his leg and arm.

Looking up at Yellow Dog, Jed spoke softly. "Tell him to yield, Cheyenne, or I'll break his neck."

"Enough." Slow Wolf stepped forward. "He is beaten, but he is Cheyenne, too proud to give up."

"No, my Chief, I will hear from Crazy Cat or his keeper, Yellow

Dog." Jed put more pressure on the Cheyenne's arm causing him to wince in pain. Jed's face showed the same fury Walking Horse had seen during the fight with the Crow, and no mercy would be given. "Say it."

"Enough." Yellow Dog spoke up. "You have won, Crow Killer."

Releasing Crazy Cat's arm, Jed rolled easily to his feet and turned from the circle of cheering villagers. He wanted away from this, away from the madness from which he did not understand. Why did Yellow Dog want this fight? He called it a contest, but from the beginning Jed knew this was more than a wrestling match. His body still shaking from anger and adrenaline, Jed turned his back on the cheering villagers and started back to his own lodge. Realizing someone was following, he turned on his heel prepared to defend himself.

"Are you okay, Jed?" Little Antelope grabbed his arm from behind, concern showing on her face.

"I am fine. Go back to your brother and husband."

"This was not Walking Horse's idea. He did not know Yellow Dog was going to do this."

"It is of no importance, go."

"You did not take the horse." Little Antelope looked up at his face. "Why? You won it."

"I do not want it."

"To not accept your prize will shame Yellow Dog."

Jed frowned as he touched the hilt of his hunting knife. "Tell him if he is ashamed he should challenge me tomorrow, but not to a wrestling match."

"You would do my brother harm?"

"Tonight, he tried to do me harm." Jed's temper was starting to cool. "Why?"

"Walking Horse is his blood brother and I am his sister."

"So?"

"He thinks you care for me. He thinks he protects me from you." Little Antelope tried to smile but she knew this could get serious. "He thought if he could shame you in my eyes, it would be finished."

"Tell him not to worry further." Jed turned and walked away. "If there was something, it is finished."

CHAPTER 6

The Sun Dance festivities were at an end and the village returned to normal, as each tribal member went about their individual routines. New hides needed tanning for clothing and lodges, and meat had to be dried and processed before the cold times returned. Still ahead, the great hunt for the huge shaggy buffalo loomed. Plans were being made for the hunt, as well as a plan to defend the people if the Crows should raid their horse herd or village. Walking Horse spoke to both Yellow Dog and Jed about the hard feelings that were caused by the match. Both men shook hands, and Jed took the black horse at Yellow Dog's insistence. Now, Jed stayed away from the lodge of Walking Horse, preferring the company of Bow Legs and the other young warriors of the Arapaho.

"There has been no sighting of the enemy." Walking Horse had called a council in his lodge and now picked at the meat Little Antelope had prepared for them.

Yellow Dog nodded politely as he waited for his host to finish speaking. "Soon, we must go back to our lands and help our people prepare for the meat taking times."

"I know, and I thank my brother for coming here to help us." Walking Horse nodded. "I understand the meat taking times are important days."

"We must leave tomorrow with the coming of the sun." Yellow Dog refused more meat from his sister. "We came for the Sun Dance and to help in case we were needed. Now, we must get back to our lands."

"You will be missed, my brother."

"I do not think the Crows will raid now. Their warriors are needed for the buffalo hunt as we are." Yellow Dog looked across at Jed and smiled. "Besides, if they come, you have the great Crow Killer here to help you."

Jed didn't know whether the Cheyenne was sincere or jesting, but he thanked him anyway. "The Cheyenne are a great people and a good ally of the Arapaho. We thank you for coming."

"I would not have missed the Sun Dance and getting to ride with you once more, my brother." Yellow Dog nodded over at Walking Horse. "I am proud you have won the black horse, Crow Killer."

"He is a magnificent animal." Jed acknowledged. "Thank you."

"I stole him from the Crows as you did the spotted one." Yellow Dog laughed. "I did not intend to lose him. I thought Crazy Cat would win."

"Next time be more cautious about who you bet on."

Yellow Dog shrugged and laughed. "You are a great wrestler."

"Thank you." Jed pulled a rolled up piece of hide from his pouch and passed it to the warrior. "This is for you, Yellow Dog. I hope it seals our friendship, and I hope we will have no further contests."

"Crazy Cat is still holding his arm." Yellow Dog laughed. "No, there will be no more contests, I promise."

Little Antelope glared at her brother, then dropped her eyes, saying nothing. Turning as the others were watching Yellow Dog unwrap the present, she stared at Jed but he looked away, refusing to meet her eyes.

Unrolling the leather bound packet, Yellow Dog stifled a surprise grunt as he looked down at a beautiful hunting knife encased in a hand tooled sheath. The blade was razor sharp, curved to skin out an animal quickly. The handle was white bone engraved with the wings of an eagle on one side and the head of a buffalo on the other. The Cheyenne was in awe, never has he seen such a thing of beauty. Looking over at Jed he smiled. "You have done me proud, Crow Killer. It is a thing of rare beauty."

"It is pure steel from the whites, Yellow Dog. It will serve you for many years."

Walking Horse shook his head in amazement. "It is indeed beautiful and sharp enough to remove a scalp with one swipe."

"I will tell you one day, my friend." Yellow Dog grinned. "We will try it out on the Crow dogs the next time I visit."

With the departure of Yellow Dog and the Cheyenne, the next morning Slow Wolf had the Arapaho warriors patrolling day and night, watching for any war parties the Crow might send into Arapaho lands. Jed was either out hunting for game to feed the village or riding circuit of the Arapaho Village, ever alert for intruders. He has never been astride a horse for such an extended period of time in his entire life. He seemed to have become one with the black horse he had won from Yellow Dog.

Both Slow Wolf and Walking Horse were worried, as the Crow had been shamed. One lone warrior had raided their village while they slept. One warrior was dead, they had lost a valuable stallion, and their chief had lost his priceless headdress. They had been shamed and with their fierce pride, they had no choice, sooner or later their warriors would come. Now, was the meat taking time for all tribes where the villages moved closer to the hunting grounds of the great buffalo herds which would bring them in closer proximity to danger. Slow Wolf worried, but he hoped Red Hawk and his Crow warriors would be busy hunting their own winter meat and not have time to think about raiding the Arapaho. Still, something gnawed at Slow Wolf. Many times during the night, Jed would see the old chief pacing the village, back and forth, unable to sleep. It was the tribal leader's responsibility to keep the tribe safe, and Jed knew this wore on Slow Wolf's mind.

"You do not sleep either?" Jed looked to where Walking Horse was passing in the shadows. "Our Chief Slow Wolf, he doesn't sleep this night."

Walking Horse stopped as Jed spoke. "Like my chief, I know Red Hawk and his pride is too strong. He will come, I feel it. Something will happen."

"Is not the winter's meat more important to his village than a horse?" Jed asked quietly. "Would he put his pride before his people?"

"You do not know this warrior." Walking Horse looked up at the bright stars. "He carries thirty scalps on his coup stick. He is very proud. Most men walk but this one struts, and now we have shamed him in his people's eyes."

"Thirty scalps?" Jed shook his head. "That should make a man strut alright."

"Thirty." The warrior nodded. "If his chief rules out a raid on us, he will come alone, but he will come."

"They can't stop him?"

"They would not try. Red Hawk is their greatest warrior, the pride of the Crow people." Walking Horse shook his head. "His people love him above all others, even Plenty Coups."

"Even above their chief?"

Walking Horse nodded. "Red Hawk is young and proud. He moves through their villages like a prince and that is how they think of him."

"Then all we can do is wait and watch for this mighty warrior."

"The village will move soon, nearer to where the shaggies are plentiful." The warrior looked off to the north where the plains and grasslands begin. "The buffalo are there, but the danger to our people will be greater, much greater."

"Why?"

"There are many tribes hunting for their winter meat on these lands, we will be close to them, and it is nearer to Crow lands. We must be watchful when the warriors ride out to hunt as the women are left undefended." Walking Horse shook his head. "There will be dangerous times ahead, Crow Killer. The thrill of the chase and the kill, but you will be needed to help protect the village, the women and children."

"I will be beside you." Jed nodded. "Have you spoken to White Swan?"

"The old one has seen nothing in the smoke." The warrior looked again toward the village. "Tell me, Crow Killer, where did you get such a knife?"

"It was another gift from Plenty Coups." Jed laughed. "I didn't tell you about it."

"Plenty Coups has lost even more." Walking Horse joined in the laughter. "Maybe, he will come himself with Red Hawk."

"Is he not an old man?"

"Maybe he is old, but do not forget he is one of the greatest Crow warriors. Do not underestimate this old man as you call him, should you meet in battle." The warrior nodded. "I fought him once many years ago when I was young and he was younger."

"What happened?" Jed was curious. "You're both still alive."

"For an old man, he was powerful and quick." Walking Horse looked thoughtful. "I knew as we fought how he got his name."

"Well?"

"I was staked to the ground with my lance. I could not run, nor did I want to. He had me beneath his knife as I looked death in the face."

"Walking Horse for Pete's sake, tell me."

"I do not know myself. He had my arm pinned and the deathblow ready when he stopped, looked me up and down, then just cut the rawhide binding me to my lance."

"How old were you?"

"Maybe seventeen summers."

"Was that the reason, because you were young?"

"I do not know, but I owe him my life."

"You've never seen him again?"

"Yes, many times, but we always turned away from each other. Now, he is an old man."

"You seem sad."

"I am, as a warrior that respects a great warrior from any tribe, more so when they get old and lose their fighting ability. Plenty Coups was one of the greatest of Crow warriors, as Red Hawk is now." Walking Horse seemed to look into the past. "He is one of a kind, and upon his passing, he will be missed."

"I have known men like that, from years ago."

"Tomorrow, I take Bow Legs and many others to hunt for the shaggies." Walking Horse looked toward his lodge. "I ask you to watch out for Little Antelope and the village."

"Am I not to go?"

"No, I need a warrior here I can trust to stay alert for trouble."

"You're not babying me again?"

"What does this word mean?"

"Watching out for me."

Walking Horse laughed. "You are a Lance Bearer now, my friend. You do not need babying any longer, if you ever did."

"I will watch."

Walking Horse cleared his throat. "You and Little Antelope have not spoken since the Sun Dance. If something has happened because of the fight, perhaps this will give you a chance to talk it out."

"We disagreed over her brother is all?"

"But, I thought, you and Yellow Horse departed friends?"

"We did." Jed smiled. "Your wife is a very stubborn lady."

"All Cheyenne women seem to change after they marry."

"I will speak with her."

"Good." Walking Horse nodded. "We should be gone eight sleeps, if we are lucky."

Dismounting tiredly after a full day of riding the perimeter of the village, Jed watched as Little Antelope carried a cooking pot to his lodge. Turning his worn out horse loose and slapping him on the rump, he greeted the small woman as she passed.

"Walking Horse has not returned?"

"No, my husband has not returned yet." She passed through the lodge opening without looking at him. "Come, I have brought you food to eat."

Sitting down across from Little Antelope, Jed took the plate of meat she offered. "Thank you, little one."

"You must be hungry." Little Antelope casually touched his fingers as she passed him the plate. "You have ridden far and you have lost weight the last few days."

Jed bit into the meat. "I gave Walking Horse, your husband, my word I would make sure no enemy nears the village while he rides with his warriors farther out onto the grasslands, searching for the shaggies."

"My husband has been gone many days to the north to look for buffalo." Her smoky eyes questioned him with worry. "When will he return?"

Jed was worried as Walking Horse had been gone too long. "Perhaps, tomorrow."

"Do not lie to me, Jed." She grabbed his hand. "I can see fear in your eyes."

"Slow Wolf and White Swan also worry about Walking Horse and his warriors being gone so long. They fear the enemy might raid our village if they find out most of the warriors are out looking for the shaggies." Jed looked across at her. "The great herds have to be found, little one, we must have meat. I am sorry; I do not know how long he will be gone."

"I believe you, and I am proud of you." Little Antelope smiled. "You have become a warrior and leader of our people in such a short time."

"Tell me, did all this happen because I defeated Crazy Cat?"

"No, you are not like others. You are truly a good man." Little Antelope looked at him. "I am sorry we quarreled over my brother and that silly contest."

Jed smiled. "I am sorry also, but Crazy Cat fought me like a crazy man wanting to do me harm. Why?"

"Many years ago when I was young, Crazy Cat was a suitor as were many others." She dropped her eyes. "Yellow Dog wanted you defeated only in wrestling to shame you. He did not want you hurt. Crazy Cat grew furious when my brother told him I liked you."

"So it was jealousy that got him riled up?" Jed nodded, then smiled over at her. "Well, I can't say I blame him for being jealous."

"I am a married woman, and both of you know that." The little woman pouted. "Married."

"Yes, we know, but you are also a very beautiful woman and my closest friend." Jed shook his head. "We are only human, you know."

"You should not be interested in a married woman. We are only friends and I am proud of you because you are my friend." She looked directly into his eyes. "We both know this is all there can be between us. Someday, you will be a great leader of the Arapaho. Now, you must forget anything else."

"I fear Walking Horse knows how I feel about you." Jed blushed, as he has never spoken so openly to Little Antelope, or any woman before. "I hope not."

She looked down. "Perhaps, but he too is a great leader. He knows you are an honorable man, a friend he can trust and respect."

"And I respect him." Jed nodded. "I would never do anything to dishonor him or you."

"If Walking Horse rode to the north in search of the shaggies, he would not return for many days." Little Antelope looked into Jed's eyes changing the subject. "Perhaps, he has not located them yet, and that is why he stays away so long."

"He has been gone many days now." Jed looked at her beautiful face. "Like you, I doubt he will return until he finds them."

"Then you should be rested when he returns." She smiled. "Providing you do not let the young women of the village catch you."

"I have no time for such foolishness." Jed shook his head and looked away. "I will rest tonight and tomorrow ride to the west."

"I think you should stay. You need rest." Little Antelope stood to leave, looking down at him. "I suppose you will do as you will. I will have food prepared for you in the morning."

"Thank you, little one." Jed studied the beautiful face, as he wanted to say more. "You are a good friend."

"Yes." Little Antelope dropped her eyes dejectedly and turned to the lodge opening. "A good friend. Come to my lodge before you leave, everything you want will be ready."

For many days, while Walking Horse was away, Jed and Big Owl rode the flat plains and smaller valleys where the Arapaho people had set up their village. They were ever on the alert for lurking enemies and watching for the return of Walking Horse and his warriors. Finally, as the sun started to dip and finding nothing, they turned their horses back toward the village. Almost at dark, nearing the heavy timber where the lodges stood hidden under the heavy foliage, they noticed several warriors gathered in front of Slow Wolf's lodge. Excitement and loud questions ushered from the warriors as the two reined in their horses and dismounted.

Big Owl rushed forward into the excited group. "What is wrong? What has happened?"

A warrior called Crooked Mouth looked shamefaced down at the ground. "We have told our chief, we found the shaggies, but the Crow found us and there were too many of them to fight."

"What else?" Big Owl studied the downcast faces. "What else?"

"Walking Horse is dead."

"What?" Jed pushed forward. "Dead? How? What happened?"

"We were seeking out the great herd when the Crow charged out of a hidden ravine and rode right at us." The warrior's eyes wouldn't meet Jed's.

All eyes were focused on the warrior. There was more; something he didn't want to speak of. "Go on, what happened?"

"Walking Horse yelled out the name, Red Hawk! We all rode away from the charging Crows as fast as our ponies could run."

"And Walking Horse, what happened to him?"

"We thought he was with us, but when we stopped to ford the Yellowstone, he was missing." Crooked Mouth's shoulders slumped, as he stared sadly at the ground. "He was not with us at the crossing."

Slow Wolf stepped closer to the warriors. "You ran away and left your leader behind to fight the Crow alone?"

"We did not know he stayed behind until we had ridden many miles, but then it was too late to return." Another warrior spoke up. "There were too many Crow warriors to fight."

"There is never too many." The chief shook his head in disgust. "Did you go back to look for him?"

"No, my Chief, we came here to tell you of Walking Horse and the Crows." The warrior, Elk Runner, spoke up. "Bow Legs waits and watches back at the river. He thinks the Crow may be on their way here to attack the village."

"My Chief." Jed looked over at Slow Wolf. "I will go find Bow Legs, then we will look for Walking Horse. Keep the rest here to move the village closer to where the shaggies are."

"Perhaps, Crow Killer is right. We must have winter meat, robes for the cold times, and our enemies are everywhere." Slow Wolf nodded. "Big Owl will ride with you. Send him back with a warning if you see the Crow. One set of eyes is as good as many. Ride with speed, my son."

Instructing Big Owl to catch the black horse, Jed hurried to find Little Antelope who wasn't in sight. With all the excitement and wailing in the village, he didn't know how, but apparently she didn't hear the news of Walking Horse yet. The warriors riding with Walking Horse had arrived at the village, ahead of them, and with the village strung out in the heavy timber, perhaps she wasn't aware of the clamor going on. Walking Horse's lodge was on the outside perimeter of the village as most of the Lance Bearers were, protecting the people from enemy raiders. His mind raced as he hurried to Walking Horse's lodge, but what would he say to her? If her husband was dead, he had no way of knowing, but likely he was from what the warriors reported about him.

Kneeling over her lodge fire, Little Antelope was absorbed in her work and didn't see him as he walked up. Studying the small back that sat hunched over the hot cooking fire, he hesitated, not knowing how to break the news. What would he say? A dry twig cracked under his foot, betraying his presence, causing her to turn where he stood, grim faced, looking down at her. Standing slowly, she looked into his drawn face and dropped the small gourd she was using to grind wild berries and seed.

"What is wrong, Crow Killer? What has happened?" She used his Arapaho name, something she had never done before. "Is it my husband, Walking Horse, what?"

Jed shook his head sadly. "Walking Horse did not return with his warriors."

"Tell me, what has happened?" She stepped closer to him with a scared look on her face. "Tell me, where is my husband?"

"I'm sorry; no one knows for sure what happened." Jed tried to avoid her eyes. "The warriors said they thought he stayed behind to fight the Crows that surprised them while they hunted for the shaggies."

"Walking Horse is dead?"

"The warriors did not know. I go now to find Bow Legs. He waits behind where Walking Horse was last seen. I will find your husband, do not worry."

"If he still lives, you must find him." Little Antelope sadly stared up at him, tears running down her small face. "Promise me."

"I promise you this; I will do my best. We go now." Jed hugged her in his arms, trying to console the distraught woman, then turned toward his lodge. "I must get more arrows and my war axe."

"I will have food ready when you return." Her small shoulders were straight as she tried her best to compose herself and show courage as she disappeared inside her lodge. "You will find him, Jed. I know."

Big Owl sat his horse and held Jed's horse as she brought out the bag of jerked meat she had prepared for their journey. Nodding, Jed swung onto the black horse's smooth back and reached for the bag. Feeling the touch of her hand on his leg, he looked down at the sad face and nodded.

"If it is possible, I will bring Walking Horse back to you." Jed touched her face. "I promise."

"Thank you, Jed." This was the first time she called him by his white name with someone listening since being renamed Crow Killer. "You will find Bow Legs also. Bring them both back to their people safe."

Their horses were tired, as two days of hard riding with little rest brought them to the mighty Yellowstone. Big Owl had hunted these lands many times so he knew the grasslands where the great herds of buffalo migrated. Here, the buffalo found the rich and abundant grasses that fattened and filled them out for the hard times ahead. He listened to the warriors who were with Walking Horse as they described to him exactly where they were attacked by the Crow, and where they should look for Walking Horse's body. Somewhere to the north, Bow Legs would be waiting. He would find them, hopefully before the Crow reappeared. Big Owl knew this land was very dangerous for two warriors riding alone, but Slow Wolf could not send more warriors. The people were Slow Wolf's responsibility and he could not endanger the village. The meat gathering time was so vital for the tribe to survive the harsh winters that engulfed the lands of the Arapaho during the months ahead. Starvation was a worse death than the Crow, and even for Walking Horse, his nephew, he could not send more.

Big Owl made sure he and Jed were well mounted, with the black and a red roan from Slow Wolf's horses. They rode the best horses in the Arapaho Village, but the horses had traveled far with little rest in their mad rush to the Yellowstone. If discovered, he doubted they would be able to outrun any pursuit by the enemy. The hunting grounds where Walking Horse had been attacked and where the huge herds grazed was only three days hard ride from where the village was set up in the timbered valley. Slow Wolf was reluctant to move the village closer to the herds, until the buffalo was located, because of the troubles with the Crow. Big Owl knew somewhere close ahead, near the river, Bow Legs would be watching for them and come to them if he still lived.

Tired from the long ride to the north, Jed and Big Owl made camp on the banks of a small stream at sundown. They tethered their horses to graze while they pulled their own food from the meat Little Antelope had prepared. Lying back against tree trunks, the two young men ate hungrily as they watched the small ripples passing in the stream's water.

"Do the mighty Arapaho warriors have any extra meat for a skinny wanderer?" Bow Legs laughed as he led his horse from the tree line.

Startled, Big Owl leaped to his feet, grabbing for his weapons. "Bow Legs, you scared me out of my moccasins."

"You should be scared, lazy one, letting one warrior sneak up on you in the shadows while you sleep."

Laughing, all three men hugged and greeted one another. "Have you found Walking Horse?"

"No, the Crows still search for him when they are not hunting the shaggies. I could not search for him as I would like." Bow Legs accepted the meat. "But, I found you."

Jed looked at the thin warrior. "How many?"

"There are only two of you."

"Crows." Jed was slightly frustrated at Bow Legs joking.

"Oh, you mean Crows, many, my brother, too many for three to fight." Bow Legs shrugged. "I think Plenty Coups grows tired of them hunting Walking Horse and not hunting the shaggies."

"What will we do?"

Bow Legs looked across at Big Owl. "If we were smart, we would return to our village, but we are not smart, I bet."

"Without Walking Horse?" Big Owl questioned. "Leave him behind?"

"If he is still alive, he will return to us."

Jed shook his head. "No, I was never smart."

"What does Crow Killer wish to do?" Big Owl asked as he handed Bow Legs the bag of jerky.

"In the morning, you and Bow Legs head for the village and report what you have seen to Slow Wolf."

"And you?"

"I will stay and look for Walking Horse, or his body." Jed thought of Little Antelope. "I cannot go back to the village without knowing what has happened to him."

Bow Legs nodded. "Then I will stay, as it only takes one to bring bad news. Big Owl will return to the village and tell what is to be told."

At sunup, Big Owl swung up on the roan, turning the horse back to the south as Jed and Bow Legs kicked their horses across the cold stream and headed north. Several hours they rode toward the vast flatlands where the buffalo traditionally grazed and several different tribes hunted each year. The great herds were immense and the land they grazed was huge, so the tribes could stay far from one another with little to no trouble. The sun was high overhead when Bow Legs finally reined in and motioned with his chin toward a small ravine ahead. Both men were on full alert, watching for any enemy as they moved further north, closer to the ravine. The same place Crooked Mouth had described when he told how the Crow had ridden out and surprised their small party of hunters.

Nearing the cold times, all tribes should be busy hunting buffalo so their women could dry the meat they depended on for the harsh winter ahead. Jed could not understand the Crow as most tribes held an unspoken truce not to attack their enemies until the great hunts were over. Buffalo meat, hides, and bones were essential for the tribes to survive these hard times, and it was not a time for warriors to ride to war. There was plenty of time to raid and fight during the warmer months. Jed also remembered Walking Horse's words of warning that Red Hawk was no ordinary warrior; he did not take orders even from his chief, a loner most of the time, but highly respected so much that others would follow him wherever he led.

"This is the place where we saw Walking Horse last." Bow Legs pointed to the ravine. "We must be very watchful, ready to ride from this place fast."

"I've come for Walking Horse, or his body." Jed shook his head. "I will not be running."

"Sometimes, my friend, the rabbit wins out over the coyote and does not lose face or his life." Bow Legs looked across at Jed.

Slipping from their horses, they walked slowly forward, alert for any movement from the ravine. Looking down into the wide gully, they could see the many tracks that cut the soft sandy bottom below. The ground was cut up by horse sign across the canyon floor, but the body of Walking Horse was not seen among them. Jed and Bow Legs studied the gorge as their sharp eyes scanned the area slowly, taking in everything in their view. Nothing but horse tracks were seen. Jed could clearly see how Walking Horse and his warriors were surprised by the Crow warriors as the site was the perfect place for a trap. An enemy hiding below could not be seen until they were right on their quarry as they exited the deep ravine.

Bow Legs closely studied the ground and the mixed tracks. "You see it is as Crooked Mouth told Slow Wolf, there were many enemies here waiting to attack."

"Yes, there were many." Jed nodded as he scanned the landscape. "No matter, we must find out what happened to Walking Horse."

"Walking Horse is no fool. He would not have fought against such odds, nor would he have put his warriors in danger trying to help him." Bow Legs walked back and forth. "There must be more. Why did he stay behind when we retreated? Maybe his horse was wounded or maybe he stepped in a hole and fell."

Sending Bow Legs off to the left of the ravine, Jed took the right, along the edge of the deep gorge. He warily led the black gelding behind him as he explored the rough ground with its wind eroded gulches. Two hours passed, Jed would not give up as he crossed and recrossed the sandy ground, looking for a clue. Finally, even Jed had to admit, they were beaten as darkness closed in, making them come together to settle in for the night. To wander around in this rough terrain in the dark could be disastrous. They didn't need to break a horse's leg or have a bad fall in this far land with the Crow warriors lurking all around.

No fire was lit as each man sat wrapped in a light robe as they chewed softly on the dried meat Little Antelope had prepared. Not a word was spoken as both men kept their thoughts to themselves, only the occasional stomping or movement of the horses was heard in the darkness. The night was pitch black; no moon showed in the night sky to light the dark, only bright stars showed overhead. Jed chewed slowly on the stringy meat, letting it sit in his mouth to soften before he tried to swallow. His troubled mind went over the day. What did they miss? If Walking Horse was taken captive, wouldn't there be signs of a struggle or something? He shook his head, what were they missing? If he had been killed, where was his body?

Off in the dark, one of the horses snorted slightly and stamped a front hoof. Both men stiffened as something startled the horse. Something was out there and has his attention. Both horses were well broke animals, almost like dogs maybe better when it came to smelling or seeing an enemy in the dark.

"What is it?" Jed whispered as he moved closer to Bow Legs.

The soft wind of the night shifted from the south blowing a slight breeze across them. "He smells something."

"What?"

"Death is on the wind, that, my friend, is what he smells."

"Death?" Jed could see or smell nothing. "Do you smell anything?"

"I too smell death."

"I can't smell anything at all."

Bow Legs nodded and grinned in the dark. He did not want to hurt Jed's feelings by telling him he was still mostly white and hasn't learned to use all his senses as his wilder brothers, the Arapaho. "The horse does not lie as death is on the wind, Crow Killer. When the light comes, we will find out what makes it."

"What is it, do you know?"

"Maybe I know. Now sleep, you will find your answer tomorrow."

Jed looked over at the place where the voice came from the dark. He knew he could trust the senses of Bow Legs, and whatever was dead couldn't hurt them now. Gathering his light robe, he rolled up in it, and fell asleep.

The welcoming, warming rays of the sun peeked slowly from the east, shining on the light frost that lay like crystals across their bodies. The two warriors stood up slowly and shook the ice from their robes. Jed chewed on a piece of meat as he followed Bow Legs and his horse to a small seep hole down in the ravine. Watering the horses, the men mounted and turned back to the rim. Both were watchful and alert as they topped out of the gorge and passed alongside their night camp. Bow Legs warily led Jed slowly down an old deep beat-out trail made by the many roaming herds of buffalo that had passed this way for centuries.

Both horses were excited as the smell of death became stronger on the wind. Bow Legs reined in abruptly and pointed. "There."

The stench came from a small mound of loose dirt ahead on the ground. Beneath the sand, a dead horse lay partly concealed in a shallow, washed-out ditch. Someone had scratched sand over most of the body to help conceal it, leaving only a small part of the body uncovered. The body of the dead horse was uncovered just enough to let the smell of death infiltrate the night air and drift on the wind. With their sensitive noses, it was what the horses scented during the night, causing them to be fretful. Dismounting back away from the smell, Jed held the horses while Bow Legs walked forward and studied the body and surrounding ground.

"It is the horse of Walking Horse. His throat has been slashed." The slender warrior announced after fully investigating the area.

"Why?'

"There is also blood on the horse's withers, but it is too high for it to be from the horse." Bow Legs looked around. "I think the blood is from Walking Horse."

"What do you think happened to him?"

"Wounded perhaps, I don't know." Bow Legs shrugged. "The signs show that Walking Horse killed the horse, then pushed him into the ditch as he fell, trying to hide the animal from the Crows so he could escape."

"Then he is alive?"

"Perhaps." Bow Legs shrugged. "The wind blew some sand from the dead animal uncovering it. I do not think the Crow ever found it."

"If he is wounded, how did he escape being killed back in the arroyo?"

Bow Legs knelt and picked up a handful of dirt. "I think he was wounded in the battle and fell from the horse. The Crow, thinking him dead, chased after the others. While they were away, Walking Horse managed to get up and ride the horse to this place and kill him."

Jed nodded. "That makes sense; he killed the horse, buried him in the gully, and crawled away."

"There is no sign of a fight here. With all the blood, I think if Walking Horse lives, he is hurt bad, if so he must be close."

Jed mounted his horse. "We will split up and search. Dead or alive, we will find him."

"Be careful Crow Killer, the enemy might be close." Bow Legs warned. "And Walking Horse may be out of his mind with pain, so go slow."

Late in the afternoon, Bow Legs finally picked up their first lead. Drag tracks of a crawling man were found on the sandy ground. Motioning Jed to follow him, Bow Legs led his horse through the rough country which was the beginning of the grasslands. If it was the tracks of Walking Horse, in his delirium, he had drug himself in the wrong direction, straight for the land of the Crows. While Jed watched and guarded their back trail, the Arapaho cautiously followed the trail of the wounded man. He knew Bow Legs was right, if Walking Horse was still alive, but badly wounded, he could be as dangerous as the Crow, if he didn't recognize the ones following him. Large boulders stacked along the ravine were the final outlying obstacle before the easier flat grasslands of the buffalo country.

Dropping the reins of his horse, Bow Legs raised his hand for Jed to leave his horse. Quietly, they slipped forward, their eyes alert for any enemy or whoever had made the tracks into the boulders. Twenty feet ahead as both men slipped around the largest boulder, they came face-to-face with a familiar figure leaning, bloody, and tattered with his back against a huge rock. Recognizing the familiar faces, he slumped forward, falling onto the ground.

"Walking Horse." Both men raced forward to help the wounded man.

"Bring water from my horse, Crow Killer." Bow Legs slowly turned the warrior and studied his wounds. "Quickly."

The water seemed to revive the wounded Walking Horse enough to let him speak weakly. Bow Legs pointed out two wounds on the man; an arrow in his side and another arrow in his left leg.

"How bad is it?'

"They are bad." Bow Legs frowned with concern. "If we can get him back to the village, White Swan may save him."

"He can't ride a horse. We need a travois to move him on."

"A travois will be dangerous. We will leave tracks and the going will be slow." Bow Legs was worried. "But, if he is to live, it is all we can do."

"You can leave me here to die in peace." Walking Horse stirred and opened his eyes. "That would be good."

"You haven't died yet, my friend. You won't die if we can help it." Jed smiled down at the wounded man. "Remember, you are Arapaho, a very strong people."

"I do not feel very strong right now."

"You were strong enough to bury that horse and crawl here, my

Chief." Bow Legs looked down at the warrior. "You are strong enough to live."

"I am not a chief."

"One day, you will be." Bow Legs stepped back. "Only a chief can do as you have done today."

Several times in the next three days, enemy warriors had been sighted as the travois bumped and lurched across the rough trail as they journeyed back to the Arapaho Village. Both Jed and Bow Legs took turns scouting the trail ahead, knowing warriors were out looking for the wounded Walking Horse, not the buffalo.

CHAPTER 7

After chasing the fleeing Arapaho warriors, Red Hawk was livid with rage as the Crow returned to the ravine where they had killed one Arapaho, only to find his body gone. For two days, they had searched the ravines and gullies looking for the warrior, but not a sign of him or his horse had been found. Red Hawk shook his head in disgust as a runner from Plenty Coups found them, relaying their chief's orders for them to return to the village. The snows were almost upon them and now was the time to hunt. Red Hawk knew his father was right, the winter hunt was far more important than one lone Arapaho.

Arriving back at the hunting grounds of the big shaggies, the Crow warriors mounted their best buffalo runners and left the village to start the hunt. During the following days, as they waited for the squaws to skin and quarter the buffalo, Red Hawk led his warriors back to the ravine in search of the wounded one. He had seen the warrior fall in the first charge as the Arapaho tried to block the Crow's charge to save his warriors. Red Hawk knew if the warrior still lived, he was badly wounded. He had seen the blood on the body that lay in the ravine, and he had to be hiding somewhere in the sand dunes. Red Hawk wanted this warrior, as the scalp of this Arapaho Lance Bearer would hold much honor for the warrior that carried it. He had seen with his own eyes, this Arapaho was a brave warrior; a great warrior.

Jed kept busy trying to brush out any signs of the travois passing, riding a circuit around the drag, and watching for Crows or any danger.

The Arapaho Village was near but Jed knew the closer they got, the greater chance they would have of running into enemy warriors prowling the hills, looking for the wounded Walking Horse. The warrior had lost a lot of blood and had become very weak. The bumpy ride on the travois was rough on him. Awake now, after coming this far, he was determined to reach the village and see Little Antelope. Bow Legs managed to stop the bleeding but they had to reach the village soon. White Swan's medicine and herbs were needed to keep the evil ones out of Walking Horse's wounds.

From high on a rim, Jed looked down and discovered several Crow warriors making their way along the small trail they had just come up. Jed counted six riders as he turned and hurried to catch up to the travois further down in the next valley. Whipping his tired horse hard, Jed raced across the valley to find Bow Legs stopped on the banks of a stream, watering his horse. Crossing the water in a hard run, Jed charged up beside Bow Legs and reined his horse in.

"Crows!" Jed pointed back over his shoulder.

"What will we do?"

"Go quickly, Bow Legs. Get Walking Horse away." Jed slid from the black horse. "My brother, Walking Horse, will have to ride. The travois is too slow and it cannot escape the fast horses of the Crow."

"And what will Crow Killer ride?"

Jed looked down at the travois. "Hurry Bow Legs, let's get Walking Horse on my horse."

Bow Legs shook his head. "Once before I left a warrior behind, never as long as I draw breath will I dishonor myself again."

Jed looked down at Walking Horse who was listening. "You will save our brother if you get him away quickly. He cannot defend himself. Go, Bow Legs, ride from this place."

Only a low moan came from the wounded warrior as they lifted him bodily onto the back of the black. "Walking Horse, can you ride? Can you sit the horse?"

Nodding, the warrior looked down at Jed. "I will see you soon, my brother."

Jed smiled. "That is the first time you ever called me brother."

"I hope not the last."

"Go now, Bow Legs. Get him away, quickly!"

Leading the black horse with its injured rider, Bow Legs stopped at the edge of the trees and looked back where they left Jed. "Look, Walking Horse, he plants his lance in the ground."

"He gives us time to get away." Walking Horse turned slowly to look. "We must go back."

"But, Walking Horse, you cannot fight."

"No, but I can die a Lance Bearer's death with Crow Killer, it is my right."

Jed pushed the lance deep into the soft ground that ran along the creek bank, then used a rawhide thong to fasten the lance to his ankle. The banks of the crossing where he waited were steep and wide enough to allow only two horses at a time to ford the water. He knew he had counted six Crow warriors from the ridge, far too many to fight. Walking Horse and Bow Legs only chance was for him to slow down the oncoming warriors, long enough for them to escape.

Turning, as the sound of hooves came up behind him, Jed shook his head. "Why? Bow Legs, why have you brought him back?"

"Crow Killer wishes to have all the fun by himself?" Walking Horse straightened on his horse. "But I think your fun may be here."

Turning to where the warrior looked, Jed watched as seven Crow warriors rode into sight, lining up their horses across the trail. "They followed faster than I thought."

"They wish to see you, Crow Killer." Bow Legs laughed. "They are in a hurry to die."

"That must be Red Hawk doing all the gesturing." Jed watched as the far rider whirled his pony and taunted them. "He seems a little agitated."

Walking Horse was weak, barely able to remain on his horse. "It is Red Hawk, the Crow."

The Crow warriors moved in a line toward them with their lone eagle feather blowing in the slight breeze passing through the trees. Jed has never seen such a spectacular and colorful display as these Crows were showing as they approached. The warriors were astride the sleek, long-legged, beautiful buffalo runners, the Crows were known for. With their tails tied up and paint covering every animal, the warriors sitting them straight and proud with every face looking right at them were a sight Jed has never witnessed before. He knew the pride of the Crow Nation, seven warriors dressed for battle, rode slowly toward them; a sight to behold.

"They are magnificent."

"Maybe, but along with their magnificence, they are here to kill you."

Jed grinned. "A man can't live forever, Bow Legs."

"Maybe not, but am I to die on an empty stomach?" Bow Legs rubbed his flat stomach.

Jed shook his head. "Maybe they will let you eat before their squaws eat you."

"They will not eat me, Crow Killer." The thin warrior laughed. "I am much too skinny."

"That's good to hear."

"But you are not." Bow Legs looked Jed up and down. "You, my friend, will make them a tasty meal."

The Crows couldn't understand what the skinny Arapaho was laughing about, maybe he was just crazy and didn't realize he was about to die. The Arapaho were great warriors, but seven against three with one wounded was no match for the Crow. Kicking their horses into a trot, Red Hawk raised his war axe to charge when suddenly, all seven warriors reined in and stopped, their attention fully focused behind where Jed and the others waited.

Turning, as the noise of pounding hooves sounded from behind them, they were all astonished as twenty warriors sprang from a stand of timber and charged toward them. Looking quickly at the warriors, then back at the Crows, Jed raised his war axe ready for the attack.

Whirling in a circle and leaping up and down, Bow Legs let out a shrill scream. "They are ours, Crow Killer. It is Crooked Mouth, Big Owl, and the Arapaho."

Blinking in disbelief, Jed smiled up at the wounded Walking Horse, and helped him from the black horse. "How are you doing?"

"Better, now that our people have come."

Racing up to their three lost warriors and seeing Walking Horse still lived, the Arapaho warriors yelled in delight, each reaching down to touch the wounded man. Several of the warriors whirled their horses and raced after the fleeing Crows.

Crooked Mouth did not follow the others. After greeting Walking Horse, he pulled Jed away, out of earshot, from the wounded man. Waiting several minutes before speaking, he finally composed himself and looked over at Jed.

"You do not seem happy to see Walking Horse." Jed was curious at the warrior's sad face.

"It is not that, Crow Killer. I have bad news for your ears, very bad."

Jed looked over where Bow Legs was talking with Walking Horse. "Tell me, what is wrong?"

"The spotted stallion has been stolen. He is not with the other horses."

"Stolen, how long has he been gone?"

"The horse guards missed him yesterday." Crooked Mouth shook his head. "We have been out searching for him. Slow Wolf sent us to find you and Walking Horse."

"You found no sign of the stallion?"

"No, Crow Killer, but that is not all."

"What else?"

"Little Antelope is missing also." Crooked Mouth looked over to where Walking Horse lay. "We looked everywhere for her. She is gone."

"Little Antelope gone, did you search the village and lodges?" Jed frowned. "Who would take her?"

"She would be a trophy captive." Crooked Mouth shook his head. "She is a very beautiful woman, and she is young and strong."

"I meant, how did they take her?"

"She has been very sad since Walking Horse has been lost. Many times, she walked alone by the river." Crooked Mouth shook his head. "Her tracks were found near the horse herd along the river. Whoever took the spotted one found her there and took her."

"What would she be doing so far away from her lodge, alone?" Jed looked at the warrior. "She knew the danger, even if she was upset."

"Perhaps she just wanted to see the spotted stallion." Crooked Mouth shrugged. "Maybe it made her feel closer to her husband."

"It was not Red Hawk, he was here today." Jed spoke the name. "If he had the horse and Little Antelope, why would he come looking for Walking Horse?"

Crooked Mouth shook his head. "I do not believe it was the Crow that came to the village and took the horse."

"I think like you, but who could it have been?"

"The tracks of many mounted horses and the spotted one lead to the west and farther north, not to Crow lands." Crooked Mouth looked to where Bow Legs and the others were laying Walking Horse on a travois. "Maybe the Nez Perce came here to get their horse back.

"How would the Nez Perce know where to look for the horse?" Jed shook his head. "How could they find one horse in this vast land?"

"The great spotted stallion is not hard to spot in a herd." Crooked Mouth mounted his horse to follow the travois. "They could have sent out runners to every village to spy out the horse herds to find the horse."

"Pull your lance, Crow Killer." Crooked Mouth looked to where the lance stood. "It is not needed now. We will take Walking Horse home."

Pulling his lance from the creek bank, Jed pushed it and the rawhide thong into his arrow quiver, then swung up on the black. "The warriors are returning, they could not catch the swift horses of the Crow."

"Walking Horse needs care badly. We will take him to White Swan." Crooked Mouth looked at the warriors. "We must get him to the village, and prepare for the buffalo hunt."

"No hunters have been sent out yet?"

"Yes, we have killed many. The women already dry meat for the cold times ahead, but we must kill more, many more."

The village was close, since Jed and Big Owl left to search for Walking Horse, Slow Wolf moved the village closer to the hunting range of the buffalo. Turning the black, Jed rode a few feet behind the travois as the column of warriors started for the village.

"What will we do, Crow Killer?"

Jed dropped his arm. "We will ride to the village. Hopefully, Little Antelope has returned."

"Hopefully." The warrior shrugged. "But, I do not think she has."

Jed smiled. "I don't think so either."

The column of warriors, dragging the travois, rode into the village almost at dark. The village immediately became a beehive of activity as news of Walking Horse being alive spread throughout the lodges. Bow

Legs hurried the wounded man to White Swan's lodge, where the old medicine man had them carry him inside. Quickly the old one ushered the warriors out and set to work on the injured warrior. White Swan worked feverishly on Walking Horse. The warrior was conscious, but no one told him of Little Antelope's disappearance, as it would have upset him and weakened him more. Walking Horse couldn't do his wife any good in his condition. White Swan predicted if the evil ones did not attack the warrior, his wounds would heal, but it would be many days before he would grow strong and some time before he could ride.

Being of no use at the medicine lodge, Jed walked over to where Slow Wolf was listening to Bow Legs and Crooked Mouth as they made their report. Every face was grim as the warriors sat around the small fire, discussing what had happened, and how the Crow had fled as they approached.

"If Red Hawk had come into our village after the horse, I believe he would have tried to steal the headdress back from our chief." Bow Legs spoke up. "He is fearless and arrogant, and he would do this no matter how dangerous."

Crooked Mouth shrugged. "I do not think it was Red Hawk or any other Crow, who took the horse and woman."

"Why do you think this?" Slow Wolf asked.

"If he had the horse, he would not have been hunting for Walking Horse, and even the great Red Hawk cannot be in two places at once."

"The Crow country is not far away." Slow Wolf shrugged. "Maybe he got the horse and woman, but still looked for Walking Horse."

"No, my Chief." Crooked Mouth argued. "As me and Crow Killer have already discussed, we believe another tribe took the horse."

"We agree; it was not Red Hawk." Jed nodded. "But who else would come here to steal the stallion?"

"Many tribes are hunting the shaggies now. All know about the horse of Red Hawk, and many would die trying to take him."

"I say it was the Nez Perce of the far northwest." Crooked Mouth was sure the Nez Perce were the guilty ones.

Slow Wolf looked at Crooked Mouth. "A guess, Nephew, are you sure?"

"I am sure, my Chief." The warrior nodded. "I would wager my best buffalo runner on it."

The council with his warriors was finished, and now, Slow Wolf sat cross-legged in front of Jed as the two talked.

"Crooked Mouth does not think Red Hawk or the Crows took the woman." Slow Wolf spoke, looking up as White Swan stepped inside the chief's lodge. "I think he is wrong, I believe it was the Crow."

"I will ride after Little Antelope today." Jed announced.

The old chief nodded slowly. "I cannot forbid you to go, but I cannot send warriors with you, Crow Killer. Tell me, why do you risk your life for a squaw? You did not mention the spotted horse."

"I feel responsible for her being taken and for Walking Horse being hurt. I stole the stallion from Red Hawk." Jed looked into the fire. "I care nothing about the horse."

"Is that all?"

"What else? She is the woman of my friend, Walking Horse, and he cannot ride to help her." Jed spread his hands. "I will go; that is all."

Slow Wolf studied the face of Jed for several moments, then reached behind him for the rolled up headdress. "Take this, it will not replace the stallion but maybe Plenty Coups will trade it for the woman, if the Crow have her."

"Tell me, my Chief, how can I make contact with the Crow and speak with them before they kill me?" Jed looked at the older man. "Remember, I killed one of their warriors."

"I remember." Slow Wolf nodded and produced a white skin from a deer's belly. "If you run into their scouts or if you reach their village, tie this to your bow and raise it in front of you as you enter their village."

"Is it the same as a white man's flag of truce?"

"I know nothing of flags, but remember it does not guarantee your safety if the Crow will not listen." Slow Wolf shrugged. "At least it will get you into the village before you are killed."

"I will ride with you." Crooked Mouth had been sitting behind Jed listening.

"No, my friend." Jed shook his head. "The people will need you here. This job must be done by one man."

"When do you leave?"

"Now, as soon as I resupply."

"I will ride with you for two days to the Yellowstone." Crooked

Mouth spoke, refusing to take no for an answer. "Then, I will return and hunt for the people."

"Good luck, Crow Killer." White Swan looked across at Jed. "I will speak to the spirits to help you."

"Thank you, Grandfather."

The cold waters of the Yellowstone drifted slowly before them as Jed and Crooked Mouth sat their horses on the gravel bank. No enemy warriors were sighted as they made their way from the village. Jed was surprised, as many had been spotted on the same trail only days before when they had brought the wounded Walking Horse home. Before departing the village, Jed had spoken briefly with the wounded warrior of the spotted stallion, not mentioning Little Antelope's abduction or his plans to look for her. Walking Horse had been told she was out with the women skinning buffalo, and since he was still delirious, there was no need for him to know more.

"Good-bye, Crow Killer, and good luck." Crooked Mouth reached out his hand.

"Ride careful going back, my friend." Jed took the extended hand.

The cool waters of the great river felt soothing to Jed's feet and legs as the water deepened around the horse. He removed his moccasins and slid from the black as they entered the river. Riding out onto the far bank, he turned the black horse and waved back at Crooked Mouth who was waiting and watching him cross. In days past, Jed had ridden to the Crow Village with Walking Horse, here to the north with Bow Legs, and now further into these lands alone. Strangely, he felt at ease, almost invincible as he swayed in rhythm with the slow walking of the powerful horse beneath him. His bare legs could feel the warm, smooth hide of the animal as he gripped the horse's sides. For two days, he moved slowly through the flatlands, staying alert to everything and anything that moved around him. He was cautious, not greatly worried as he had great faith in the black's speed. If discovered, he felt he could outrun the best horses of his enemies.

Sundown of the third day found Jed hidden in a deep stand of mountain spruce, overlooking the Crow Village of Plenty Coups and Red Hawk. Several times, he watched from concealment as Crow warriors passed him, unaware they were being watched. He sat patiently throughout the next day, his eyes focused on the activities going on below in the large village. Their huge horse herd grazed all around the village under the watchful eyes of younger boys. Jed was astounded as he lost count, but he knew there must be several hundred horses roaming the vast grassland surrounding the village. Yes, the Crow people were rich in horses, great horsemen, and their herds contained some of the best animals of all the tribes. He was also amazed at the packs of mongrel dogs roaming the village, almost a dog for every person.

Moving back to where the black horse was grazing, Jed unrolled his warm robe and pulled out a piece of jerked meat. His strong teeth bit into the tough meat absently as he studied on the idea of what his next move should be. Little Antelope might not even be in the village, and if she was, where would she be? The village was huge. He could see the movement of bodies around the glowing cook fires as the villagers prepared to retire for the night, but he was too far away to discern individuals. Where should he start and where should he look for the woman? Troubling too was that he hasn't seen the spotted stallion anywhere in the village or horse herds.

Rising and rolling his robe up as the night darkened, he removed the hobbles from the black and swung up on the animal. Considering his options, Jed finally decided on what he should do. Nudging the horse, he moved toward the horse herds. Somewhere below, he would find one of the young herd guards, then maybe he would find out what he needed to know. Slipping from the black, he tied him securely, and then on foot he started forward, searching out one of the night herders guarding the herd. Finally, he came upon his quarry, and it was as he figured, the guard was young and inexperienced. Jed found him fast asleep, sitting atop his horse, unaware an enemy was anywhere near as he reached up and jerked the guard bodily to the ground.

Surprisingly, despite his youth, the boy did not cower or yell out, as he boldly struggled back against the powerful hands that gripped him. The youth fought hard trying to break free, but was no match for the stronger hands that held him fast. Finally, feeling a knife touch his throat, the youngster ceased to resist. Now, he was scared and knew his life was about to end. His fate was now in the hands of the warrior that knelt above him, blanketed in the darkness of night. The young guard did not whimper a word as the rising moon showed the dim face that threatened him.

"Do you understand my words, young one?" Jed pulled back the knife. "Speak."

"I understand some of what you say."

"I come here for a squaw, an Arapaho woman, very young." Jed could barely make out the face of the youngster lying beneath him. "Is she in your village?"

"I have seen no such captive in our village."

"Do not lie to me, if you do, I will leave you here for the coyotes."

"I do not lie. I have seen no such woman."

"Red Hawk, where is his lodge?"

Silence came from the young guard. He was not yet a warrior, but he was no coward and would not betray the great warrior Red Hawk. "This I will not say."

"You will tell me or die." The knife brought a small trickle of blood. "I will only ask you once more."

"Why should I tell you anything?" The guard's face was deep red from the tight hold Jed had on his throat. "I am dead already."

"Speak and I will let you live."

"I will tell you this only; Red Hawk left our village yesterday riding to the northwest."

"Why would he do that?" Jed pulled back the sharp knife.

The young guard raised slightly on his elbow. "Our scouts came in and reported seeing warriors of the Nez Perce leading his spotted stallion to the west."

"And the woman?"

"They said nothing of a woman." The boy felt of his throat. "We Crows have many pretty women."

"How many went with him?"

"He rode alone. Plenty Coups refused to send warriors with him as he needs them for the great hunt." The youngster studied the knife. "The stallion is valuable, but our chief thinks of his people first. I speak the truth."

Jed studied the dark face of the young horse guard and didn't believe the boy to be lying. If the horse had been sighted by Crow scouts, then

Little Antelope must be with the same warriors, unless she was already dead. If the warriors were Nez Perce, they would be traveling further west and north, to their country. No, the youngster wasn't lying, he was too scared. Flipping the guard on his stomach, Jed pulled his arms behind him and lashed them tightly with rawhide strips.

"You are going to kill me?"

"No, take this bundle to Chief Plenty Coups." Jed produced the bundle with the headdress Slow Wolf had given him. "Tell your chief that Crow Killer sends it back to him. Tell him I follow Red Hawk, but not to kill him. I only want the woman back, nothing else."

"What else do you wish me to tell Plenty Coups?"

"Tell him not to send warriors after me, if he does they will not return to your village."

"How do I do all of this if you tie me up?"

"You are lucky, young one, I do not cut your throat." Jed touched the knife to the youngster's throat again. "Maybe I will, you deserve to die for sleeping on watch."

"I believe you." The youngster swallowed hard. "I will tell my chief what you say, when I get loose."

"You do that."

"You are Crow Killer?"

"That is what I am called."

"Thank you, Crow Killer." The youngster nodded in the dark. "My people have heard of you."

"For what?"

"My life, and you taught me a good lesson."

Jed was curious. "What?"

"Never to sleep on guard." The youngster felt of his throat again. "A good lesson and one I will never forget."

The black horse was tiring, strong as he was; the mountain ranges to the west were looming taller and taller, and the trails rockier with much more difficult places to climb. Slipping to the ground, Jed led the horse on foot, letting the animal rest. His sharp eyes took in the horse tracks along the narrow trail that led up and over the mountain. Several riders had passed this way in the last couple days. Jed couldn't tell if Red Hawk was following them as the tracks were mixed up and he had no way of knowing one horse track from another. Whoever made the tracks had taken the most difficult path, straight to the west and north, over the most difficult passes to throw off anyone following. Jed knew little of the tribes, but Crooked Mouth had said it could be the Nez Perce tribe that had taken Little Antelope and the spotted stallion, and the Crow youth had said the same. Jed knew the Nez Perce lived to the far west and north and even Lige Hatcher had spoken of them at times. Now, he was heading west, maybe Crooked Mouth was right.

With the coming of dark, after three days on the trail, Jed found himself standing on a lower slope at the edge of a stream that flowed swiftly through jagged rocks and down small waterfalls. Maybe he was just thirsty from the long trail, but the pure clean water was better than any water he has ever tasted. It was crystal clear coming down from the tall mountains and ice cold from passing through the frozen underground higher places. Watering the black, Jed hobbled him in a small pocket of bunch grass that grew alongside the stream, then tossed his robe on the ground. After several long days, he was dead tired and couldn't help himself as his head hardly touched the ground before falling fast asleep.

A snort from the black brought Jed abruptly awake, springing straight up with his eyes wide open. Across from him, not ten feet distance, sat a warrior with his legs crossed, and Jed recognized him right off as Crow. He knew this red-shirt warrior was Red Hawk; the warrior he had heard so much about, the one Walking Horse had spoken of so often.

"You are foolish, Arapaho, to sleep here in the open in a strange land among enemies." The warrior was everything Walking Horse had described. Not as tall as Jed, but heavily muscled, straight and strong as a tall oak. Jed studied the war axe resting lightly across the warrior's lap.

"I was tired and needed rest." Jed nodded, studying the smooth face of the warrior. "You are Red Hawk. You could have killed me while I slept."

"I can kill you now."

"Perhaps, but it will not be as easy, now that I am awake."

Red Hawk studied the feathered lance lying beside Jed. "I see you are a Lance Bearer of the village of Slow Wolf."

"Yes, I am from Slow Wolf's village."

"I saw you one time with Walking Horse when the spotted stallion was stolen from my people." The warrior studied Jed. "We almost ran you down."

"Walking Horse said you would recognize us." Jed nodded. "And you are right, you almost ran us down."

"The eyes of a Crow warrior are like the hawk's, sharp."

"As the Arapaho's are."

"Tell me your name and how you knew to follow me to these mountains before I kill you, Arapaho." Red Hawk stood up with the war axe clenched tightly in his hand.

"Four days ago, I returned the eagle bonnet to Plenty Coups. A young horse guard, I captured, told me you had ridden this way after your warriors spoke of seeing the stallion being led off to the northwest." Jed rose to his full height. "My name is Crow Killer."

"You have killed my people." Red Hawk nodded. "I have heard of you."

"One, in the lower valley."

"He was a young warrior, too young to die."

"It was his choice. Walking Horse told him to leave Arapaho lands." Jed shrugged. "He chose to fight that day. He challenged me."

"His name was Wild Wind; he was proud." Red Hawk nodded. "Perhaps, too proud for his years."

"As Red Hawk is proud, and now Red Hawk chooses to fight instead of riding away." Jed picked up his war axe. "Now, one of us will die because of pride."

"You are not afraid, Lance Bearer?" Red Hawk looked curiously at Jed. "Do you have pride, Crow Killer?"

"I reckon I have pride." Jed laughed lightly. "But, a great warrior told me once never to fear just one Crow."

"I think we wounded this warrior many days ago." Red Hawk guessed who Jed spoke of. "We searched for him but could not find him. Is he dead?"

"No, Walking Horse lives."

Red Hawk was curious. "Why do you come to this place? Is the spotted stallion so important to you?"

"It is not the horse I come for."

"What then, me?" Red Hawk waited ready. "Because I attacked your friend?"

"These warriors who took the stallion also took one of our women." Jed gripped the axe hard. "I have come for her and I will kill the ones who dared take her."

Red Hawk could feel the rage in Jed's voice as he spoke. "She is your woman?"

"No." Jed shook his head. "She is the wife of Walking Horse. He was gravely hurt by your hand, Red Hawk. He could not come."

"Your face says different, Crow Killer." Red Hawk smiled sadly. "You have feelings for this woman."

"Little Antelope is the wife of Walking Horse, sister to Yellow Dog the Cheyenne, and my friend." Jed shrugged. "That is my feelings."

"I know of Yellow Dog. He is as Walking Horse, a brave enemy." Red Hawk studied the dark face before him. "I fear if the woman dies many of my tribe will pay in blood by their hands."

"That is why I am here, Red Hawk." Jed looked across at the warrior. "So, she will not die."

"I know nothing of the woman. I come after the spotted stallion." Red Hawk braced himself. "Tell me, Lance Bearer, did you kill the young horse guard who told you where to find me?"

"No, he carries the headdress and a message to Plenty Coups for me."

Red Hawk hesitated as he felt the one before him spoke the truth, but he was still an enemy from the Arapaho Nation. "We are enemies, Arapaho. Perhaps we could become allies until my horse and your woman is recovered."

Jed was surprised, as this was surely not the great bloodthirsty warrior of the Crow that Walking Horse had spoken of being so cruel. "You would do this for an Arapaho woman?"

"We will be two against many, and I want the stallion back." Red Hawk stepped forward offering his war axe to Jed who in return gave the Crow his own, a sign of giving their word. "When they are rescued, we will fight each other or go our own ways, and we will no longer be allies; do you agree?"

Jed touched the axe. "I agree, until it is finished, we will fight together."

"You are very young to be a Lance Bearer, the greatest fighters of the Arapaho."

"I can fight, do not worry." Jed frowned. "And, I'm not that young."

"I know this, if you couldn't fight, you wouldn't have the lance you carry." Red Hawk nodded. "We are outnumbered in this strange land. We are here to recover the horse and squaw anyway we can. We leave our honor, glory, and coup counting behind, and get them."

"I agree."

The two warriors were of different tribes, and rode together for three days, following the trail of the Nez Perce doggedly. In spite of himself, Jed had come to like and trust the Crow warrior, Red Hawk. The warrior almost mirrored Walking Horse in mannerisms and bearing as he clung to the trail of the Nez Perce like a wolf after game. Red Hawk was from an enemy tribe but still Jed trusted the warrior as he would Walking Horse. One day, they might fight each other in battle. Today they became close, not so much as old friends, but as comrades who were compelled to depend on each other.

Jed stiffened as the ears of both horses stood straight forward as they sensed something down the trail. Both men kicked their horses hard and jerked their heads as they felt a nicker starting to come forth. Up ahead, close enough for the horses to detect, someone or something was on the trail ahead of them. The trail they were traveling had high sloping ridges on each side and covered with adequate places to conceal a large force, perfect for an ambush.

"Hold the ponies. I will check the trail ahead." Red Hawk slipped from his horse and quickly turned down the trail. "Be ready to retreat fast if I get into trouble."

"I will be here." Jed took the reins. "I will not leave you."

Red Hawk nodded. "I believe you."

Almost an hour had passed since Red Hawk slipped away, leaving Jed behind with the horses. Craning both his eyes and ears, he watched and listened closely, trying to see any sign of the Crow returning. Even this high in the mountains, the day turned warmer, and it was almost midafternoon before Jed spotted the Crow trotting tiredly up the rough trail. The Crow people were horseback warriors so most were bowlegged from being on a horse all their life and not used to traveling afoot long distances. Still Jed had to admit, the warrior trotted all the way up the rough trail without stopping.

"I found them." Red Hawk took a long breath. "They think they are safe in these mountains they call home. They camp below at the river."

"Did you see Little Antelope and the stallion?"

"Both are there. The woman is not harmed." Red Hawk looked up at the sky and sat down. "She seems very tired but not touched."

"What will we do?"

Red Hawk took the jerky Jed offered. "There is a white man with the Nez Perce."

"A white man?" Jed looked down the trail. "Where did he come from?"

"A few white trappers live in the land of the Nez Perce. Sometimes they go on the war trail with them in the warm times, when it is too warm to trap for furs." Red Hawk bit into the meat. "Some of these whites are cruel and evil, even more so than the Indian."

Jed knew Lige Hatcher had lived with the Arapaho for some time and he wondered if this was Hatcher with the Nez Perce. "A small white man with a dark beard?"

"No, a big red bearded white, very strong looking." Red Hawk swallowed. "He has claimed the woman you come for, as his own."

"What?" Jed couldn't believe what he had just heard. "She is married to Walking Horse."

"She was, now she is a slave of the redheaded one."

"Has she been hurt?"

"No, for now, she does the camp work until the warriors return to their village, then she will be the woman of the evil one." Red Hawk shrugged. "It is their way, he has traded for her."

"Why do you call him evil?"

"He has an evil heart." Red Hawk shrugged. "I have seen his eyes, and the way he treats the woman."

"What can we do?"

"The Nez Perce have a few guns, mostly bows and arrows as we do."

"And they outnumber us."

"I want my horse back, as you want the woman."

"How do we fight so many?" Jed looked down the trail.

"We will slip in after dark when they sleep and use our knives quietly." Red Hawk watched Jed's face. "It is not honorable but it is the only way. If we ambush them on the trail we may get a few but there are too many to win in open battle."

"That's cold-blooded murder." Jed shook his head thinking of what the Crow was suggesting. "Cold."

"They came to your land and stole the woman. Now, they pay for their foolishness." Red Hawk's face hardened. "Now, they die. It is not murder, it is war."

Jed nodded. "I know it is one way to save Little Antelope. I'd rather sneak her out and take our chances."

"And the stallion?" The warrior questioned. "Will we sneak him out too?"

"Does the horse mean that much to you, Red Hawk?" Jed looked over at the warrior. "To kill for?"

"Yes." The warrior nodded. "There are many women in our village, but only one spotted stallion like him in the whole nation."

"There is only one woman like her." Jed muttered to himself quietly, but Red Hawk heard the faint words.

"You say you don't care for this woman, Crow Killer." Red Hawk smiled. "I think you lie to yourself. I think this woman holds your heart."

"I told you, she is just my friend."

"Yes, you told me that."

"When do we leave?"

"They think they are safe so they rest along the banks of the big river. We will move close to them after the sun sleeps."

"Then we will attack."

"Not attack, kill."

"I'll be ready." Jed agreed. He didn't like it, but it was the only way Little Antelope would stand a chance of being reunited with Walking Horse.

"Get some sleep, you will need your strength tonight." Red Hawk looked back down the trail. "Tell me, Crow Killer, have you ever killed up close with the knife?'

Jed thought of Little Antelope. "I can kill. I'd rather do it my way."

"Your way, Arapaho, would get us both killed within two days." Red Hawk rolled into his robe. "They would run us down, and there are too many of them."

The horses were left hobbled behind them so they could graze and get water, but if something should prevent them from returning for them, the horses would eventually work the hobbles off. Red Hawk was determined to get the spotted stallion back, if he failed, he would have no further use for a horse. He could feel the young Arapaho, whom he had begun to trust, felt the same about the Arapaho squaw. Though the young warrior of the Lance Bearers denied his feelings for the woman, Red Hawk sensed there was more than friendship in their relationship. The sound of his voice and the look in his face when he spoke of her was more than just friendship. The Crow wondered, did the great Walking Horse know of Crow Killer's feelings?

Red Hawk was right, the Nez Perce felt safe and didn't even bother to put out sentries or horse guards around their camp. They sat in circles, laughing and joking while smoking their pipes, telling stories about their bravery and exploits against their enemies. Enjoying themselves, none of the warriors sensed the two sets of dark eyes watching them from the perimeter of the camp, taking in every movement, waiting for the fire to dim, and for the Nez Perce to turn to their robes. Jed felt guilty about what Red Hawk intended to do to the unsuspecting warriors, as he sat watching Little Antelope carrying water and fresh cooked deer to the warriors. Only hard blows and laughter came from the Nez Perce as she fell to the ground, then she proudly stood back up and brushed herself off. The white man, Red Hawk spoke of, did not appear in the firelight so Jed was not able to get a good look at him.

"Soon, they will sleep." Red Hawk lay on his stomach, observing the warriors gathered around the fire. "Then we will do to them the same as they do to the woman."

Jed was about to answer the warrior when his attention was diverted as a muscular white man stepped into the light with shaggy red hair and bloodstained hunting shirt. Angry words spewed from the Nez Perce as the redhead grabbed Little Antelope roughly.

"This is good, maybe they will fight over the woman." Red Hawk watched as the warriors stood up. "Maybe they will kill each other."

"Billy Wilson." Jed mumbled low in shock.

"You know this white man?"

"No, I can't be completely sure. I cannot see his face plain enough, but the red hair." Jed squinted through the dark at the large figure holding Little Antelope. "If he is the one I knew, he has grown some."

"When did you know this white?"

Jed thought back, how long has he been with the Arapaho now? "Maybe three years ago, he was with a wagon train heading west."

"You would know this white man with the red hair?" Red Hawk queried Jed. "Many whites come west, and there are many fur trappers who live with the Nez Perce people."

"Not any like Billy Wilson, I'll bet."

"Is he a warrior?"

"He was younger when I seen him last." Jed could still see the troublemaker, Billy, with his silly grin. "Even back then he was trouble."

"Maybe it was not this one you saw."

"Maybe." Jed couldn't be positive.

More loud and angry words came from the campfire as the warriors threatened Little Antelope with bodily harm after the redhead interfered with their fun. The white man pushed her slowly behind him, backing away from the angry warriors with her in tow. Jed and Red Hawk watched as the warriors settled back down around the fire. Jed breathed a sigh of relief, for the moment, Little Antelope was out of danger. Soon, it would be time to do what they came for.

"The redheaded one shows no fear." Red Hawk nodded.

"If this is Billy Wilson, he's not a coward."

"We will kill the warriors first. I will let you kill the redhead, then we will take the stallion and the woman." Red Hawk slipped his sharp skinning knife from its scabbard. "I know what you think of this kind of fighting but there is no other way. If we let them live, they will run us down with the coming of the sun."

"Then we will be dead as will Little Antelope." Jed finished the sentence.

Red Hawk rose quietly in the pitch dark. "Wait until I make the call of the owl, then start over there. We will meet in the middle."

"If the alarm is given, what then?"

"Then you can use your lance. We will fight and maybe live, or perhaps we die." Red Hawk placed his strong hand on Jed's arm and repeated himself. "I know killing like this is not the way of the warrior, but I want the spotted one. It is our only way, if you want the woman back alive."

"I know." Jed's voice was hoarse. Killing like this, to him, was cold-blooded murder. With so many against them, they had no choice. It was either the lives of the warriors lying around the dead fire, or Little Antelope. Jed figured they could just slip in and get the woman and the horse. However, as Red Hawk said they were so far from their villages and saddled with the exhausted Little Antelope, the Nez Perce would run them down within two days. Pulling his knife, Jed turned and worked his way carefully to the first sleeping body, waiting for the signal.

"The white man is gone." Red Hawk took Jed by the arm before he reached his first victim. "So is the woman."

"It is dark, are you sure?"

"They are gone. The redhead and the woman were lying there." Red Hawk pointed at a vacant spot nearby. "This white is smart, as he has slipped away with the woman while the others sleep."

"Burdened with Little Antelope, how could he hope to escape?"

"The redhead has probably taken the stallion too." Red Hawk looked about in the dark. "The woman is light, even riding the spotted stallion double, no horse in these mountains could catch up with them and he knows it."

"Why would he want her bad enough to break with the Nez Perce?"

"The warriors would never have given her to him, here on the war trail, and he knew it at the fire so he slipped her away from them." Red Hawk laughed lightly. "After they return to their village, the redhead could give the spotted stallion back to the warriors in front of the whole village. With their women watching, they would have to accept, they could not show their anger over an Arapaho squaw."

Jed nodded solemnly. "Yeah, you're right, they couldn't do that."

Billy Wilson, Jed remembered the youngest redhead, always figured out a way to get whatever he wanted. Back when they were young, he would do whatever needed to get his way, no matter what it took. Deserting the Nez Perce, stealing the horse and woman meant nothing

to Billy as long as he got what he wanted, and that was the woman. Jed
knew if this was indeed Billy Wilson, winning was like a sickness to him.
It wasn't that he really wanted something as much as he just had to win.
In the end, if the Nez Perce got the valuable horse back, the woman
would soon be forgotten, they would be his friends again, and Billy
would win as usual.

Forgetting the sleeping warriors, Jed and Red Hawk quickly retreated
to where their horses were hobbled and gathered their robes and jerked
meat. Red Hawk wanted to run off the horses of the Nez Perce, but to do
so would arouse the camp. Left asleep, Jed knew they could be on the trail
of Wilson and the girl several hours before the Nez Perce woke up. The
horses were rested so now they hurried to find which trail the redhead
was taking down the backside of the mountains. Two years earlier, Red
Hawk had ridden these trails on his way west to steal the spotted horse.
If the white was heading back to the Nez Perce villages, he would take
the fastest route. Now, Red Hawk was leading Jed to the same trail. The
moon lit up the trail slightly, but it was steep and treacherous in places
and the going would still be slow until the break of day.

At first light, Jed slipped from the black and let him drink as Red
Hawk stopped his sorrel alongside a rushing stream. Kneeling, Red
Hawk pointed out the fresh tracks of the spotted stallion entering the
small stream.

"The redheaded one has been slowed, the same as us, by the darkness
and the rough trail." The warrior shook his head. "Still, the fool does not
even stop to let the spotted one drink and rest."

"He hurries, as he knows the same as we do." Jed looked up at the
breaking haze in the east. "The ones behind us will be coming soon."

Red Hawk nodded. "We must catch up to the white quickly, and
take the woman and horse, then circle around and stay ahead of the Nez
Perce for many days until we get back to our hunting grounds and safety."

"Surely the Nez Perce wouldn't take a chance and follow us back to
the east, just to get the stallion back."

"Yes, they will not give up on the spotted one." Red Hawk smiled
grimly. "I don't blame them; I haven't."

Tossing the bag of jerky at the warrior, Jed nodded. "Then let's ride."

CHAPTER 8

Following the rough mountain trails proved Red Hawk right about the redhead setting a direct course, straight to Nez Perce Country. The deeper they went into these lands, the more Jed and Red Hawk knew they would have to be very alert. The white ahead, whoever he was, did not have to worry, as he was at home in these lands. Any warriors he met would be his friends or at the least he would know them. Now, he had burdened himself with the woman, and being exhausted, she would slow him down. Even the weather was against him, as the sky was overcast and rain had been falling in the mountains all day, leaving the trails muddy, slick, and difficult to navigate. Following the white now was easy, as the tracks of the spotted stallion cut deep with the extra weight of carrying two.

"We are closing in on them." Red Hawk pointed at the fresh tracks still seeping with water. "The woman is tired; she slows him. We are close and soon we will catch up to him."

"How far behind are the ones that follow?"

"There is no way to know." Red Hawk shrugged. "Their horses have traveled as far and fast as ours, but hopefully we are better mounted."

"I hope so." Jed patted the neck of the black as he looked about. "I want to catch Mister Billy Wilson; I want him bad."

"You said you were not sure the redhead is this Wilson."

"I ain't, but I want it to be him." Jed thought about Little Antelope being in Wilson's grasp.

"Ahead, there is a big river, deep and swift. The white will have to rest the stallion before swimming across." Red Hawk studied their back trail. "The woman looked exhausted back in the camp. She cannot swim and the stallion cannot carry her across the river on his back without rest. She would be too much weight for him to swim with."

Jed remembered Billy swimming, trying to dunk him in the creek back home. "If it is Billy Wilson ahead, he's a strong swimmer."

"No matter, he will rest the stallion, just as we will rest our ponies before crossing the river. The current is very powerful and we cannot afford to lose one of them."

"How bad is it?" Jed was worried Little Antelope could drown attempting to ford the wide river. "Can the stallion cross safely if she hangs onto him?"

"The river is always swift and deep. The stallion will be swimming in water as soon as he goes a few steps. He cannot carry even one on his back crossing that far." Red Hawk remembered the treacherous, swift water. "And we do not know how much rain there has been upriver to raise the river and strengthen the current."

"Little Antelope could be in danger." Jed kicked the black forward as he worried. "If we hurry, maybe we can reach the river before the redhead tries to cross."

"Do not worry, he will stop and rest. He thinks he is safe." Red Hawk cautioned Jed. "He knows the Nez Perce are hours behind him, and he does not know anyone else follows him."

Red Hawk pulled his sorrel in and looked across the wide sandy bank leading down to the river's edge. Two figures were in view alongside the rushing river. The small figure of Little Antelope lay collapsed on the ground with her face covered by one arm. The redhead was examining the spotted stallion, running his big hands over the tired animal. Carrying two people, the horse had been ridden hard without graze or rest since sneaking away from the Nez Perce. Even with the stamina and breeding of the stallion, the extra weight and lack of feed and water had taken its toll on the great animal. An ordinary horse would have already given up and laid down. Red Hawk could plainly see, even from a distance, the animal was exhausted. He watched as the white examined the horse and looked out across the broad river. As the big white man studied the current, Red Hawk knew what he was thinking. He wasn't sure the spotted stallion could swim the powerful river in his condition, but he did not have a choice, he had to cross. Looking behind him, down his back trail, he didn't see the two figures hidden behind the trees, their black eyes taking in everything he was doing. Normally, the stallion would have sensed the strange horses were there and given a warning, but now his head drooped as he was too tired.

"He cannot escape us now, Crow Killer." Red Hawk mounted his sorrel. "He is ours to kill."

"We must be careful. If he is Billy Wilson, he's an excellent shot with his rifle." Jed remembered shooting was the one thing Billy could best him at always, the redhead could shoot.

"He has time for only one shot before one of us is upon him." Red Hawk argued. "There is little choice we must go now as the Nez Perce that follow will be here soon."

"Red Hawk, it is Billy Wilson." Jed finally got a good look at the face of the white standing beside the stallion. Even with the heavy red beard there was no doubt, it was Wilson. There could be no mistaking the ugly, hateful features of the man. Nodding slowly, he fingered his war axe, then swung upon the black. "He is mine to kill."

"Be careful, my friend, he looks very strong."

"You slip downstream and cut him off if he tries to flee that way." Jed nodded at Red Hawk. "I will go straight at him."

"The spotted one has no run left in him." Red Hawk's eyes flamed. "He will die for misusing my horse the way he has."

"Remember, he is mine." Jed looked to where Wilson had just kicked Little Antelope viciously, causing her to roll sideways. "I will kill him."

"Be careful, Crow Killer, this one is evil."

Jed waited several minutes for Red Hawk to get in position downstream, prepared to cut off Wilson's escape, before riding out from the tree line into plain sight. Even from this far distance, their eyes locked immediately, studying each other. Wilson didn't recognize Jed, only that the warrior charging toward him was Arapaho, not Nez Perce, probably the husband or relative of the Arapaho woman. Jerking the girl roughly to her feet, he pointed his rifle at the lone warrior and laughed as he shoved her toward the stallion. Little Antelope focused her eyes on the oncoming warrior, letting out a shriek and turning on Wilson, fighting him with all her might. Jed watched in horror, helpless as the meaty fist took the girl by her throat, crashing his rifle against her skull. He knew the way she collapsed without moving, she was dead.

At the sound of another horse running behind him, Wilson turned his attention, focusing downstream at another warrior charging him. Raising the rifle quickly, he snapped off a shot, knocking the red-shirted warrior from his running horse.

"Now, it's your turn, Arapaho." Wilson mumbled the words as he quickly reloaded and fired at the hard charging black horse.

Seeing the big horse fall, he whirled toward the stallion, swinging upon the back of the horse as he tossed everything but his rifle, powder, and shot to the ground. Entering the river, he looked over his shoulder to see the Arapaho racing toward him afoot. Unable to reload, he slipped from the horse as it reached swimming water and hung onto his tail as he started across the river, away from the screaming Arapaho.

Jed had his arrow ready to shoot, but was afraid to let loose for fear of hitting the spotted horse. Lowering the bow, he unnotched the arrow and raced to where Red Hawk raised to a sitting position.

"Are you hurt bad, my friend?" Jed examined the bullet wound that ripped into the warrior's side. Tearing part of Red Hawk's shirt away, he quickly packed the wound and bound his side tight, stopping most of the bleeding.

"It is not a great wound." The warrior looked down at his side, then back across the river. "Is the woman dead?"

"Yes, his rifle did its work."

Red Hawk pointed to where Little Antelope lay. "Crow Killer, a dead body does not move its arms."

Jed turned his attention to where the girl raised her hand to her head. Rising to his feet in disbelief, he raced to her side and knelt down. "You are not dead, Little Antelope!"

"No, my head hurts terribly, and my eyes seem blurred. I cannot see you plainly." The voice was feeble. "It is you, Jed? I recognized you when you charged the white."

"Yes, it is me, little one." Jed cradled her head and wiped the blood from her eyes. "You saved my life when you fought with him."

"I did not think anyone would come for me." She looked up at him, shaking her head. "And my husband, Walking Horse?"

"He lives. He is back in the village badly injured but he will live." Jed could see the look of relief that crossed her beautiful face.

"Sit me up, Jed."

"The redhead escapes with the spotted one!" Red Hawk looked across the river as he staggered up behind them unseen, listening to their conversation, and watching Jed's expression as he looked down at the girl.

Little Antelope looked up at the wounded man and drew back as her eyes widened, taking in the red shirt and hawk feathers. "You are Crow. You are Red Hawk, hated enemy of the Arapaho."

"Her tongue is as sharp as she is beautiful." Red Hawk laughed.

Jed touched her softly on the shoulder. "Yes, little one, it is Red Hawk but he is no enemy, he is my friend. He helped me rescue you."

"Friend, a Crow?" She spat disgusted. "No Crow is a friend of the Arapaho, never."

"He is." Jed turned his attention to where Wilson and the stallion passed the halfway mark, crossing the river. "The stallion is still very strong. I think he will make it across safely."

"The spotted one has a mighty heart." Red Hawk stared sadly at the horse and man's bobbing heads as they made their way slowly across the water. "I hate the thought of losing him."

"You haven't lost him yet, my friend." Jed looked at the warrior.

"I am wounded and cannot go after him for several days, by then he will have reached the Nez Perce or found safety with the whites that have settled to the north."

Jed walked to where Wilson had discarded two pouches and examined them. Nodding, he dragged the leather pouches to where Little Antelope and Red Hawk waited. "We are in luck, Wilson left enough jerked meat to last you two several days, long enough for Red Hawk to recover and be able to hunt."

"And what of you, Crow Killer, where do you go?"

"You helped me rescue Little Antelope. Now, I leave her in your care and go after the stallion." Jed looked at the two disbelieving faces staring at him. "You will be safe here. I know you will help each other."

Little Antelope turned her head toward Jed in shock. "You are leaving me with this Crow? He is our sworn enemy and he will probably scalp me when you leave."

"He is my friend." Jed stared down at her. "You will be as safe with him as you would be with me."

"He was probably the dog that wounded Walking Horse."

Red Hawk smiled. "I was, and it would probably be easier than scalping you or taking care of you will be."

"What, you take care of me?"

"Like I would a papoose."

"Papoose, am I?" A hard glare full of hate came from her face.

"Enough!" Jed raised his hand. "We must find a place to conceal you before Wilson gets too far away, or the Nez Perce get here."

"Yes, we must hurry. Crow Killer must be across the river and out of sight before they arrive at this place."

Helping both of them onto Red Hawk's sorrel horse, Jed led them to the shelter of the timber. He had to find a place of concealment for them. A place Red Hawk could recover from his wound, hopefully without being discovered until he was able to defend them. Leaving them sitting on the sorrel, he walked the heavy thickets of the riverbank. Searching along the river, he finally stumbled on a small washed out cave, just big enough for two people to slip into comfortably. Leading the sorrel into the timber, where the cave lay concealed, he helped both of the wounded ones to the ground.

"I found a place for you." Jed shouldered the pouches, Red Hawk's weapons, and walked away toward the cave. "I will return for you."

Jed quickly washed their wounds from his water pouch, rewrapped Red Hawk's wound, and made sure they both had robes to keep warm. "You have food and water; I must go."

Red Hawk lay propped up against a clay wall. "Have you erased all signs of our passing?"

"All except where the horses entered the water and I could do nothing about the black horse's body."

"Good, now go. You must get across the river before they get here." Red Hawk looked over at the girl. "I will protect her with my life."

Jed knelt beside Little Antelope. "You will be safe. Red Hawk will get you back to the village safely."

Her small hand raised, touching his face gently. "It is you, I worry about now, Jed. Come back to me safe."

Red Hawk watched the way she looked up at him. "Why does she call you such a name?"

"It is just a name."

"You do not have to go after the stallion. I think getting the woman home is more important to you."

"No, Red Hawk, you saved Little Antelope. Now, I will get the stallion back for you." Jed shook his head, not mentioning his desire to catch Wilson. "She is in safe hands with you, I know this. Helping a friend who has helped me is important to me also."

"Good luck, Crow Killer." The warrior nodded. "I hope you are a good swimmer."

"I am." Jed nodded. "Is the sorrel?"

"He is."

Red Hawk and Little Antelope watched from their hiding place as Jed brushed out his tracks and made his way back to the same place where the redhead had entered the river. Searching the tree line for any sign of the Nez Perce, he swung onto the sorrel and kicked him into the water. Sliding from the horse's back as he hit swimming water, Jed grabbed the sorrel's tail and kicked hard, helping the animal as it pulled itself powerfully through the deep water. Dripping water from his leggings as he tiredly exited the river, Jed inhaled deeply, as it was a long hard crossing. He was amazed the spotted stallion in his exhausted state was able to make the long swim with the heavy Wilson dragging him down.

Quickly retreating from the riverbank, out of sight from the far bank, Jed found the tracks of the spotted one pointing due west, away from the river. Red Hawk had figured him to turn north, maybe toward the white settlements, but instead he had ridden west. The tracks were plain in the damp ground, as Wilson was leading the tired stallion, trying to let the horse regain his strength. Normally, the crossing would have caused the stallion little trouble, but the long ride carrying two people had sapped his abundant strength. The sorrel was tired too, but he hadn't been worked near as hard as the spotted horse.

"Now, I will run you down, Billy Wilson." Jed mumbled as he led the sorrel, following the tracks the stallion left in the soft ground.

Red Hawk watched from his vantage point, inside the cave, as the Nez Perce warriors stopped alongside the black horse, studying the signs that had been left. He could hear the excitement in their voices as they rang out from where they sat their horses. Red Hawk thought he could make out the word, Arapaho, as the warriors pointed at the tracks left in the soft dirt. He knew he was probably just imagining he could hear them, but each tribe could identify another tribe by the curve or design of their moccasins. The Nez Perce lands were too far distant to be blood enemies of the Arapaho as were the Blackfoot. Nevertheless, they had taken the horse and woman from the Arapaho, and they were surprised that one lone enemy would follow them.

"He is across safely, woman. Now, if he can stay ahead of these warriors and catch up to the redheaded one." Red Hawk shook his head. "It would be difficult for an older warrior, but an untried youth and a white man; it will be very difficult indeed."

"He is a Lance Bearer of the Arapaho." Little Antelope looked over at the Crow. "He is not white or untried."

"Maybe not anymore."

"He is brave and strong."

"I know he is brave, but he does not have the experience these Nez Perce warriors have." Red Hawk watched the warriors as they prepared to enter the water. "Did you see the big warrior that led them, the one on the black and white piebald paint horse?"

"I saw him." Little Antelope nodded. "Why?"

"I think that was Black Robe, a great warrior of the Nez Perce." Red Hawk watched the river. "I believe they will run him to the ground very quick."

"Then you would lose your horse, wouldn't you?" Little Antelope frowned at him. "Have faith, Crow. I tell you, he will return with the stallion, you will see."

"Who do you care more for, your husband or Crow Killer?"

"That is a foolish question, even for a Crow."

"Is it, woman?"

Little Antelope blushed lightly. "My husband is all I want."

"And all I want is a nice fresh cooked buffalo tongue right now." Red Hawk laughed. "One of us is lying, and I know I am hungry."

"In our lodges, we hear the Crow never tell the truth."

The warrior rose slightly as he watched the river. "Now, I tell the truth. The Nez Perce are crossing the river."

"How long will we stay here in this place?" Little Antelope moved closer beside Red Hawk to watch the river and the swimming warriors. "We must do something to help."

"Not long, just until we are both stronger, strong enough to walk back to our villages." Red Hawk stared across the river. "Right now, neither of us are in any shape to help anyone, including ourselves."

Little Antelope nodded. "Perhaps, we should try to get along with each other that would help some, at least until we return to our own lands."

"I agree the sharp tongue of a woman, even a pretty Arapaho, is hard to listen to." Red Hawk laughed again lightly, infuriating Little Antelope. "But, easy to look at."

"I am a married woman." She frowned. "Keep your eyes to yourself."

"You are safe. You are the woman of my friend, Crow Killer." Red Hawk laughed. "But, my eyes seem to rove where beauty sits."

"I am his friend, not his woman." She frowned. "Tell me, Red Hawk, how can a Crow be the friend of an Arapaho?'

"We had an agreement; until you are safe, we ride together as one." Red Hawk watched her face. "Whether you believe it or not, I have come to respect the young warrior as a friend."

"Until I am safe, but watch your roving eyes." She nodded.

"Crow Killer thinks much of you. He would give his life for you." Red Hawk looked at her closely. "I think you feel the same about him."

"You think too much."

Jed tried to figure how much of a lead Wilson had on him. He knew it had taken at least two hours to find the cave and transport the wounded ones there, and then erase all signs of their passing. In the back of his mind, he worried, did he erase everything, leaving no tracks for the Nez Perce to find and lead them to Red Hawk and Little Antelope? He worried, should he have stayed behind to help them, if he was needed. Did he truly come after the stallion or did he come after Billy Wilson? He always thought Wilson had pushed him purposely from the wagon. Perhaps it had been an accident, but Jed knew Wilson and how vicious he could be.

Two days passed as Jed followed the tracks of the spotted one. Wilson had remounted the animal and was once again pushing him hard. Jed was worried, even if he did recover the animal, would he be crippled for life or trail foundered from all the abuse he had suffered over the many miles he had been pushed? Jed's attention focused on the trail that slowly wound down into the lower valleys of the western mountains. Jed was not familiar with this part of the country. It was beautiful country, abounding with game, tall green grass, flowers, and flowing waters. On his journey west, since falling from the wagon train, Jed was astounded by the magnificent mountains and valleys he had crossed. Lige Hatcher had told him many times of the vast and beautiful land to the west, but Jed thought he was exaggerating as Lige was often prone to do at times.

Crossing another captivating valley, his mind absorbed in its beauty, Jed did not hear the two warriors who had ridden up from the trees behind him. Hearing the drumming of the hard running horses, Jed whirled the sorrel hard to face the two charging warriors. Grasping the heavy war axe, Jed kicked the sorrel into a hard run straight at the warriors, who were almost upon him. This was a battle that Jed could not, and did not, intend to lose. Attacking the warriors with a fury, he unseated the first one. He passed with a vicious swing of the heavy axe that almost caved in the warrior's chest as it passed through the heavy, buffalo-hide shield he carried. Seeing his friend fall, the other attacker tried to retreat, only to have Jed bring him down from behind. The war axe bit deep into the warrior, killing him as they rolled across the ground. Rising quickly, Jed raced to the sorrel and remounted, looking around for any other warriors. The attack happened so fast, he didn't have time to think. Now, his heart raced with adrenaline as he thought about the attacking warriors. Daydreaming, he was caught completely off guard and lucky he wasn't killed. From now on, his mind would stop studying the landscape like a child and focus on following the trail, watching for any enemies riding the mountains.

The trail near the west end of the valley split in two. Wilson changed direction again, taking the right trail, veering off suddenly to the north as Red Hawk had predicted. Both trails started to climb up and out of the valley. Now, Jed was uncertain; did the trail lead to the Nez Perce Villages or north to the white settlements? Jed was new here in the west and knew nothing of the tribes in this area, nor did he know the locations of the various villages. He knew what lay behind him, but to the northwest he was at a loss, and all he could do was follow the tracks of the spotted one wherever they led. Jed had given his word to Red Hawk; he would follow Wilson plumb to the gates of hell, if that is what it took, and not quit. Wilson knew the Nez Perce warriors would be following him, but he probably had no idea Jed had crossed the river and was close behind him.

The Nez Perce warriors rode around the bodies in a small circle, trying to figure out what had happened to the warriors. They recognized the bodies as the dreaded Blackfoot but they had not been scalped, and nothing had been taken, not even their fine horses. They could not understand what kind of warrior would leave such plunder lying on the grass untouched. How would this warrior count coup or brag on his kill? They were almost spooked, knowing the Blackfoot were great warriors and this lone Arapaho had killed these two easily. Was this some kind of mysterious being, riding the hills dressed like an Arapaho? They had heard of such demons, but they had never experienced anything like this in their days on the war trail. No warrior would leave such things as scalps, horses, and weapons behind after a great kill. Some of the younger Nez Perce were superstitious, wanting to quit the trail and head for their home lodges, while the older men only laughed, cussing them for women. Finally, shamed into following the older warriors, they relented and followed their elders into the valley.

"You see, it is the same horse that we have been following since leaving the river." A huge warrior, called Black Robe, chided the others.

"It is only the Arapaho we saw back at the river. He follows the redhead. He is no demon."

"Let us turn away and go to our lodges." Another spoke up. "Leave the white to the Arapaho."

"No, we will follow this trail and kill both of them." Black Robe looked at the weapons and horses of the Blackfoot and nodded. "We have much plunder to show for this trail. Soon, we will have more; the woman, scalps, more horses, and the great spotted one."

"Or get ourselves killed. I think this one is an evil spirit with much power." The warrior spoke again. "I fear the evil ones have reached out their hands for us."

"Is Squirrel Tooth a coward?" Black Robe scolded the younger warrior. "He speaks like a fool. Our enemy is in our grasp and you want to run home."

The younger warrior blushed deeply from the insult.

"Enough!" Another warrior spoke up. "I say this, the ones of us that wish to ride with Black Robe, stay. The others that want to return to their lodges like scared rabbits, go."

For several seconds, not a word was spoken as the warriors sat their horses. No one wanted to ride away and be thought of as a coward. Most believed like Squirrel Tooth, this was a dangerous enemy they followed, and something was amiss here in these mountains. Each warrior thought the Arapaho, if he was an Arapaho and not a demon, was a great warrior. To kill two full-fledged Blackfoot warriors so easily, either way, the warrior or demon was a dangerous enemy.

Finally, Black Robe spat disgustedly and turned his horse, cutting his eyes so none could see, grinning self-satisfied as all the Nez Perce fell in line behind him. The large warrior laughed to himself, as his will won out, shaming the others. Cold shivers went up the younger warrior's backs as they rode away from the dead bodies.

From high on a mountain ridge, Billy Wilson studied the valley floor below. Nothing stirred below, only the slight breeze of the mountains moving the grass and limbs on the trees. He was tired, as he had ridden far, crossing valley after valley in his nonstop effort to put many miles between himself and the Nez Perce warriors, he knew were following. The spotted horse stood with his head down, jaded and drawn, with his great strength almost played out. Wilson looked at the horse with no show of emotion, sympathy, or guilt coming from his cold eyes. He knew the horse was almost finished, needing rest and graze badly to regain his strength. The great animal was valuable to the Nez Perce, even to the Crow, who had ridden so far in these mountains years ago to steal him. However, to the redhead, he was just another horse. Wilson put value on furs, trade goods, and even the woman, who lay alongside the great river where he had left her for dead, but the spotted horse was just a beast of burden to him.

For several minutes, Wilson studied the valley while the horse cooled enough so a small amount of water would not founder his overworked and heated body. Leading the tired horse to the small mountain stream, he let the animal swallow several sips of water, and then moved him back into the tall grass to graze.

Wilson shook his head, as if in shock, as a nagging question soaked into his tired mind; why did he steal the horse and woman? Yes, she was the most beautiful thing he has ever seen and the horse was one of the great spotted stallions of the Nez Perce people. But, now he has lost the trust and friendship of the Nez Perce warriors by stealing two things they prized greatly. They had already agreed to give him the woman for many trade goods when they returned to their village, but Wilson didn't want to share her with them until then. But, why did he take the horse? He knew they would follow like a swarm of bees. The warrior called Black Robe was one of the greatest of the Nez Perce warriors, having counted many coups on his enemies, and was the warrior who owned the spotted stallion. He would not give up the horse and return to the village without him, as it would shame him in front of the people. If he had only left the stallion behind, perhaps the warriors would have returned to their village when they reached the fork in the trail leading west.

Wilson knew the answer and it was the same as always, in all his actions, he had to win. He had to do as he liked, when he liked and to whom he liked. In all his life, he had done as he wished, whipping, even killing men, white or red, stealing from trap lines, and taking whatever he wanted. The few trappers, who knew of him and his deeds, had been found suspiciously dead. Wilson was dangerous and smart, and he left

142

ALFRED DENNIS

no witnesses behind to tell of his crimes. Back home, in the settlement where his father and brother farmed, he was merely a trapper who came in from time to time to rest and resupply with trade goods. No one would ever guess the brutality he had been involved in. Even his Nez Perce or Blackfoot brothers did not know of his dark side. They only knew he was a good man to have on their side, if he was needed.

As his stomach growled hungrily, Wilson cussed himself for abandoning his supply of jerked meat back at the river. He looked to where the stallion grazed hungrily and started to hobble the stallion, but seeing how the horse was cropping at the tall grass, he changed his mind. Why bother, the animal was too hungry and tired to wander far. Picking up his rifle, he turned down the ridge, he needed something to eat or he would be in as bad a shape as the horse. His mouth watered at the thought of a buffalo steak or tongue roasting over a hot fire. Wilson was a big man and his huge body demanded much food to sustain him.

Jed knew he was making up ground on Wilson when the tracks of the spotted one started showing drag marks at times, not the firm steps of a horse who wasn't tired. The sorrel had made the same tough miles, but on the steepest and roughest parts of the trail, Jed trotted most of the way alongside the horse, leading him to conserve his strength. Wilson was of a different nature, the man was cruel to everyone and everything that crossed his path. The spotted stallion was no different and he thought little of the stallion, other than a means of escape from the Nez Perce. He would not slow down or show the animal any mercy until the horse finally collapsed under him. Jed cussed, thinking of the great horse being used so cruelly.

Stopping atop a ridge on the trail, he slid from his horse and studied every hiding place a man could conceal himself before moving forward, down the hill into the open valley. He knew Wilson couldn't be too far ahead. The man he knew was shrewd and crafty, trusting nobody only himself, and suspicious of everything. Jed knew Wilson would be watching his back trail carefully as he pushed hard to the north, even if he had to slow down and backtrack. Jed had to be sure Wilson didn't discover him following, but he had to close the gap and get close to him so he wouldn't be able to use his long rifle.

Seeing nothing in the valley, Jed swung back onto the sorrel's back, kicking the horse forward. Jed knew somewhere behind him, and maybe very close behind, followed the Nez Perce, and he knew they would follow the spotted stallion until he was recovered. They had ventured far into enemy lands to find the horse, and now in their own lands, they wouldn't quit their quest for him. He knew he needed to throw caution to the wind and overtake Wilson before the Nez Perce closed the gap on them.

Two days passed, and still the great stallion kept ahead of him and the sorrel. Jed had seen Wilson's tracks alongside the stallion's so he knew Billy finally realized the horse was exhausted and couldn't carry him any longer. Jed could sense, almost smell the man and he knew Wilson was close. Eagerly, he strained his eyes, searching out the trail ahead, watching for any movement that would give away the whereabouts of the redhead. Jed was worried as he was almost out of food and soon he would have to hunt, taking precious time away from following his quarry. He didn't want to admit the hunt for Wilson, which he thought was coming to an end, was now in doubt. The man, laden down and mounted on an exhausted horse, was still managing to stay ahead of him. He ran his hands over the sorrel as the horse drank his fill from a stream that meandered through the valley. The horse was starting to show signs of tiring, as he too had been pushed hard for several days. Jed considered leaving the animal and pushing forward on foot. However, if he managed to catch up with Wilson and get the stallion back, he would have to avoid being caught by the oncoming Nez Perce and that would require both the sorrel and spotted stallion.

Again, Wilson turned his direction, this time he took a trail leading due north, away from Nez Perce lands. Jed figured the trail would take Wilson over the mountain divide and into the settlements the whites had laid out in the fertile valleys of the northern territories. Jed studied the trail ahead and knew he would have to gamble if he was to catch Wilson before he reached the white settlements and help, or before the Nez Perce caught up to them. Kicking the sorrel, he followed the trail Wilson left in the soft dirt and rode north.

Loping the sorrel across an open valley and up a small rise that was covered with trees, suddenly behind him, Jed spotted warriors emerging from the far tree line. Slipping quickly into a stand of mountain cedars, Jed was shocked when a second band of warriors emerged, following his tracks less than a quarter mile distance from the others. Jed watched both groups of warriors as they converged on each other as they made their way north, down the valley. This was far more Nez Perce warriors than Red Hawk had reported seeing back at their first camp. He knew now, there was no chance of overtaking the stallion because the one band of warrior's horses acted fresh as they pranced across the grass matted valley. Jed strained his eyes, but the warriors were still too far out on the valley floor to identify or even get a close look at them, but they seemed different.

He knew with so many warriors tracking him, he would have to leave Wilson's trail and find a place to hide. Watching the two groups as they crossed the valley, Jed looked around for a better place of concealment. The sorrel was spent and had been on the trail too long to outrun fresher horses. Jed watched as the warriors below suddenly pulled their horses to a stop, with less than fifty yards separating them. He watched in disbelief, as the warriors worked themselves into a frenzy screaming across at each other. He breathed a sigh of relief as he realized they were not of the same tribe and acted as if they were enemies. Suddenly, shrill war cries sounded as both groups charged straight at each other. Jed had no way of knowing as he watched the battle that the Blackfoot were the second group. The Blackfoot warriors thought the Nez Perce were responsible for killing the two Blackfoot warriors, he had killed back in the valley. The Blackfoot had taken a shortcut over the mountain trails to overtake the Nez Perce quickly.

The battle raged as both sides fought viciously as this wasn't a game to count coup, this was a battle to kill because of the dead warriors the Blackfoot had found. Jed nodded as he watched as each side drew blood and warriors fell from their horses. This was good, doubting the Nez Perce would follow him further into enemy lands after this fight, and the Blackfoot didn't know he was here. Now, he could escape and go after Wilson. Pulling the sorrel around, he took one last look to where the fight was raging and rode the horse away. Today, he knew he was lucky, where fate stepped in and took the Nez Perce from his trail.

The trail was getting more difficult to follow as the ground became rockier and the stallion was leaving very little sign to see. Almost at sundown of the second day, Jed was becoming discouraged and wasn't sure he was even on the right trail, the ground was completely rock underfoot. Suddenly, Jed straightened as somewhere ahead, he heard a rifle fire. He was exhausted but he knew it was not a figment of his imagination; he heard a rifle shot. Was it Wilson or another hunter out hunting for game? Whoever fired the shot was close and Jed had him located. Kicking the sorrel, he circled away from the sound of the shot, circling along the trees lining the valley so he could come in behind the shooter unseen.

Leaving the sorrel hobbled in a grove of trees, Jed slipped silently to a crest of a small ravine, and crawled the last few yards to the top. If he guessed right, the gunshot came from just below this ridge. Bellying up to the top, he peeked cautiously over the rim and looked down in the valley below. "Billy Wilson!" Jed was shocked, there before him, less than fifty yards, stood his redheaded stepbrother bending over a small deer.

The redhead was engrossed in skinning the animal, too busy to watch for enemies which he should have been doing. Jed looked around for the stallion as Wilson had apparently left him somewhere ahead when he slipped back to search for game. Quickly retracing his steps to the sorrel, Jed turned to the north, circling away to keep out of Wilson's sight as he made his way to where he figured Wilson might have left the stallion. He had time to find him as Wilson would be kept busy skinning out the animal for some time. The redhead didn't realize Jed had found him and the Nez Perce were close, fighting for their own lives in the nearby valley.

Quickly quartering the ridge above the north end of the valley, he spotted the stallion grazing hungrily alongside another one of the small streams that dotted the mountain valley. Tying the sorrel back in the timber so he wouldn't call out to the stallion and warn Wilson, Jed trotted softly toward the horse. The stallion was tired and hungry, and didn't look up as Jed approached him. Slipping his hand around the horse's neck, he quickly gathered the lead rope hanging down from the stallion.

"Well, old son, I have finally found you." Jed patted the horse's neck. "Sorry to take you from your dinner but we must leave this place quickly."

Jed dismissed his desire to kill Wilson, still remembering his step-father, Ed Wilson, with affection. The man had been good to him after his mother's passing. He had known little of the badgering and the constant pranks Jed had endured at the hands of Billy and Seth. Today, Billy Wilson would live only because of his father. Plus, he couldn't be sure the Nez Perce lost the battle in the valley and they could arrive here any minute. He had to get back to Little Antelope. He didn't have time for Wilson; it could wait another day.

As Jed gathered the horses, he took one last look at the valley where he last saw Wilson, but the redhead had not yet come into sight. Slipping quickly onto the sorrel, Jed started to the north with the intention of turning back to the east, back to Red Hawk and Little Antelope as soon as he was away from this valley and Wilson. Now, the situation was reversed with Jed the hunted, the one on the run, and Wilson the hunter, if he chose to pursue Jed on foot. With any luck, the Nez Perce were defeated by the Blackfoot, at least he hoped so. Now, all he had to do was elude Billy Wilson and find another trail that would take him back to the river where he had left Red Hawk and Little Antelope.

Wilson stood looking about the spot where he had left the spotted horse. Blood dripped from his hand as he held the warm liver of the deer, he had just butchered. Distracted by the absence of the horse, Wilson ripped a piece of the liver with his strong teeth and ate the meat raw. His blue eyes scanned the valley floor for the horse. Finally, cussing his bad luck, he flung the bundle of deer meat, he had wrapped in the hide, onto the ground. Slowly, he studied the ground where the stallion had been grazing until he discovered the tracks of the stallion being led to the north. Wilson cussed, whirling in a rage as he flung the liver.

"You waste good meat, Redhead." The deep voice caused Wilson to whirl and face four warriors who had come up, unseen, behind him.

"Black Robe!"

"Did you think I would not follow?" The warrior stepped closer. "Where is the stallion?"

Wilson could see the warriors had been in a fight. Bloody scalps hung from their game belts and two of the men had slight wounds. "I do not know. While I hunted, someone slipped into my camp and stole him."

"The same way you stole the stallion and woman, when you took them as your friends and brothers slept?"

"The woman was mine, we traded."

"And the stallion?"

"I needed him to carry the woman to our village, your village."

"Why did you slink out while we slept, like a coyote in the night?" Black Robe raised his arm and pointed north. "This path does not lead to Nez Perce land, it goes to the white settlements."

"I feared my friends would not understand my feelings for the woman." Wilson could see the wildness in the big warrior. The warrior wanted to kill and Wilson could feel it as he spoke. "I only took this trail until the next turn back to Nez Perce lands."

Black Robe tried to shake off his rage. "We will get the horse and squaw back. They couldn't have gotten far."

"Squaw?" Wilson was shocked, but surely they had seen the body of the dead woman on the riverbank.

Black Robe walked around Wilson, his eyes casting around the ground, looking for signs of the spotted stallion. The woman meant nothing to him, in the Nez Perce villages, squaws were plentiful, but horses like the spotted stallion were not. The Nez Perce bred the great spotted horses that all other tribes wanted, and this stallion was the finest in all the Nez Perce nation. Size, color, strength, speed, and deep chested, all traits he possessed, traits the Nez Perce bred for and they wanted this stallion returned to their people. It had taken many moons for them to locate and find who had stolen the stallion from their herds. No one would have thought a Crow from a far-off land would have dared to travel so far just to steal a horse. Black Robe had sworn an oath to return the stallion to his people. He had lost six warriors on this trail. Now, he was close and he was mad. If it hadn't been for the redhead, the horse would already be back in his village and his warriors would still be alive. They were brave warriors that had given their lives fighting the Blackfoot who had been beaten. Now, six of his friends were dead and he blamed Wilson.

"His tracks lead to the north." Wilson stepped forward, pointing at the ground.

Black Robe fingered his knife, as the warrior called Squirrel Tooth stepped closer and whispered. "Let him lead us after this demon, Black Robe. Let him die first."

Nodding, the big warrior turned to Wilson wanting to placate the warrior. "You will follow the trail of the stallion."

"All right, it's my fault he has been lost again." Wilson grunted, as he didn't trust the warrior and didn't want to turn his back on the man.

Only a nod came from Black Robe. "Go."

"I have traveled far, and I need a horse." Wilson eyed the extra horses of the Blackfoot being led by the Nez Perce.

"Walk, Redhead, you have lost the right to ride with warriors." Black Robe raised his huge arm and pointed north. "Be content you still live."

Jed led the spotted stallion behind the sorrel while his eyes searched for a game trail leading to the southeast in the general direction he had left Red Hawk and Little Antelope. The trail he looked for appeared in the early afternoon, turning due east, almost directly back toward the river. Jed figured he was at least five miles north across the mountains from the valley trails he had taken while following Wilson to the north and west. A mountain range they had ridden across paralleled but separated the two trails. He seemed to remember passing a trail similar in size to the one he now rode only a few miles from the river where Red Hawk and Little Antelope lay hidden in the cave. He wasn't sure of the trail's destination, but at least it was heading east and that was the direction he wanted to go. Behind him, without a rider, the spotted stallion was moving well. The horse was just tired and didn't show any signs of being crippled. Jed knew with rest and feed, he would recover his strength in a few days and be as strong as ever. For the next few days, the horse wouldn't carry any load, at least until they reached Little Antelope and Red Hawk.

Unwrapping the last of the jerked meat that he had taken from the dead Blackfoot warriors back in the valley, he pushed the hard greasy meat into his mouth. Chewing slowly on the tough meat, Jed focused his attention far across the flower covered valley he was fixing to descend into. This was fertile land with the deep rich soil, a farmer or rancher's dream, and all a man could want. Mountain peaks, valleys, clear running streams that rolled on forever, and grasses that grew belly deep on the elk and deer that lived here in the high valleys. Aromatic flowers of every size, color, and strain grew abundant along the trail in the deep rich loam, emitting their fragrances as the horses brushed their legs and hooves through them. Somewhere, north of here lay the wagon road, the immigrants with Wilson and his sons had followed to the west, eager to build their homes and start their farms in this new land. Jed wondered if the land they had found was as rich as this land. He doubted it, as he has never seen nor could he even imagine so beautiful and spectacular a land anywhere.

Hobbling the tired horses on a small patch of grass as he passed out of the valley before starting up the mountainside, Jed walked further up the trail to a tall oak tree. Stripping down to his breechcloth, he reached for the first limb and pulled himself with sheer strength onto the bottom limb, starting his climb to the tall branches overhead. As kids, he and the Wilsons climbed trees back in Tennessee to spy out the game that stalked the wild. Today, he wasn't looking for game, only Wilson. He didn't figure the redhead would remember when they climbed trees to watch the trails. The dark eyes surveyed the valley and his back trail leading down into it, looking for movement of anyone following. Jed knew Billy Wilson, the one he knew as a boy, now a man, wouldn't give up without a fight.

CHAPTER 9

Yellow Dog sat cross-legged beside a small fire that separated him from Walking Horse, listening as the wounded warrior spoke weakly from his buffalo robe bed. Days earlier, Slow Wolf had sent runners to the Cheyenne telling of the wounding of Walking Horse and Little Antelope's abduction by the Crow. Bow Legs had proved his chief wrong by tracking the raiders to the northwest, away from Crow lands. Returning to the Arapaho Village, he sounded the alarm that it was possibly the Nez Perce who had taken the stallion and the woman. When Yellow Dog arrived days later with his warriors, Walking Horse still had a fever. In his delirium, the warrior was accusing the hated Crow for her abduction. Out of his mind with fever and worrying about his wife, Walking Horse was not thinking clearly as he spoke with his brother-in-law. After speaking with Walking Horse, Yellow Dog took Bow Legs aside and listened as the warrior told him of tracking the raiders for two days due west before returning to the village to report. He was sure there was no doubt it was either Nez Perce or Blackfoot warriors who were responsible for stealing Little Antelope and the stallion.

"You have done well, my friends." The Cheyenne thanked Bow Legs and Crooked Mouth.

"You will go after your sister?"

"If I can get some fresh horses from Slow Wolf, we will leave immediately."

Bow Legs waved at a youngster sitting a horse near the Cheyenne warriors. "You will have your horses and supplies for several days."

"This is good, we will leave when they get here."

"I will go with you to show you where I turned back and left the raiders trail. It will save you much time." Bow Legs nodded eagerly. "Crooked Mouth will remain here. Slow Wolf will allow no others to leave the hunt."

"With you, Bow Legs, we have plenty." Yellow Dog nodded. "I understand, the meat taking time is now and very important."

Wilson was exhausted as he had trotted ahead of Black Robe and the Nez Perce for two days since leaving the valley where they had come upon him. Finally, seeing they were losing time making the redhead walk, Black Robe ordered him onto a horse.

Exhausted, Wilson hauled his heavy body aboard the animal and kicked him down the rocky trail, straight into the valley where Jed had climbed a tree. Wilson was no fool and he knew he couldn't trust the Nez Perce warriors riding behind him. He had betrayed their trust for a woman and had stolen a prized possession from them. He was caught, so now, there was little he could do to get their trust back. They mounted him on the slowest horse they had, in case he tried to escape, they could run him down easily and kill him. He knew their contempt for him was bad but they allowed him to keep his rifle for now. All he could do was follow the trail of the one who had stolen the horse and hope to find a way to escape Black Robe later. Once, he had been a trusted ally of the Nez Perce. Now, he was almost the same as an enemy, maybe worse. He knew with the loss of the dead Nez Perce warriors, his fate was sealed and he was lucky they hadn't killed him already. Wilson was mean but no fool, when they recovered the stallion, the Nez Perce would have no further use for him.

Jed walked the horses slowly, letting them rest in case they needed their strength. He had no intentions of losing the spotted stallion again after all the trouble he went through to get him back. He was now many miles east of the valley where he had rested and climbed the tree, hours before Wilson and the Nez Perce came down from the high country. From his perch in the tree, he watched for an hour without seeing anything, while the horses rested and grazed. Climbing down from the tree, Jed managed to kill a small deer walking by the horses, unaware a human was close. The quick bow shot was a lucky one, but he ate a badly needed meal that he hastily cooked over a small fire before taking to the trail again. Some of the meat he wrapped for the long ride ahead, the rest was buried and covered with dirt and leaves, hiding it from whoever followed. Jed rode slowly, saving the horses. The valley he passed through was so beautiful, but now he had to keep his attention focused on the trail, front and back. Wilson was out there somewhere.

Bow Legs led the Cheyenne in a steady lope back to the west to the spot where he had stopped tracking the raiding party that had taken the stallion and Little Antelope. He knew the country, as he had hunted it many times with Walking Horse. It was not Arapaho lands, but it was heavily populated with all kinds of game, tempting different tribes to go there on their hunts. Many tribes hunted and raided in these mountains, making it a very dangerous and bloody land for any warrior caught unaware. Sometimes, the bleached bones of both game animals and human remains littered the ground where they had fallen.

Circling the tracks, Bow Legs pointed due west. "This trail they ride will lead us to the big river. If these warriors are Nez Perce, they will cross at the slick slopes ahead."

"How far?" Yellow Dog was eager to catch up with the warriors ahead who had stolen Little Antelope.

Bow Legs shrugged. "Maybe two days."

"Lead us, Bow Legs; get us to the river." Yellow Dog nodded forward. "I wonder, where is Crow Killer?"

"Crooked Mouth said he headed for the Crow Village when he left him back on the Yellowstone." Bow Legs shrugged. "He could be anywhere now, even dead."

Jed didn't know the strange country he passed through, but he figured he couldn't be more than two hard days ride away from the river. He walked and led the horses, letting them graze as he passed along the trail. He knew taking his time like this to let the horses regain their strength was dangerous, but he had no choice. If Wilson or the Nez Perce caught up to him, he knew he would need the horses rested to outrun them. If his luck held and he reached the river, the horses would have to carry the wounded Red Hawk and Little Antelope back to their villages. Either way, he would need the horses soon.

Hitting a slow jog with the horses trotting behind him, Jed kept up the pace for most of the morning, finally stopping alongside a small creek. Letting the horses water, he moved upstream from them and drank his fill. Rising to his feet, he swung upon the sorrel and started east, descending the mountain trail toward another small valley, hopefully the last before reaching the river and Little Antelope. Far ahead, over the crest of the hill, Jed could see what he figured to be large oak and willow treetops growing along the riverbank. Taking his time, moving easily down the steep grade of the hill, Jed knew the brief rest and grass revitalized the horses. The sorrel moved and felt stronger under him as they made their way along the mountain slope.

Wilson slid from his horse and examined the tracks in the soft ground of the valley. The warrior ahead was strong, as he had walked for almost two full days, leading and resting his horses.

Wilson looked to where Black Robe sat his horse. "This warrior is a good runner."

"He cannot run fast enough to escape, and if he does, you will pay with your life."

Wilson shook his head. "I will catch him. I know where he's headed."

"Then go, and hope you are right, Redhead."

Wilson knew these mountains and valleys like the back of his hand. Ever since he had left his father and brother behind on their farm to take up the life of a trapper, he had traveled through these mountain passes on many occasions as he trapped and traded with the different tribes. Studying the tracks, he figured the warrior that had taken the spotted stallion couldn't be more than two hours ahead, making him at least a day from the river. Wilson knew, one day, was all the time he had left to figure a way to escape from Black Robe and get himself out of these mountains. Why they kept him alive this long, he couldn't understand, but he did hear the warrior Squirrel Tooth say something to Black Robe about a demon. For some reason, they thought the warrior ahead of them was a demon of some kind. Wilson knew the Nez Perce mind, as he knew many of the tribes, and all were superstitious about anything they didn't understand. Apparently, they kept him alive to help kill this warrior they thought to be a demon. Maybe they thought they needed his rifle to kill the evil one. He shook his big head, no white man could ever understand an Indian's way of thinking.

Billy Wilson was still a youngster by some standards, not yet twenty years old, but by the standards the Nez Perce judged a warrior by, he was already a man. Since crossing the Platte, three years prior, he had aged beyond his years, growing taller, spreading wide through the shoulders, and honing his senses mostly at the expense of others. Other trappers knew him to be smart and cagey, a man to stay clear of in any kind of dealings. Some thought him to be a killer but the accusations were not proof in these mountains, and none dared confront him, face-to-face. Most free trappers hunted the mountains with a partner for safety or companionship, but Wilson had always hunted alone and being a loner, he preferred it that way.

The redhead pretended to study the horse tracks as he followed the trail to the east, but his mind was actually calculating his chances of escape. He had to make his move before the warrior ahead was seen. When the Arapaho was dead, it would be too late to make his escape. Four Nez Perce warriors were too many for Wilson to try to fight. Maybe two, but four; his mind raced as he tried to come up with something quick. He was still young, but the men he had trapped and traded with sometimes compared him to a lobo wolf when he found himself in a tight spot. They didn't think of Wilson as a coward, only a man who could go kill crazy when scared. Wilson dared not look back at the warriors, afraid the wildness in his eyes would betray him and they would recognize he was planning some escape route. Only as a last resort, would he dare fight all four warriors and if no other resort presented itself, Black Robe would be his rifle's first victim.

Black Robe kicked his pony and moved beside Wilson, pointing down at the tracks. They were moving down into a small valley, heavily wooded with beech, hardwoods, and abundant underbrush, making it hard to see over twenty feet to the side of the trail.

"We are closing in on the Arapaho." The big warrior grunted in his native voice. "Perhaps, we won't need you much longer, Redhead."

Wilson looked over at the sneering Nez Perce. "We had a deal, Black Robe, will you break it?"

"That is a funny question, white man. You have stolen and lied." The warrior frowned. "You have never kept your word. You have caused me to lose many warriors."

"I told you the truth."

"You kill this Arapaho, then we will see if you live or die." Black Robe pulled his horse in and waited for his warriors to ride up to him. "Kill him, then we will see, Redhead."

The warrior was a poor liar, as Wilson knew he wanted to kill him here and now. However, there was something holding him back and something about the warrior who rode ahead of them. He hunted and raided at times with the different tribes. He didn't respect them as civilized men, thinking they were a barbaric and ignorant race of people, completely without scruples of any kind. Wilson had traded for and married two wives, one Blackfoot, the other Flathead; they had helped him, keeping him in good graces with the tribes. When out trapping or trading, he left them behind in their own villages so neither knew of the other. The other trappers knew of his arrangement and knew he was a scoundrel, but none dared speak of it. Billy Wilson was young, strong, smart, and a natural killer, so nobody wanted him mad at them. One story floated around the mountains, told of Wilson tracking another trapper for a whole month for calling him out over some stolen pelts. When the trapper's remains were discovered, his head was stuck on a pole and his bones arranged in a circle around it, but no one could prove it was Wilson.

Squirrel Tooth watched as Black Robe rejoined them and shook his head. "We should have caught this warrior before now."

"You still say he is a demon, Squirrel Tooth?"

"How can one lone Arapaho stay ahead of us for so many days?"

"He is better mounted. He has the spotted stallion."

The warrior was just about to respond when a brown shadow roared out of the underbrush, causing Wilson's horse to rear and shy sideways, throwing the redhead sideways, right into the huge bear's path. The Nez Perce warriors pulled back on their spooked horses that had turned and bolted in a crazed frenzy, running away from their age-old enemy, the grizzly. Finally, getting their horses under control, the warriors pulled them around roughly, just in time to watch as the huge beast tore at the screaming Wilson.

"It is him." Squirrel Tooth raised his bow and pointed at the bear.

"Who?" Black Robe couldn't remove his eyes from the form of Wilson being ripped and rolled around on the ground. "Who do you see?"

"It is the demon who attacks the redhead."

The horses were shying and frightened, refusing to go any closer to where Wilson was being mauled and slashed by the huge front claws and powerful jaws. Black Robe yelled and waved his bow at the enraged animal, trying to distract it from Wilson. Rising onto his hind legs, the huge animal sniffed the air, trying to locate where the noise came from. Finally finding the warriors on the shifting breeze, it roared and charged a few feet toward them, causing the warriors to ride their horses hastily further back up the trail.

Finally getting his crazed horse under control, Black Robe turned and watched as the bear retreated out of sight. Her cubs came out of the underbrush, where they had concealed themselves, following after her. The great Nez Perce warriors of the north feared few things but an enraged grizzly with cubs was one of their worst fears, and this bear had two young ones at her side.

"It was no demon." Black Robe sneered at Squirrel Tooth. "Just bad luck for the redhead to ride so close to a bear with cubs."

"What do we do now?" Another warrior, still shaking, looked at Black Robe.

"The spotted stallion is close; we go after him."

"Is this wise, my Chief?" Squirrel Tooth spoke up, more frightened of the demon than he was of Black Robe. "Our luck has been bad since we crossed the river."

Black Robe glared at the warrior. Their luck on this trail had been bad, but he wasn't about to return to his village to face his people without the stallion. "Squirrel Tooth is as a woman."

The dark face blushed as the big warrior scolded him for his weakness. "This is bad medicine."

"We go! Squirrel Tooth, you return to the village in shame if you want to."

"How do we get past the bear?" The other warrior, Many Feathers, spoke up. "The bear could be waiting for us to approach closer. If she is there, the trail is too narrow to get away from her."

"I will go first, and you will see the bear has left." Black Robe kicked the nervous piebald horse hard, forcing him forward. "Follow me; we must ride fast to the river. We must catch the Arapaho before he crosses."

"He will kill our ponies at this pace if he keeps it up." Squirrel Tooth kicked his horse trying to catch up with Black Robe.

"He is crazy with lust for the spotted stallion." Many Feathers shook his head sadly.

"The signs were on the moon last night." Squirrel Tooth reluctantly moved forward, watching as Black Robe dismounted and picked up the rifle of the dead white man. "Did you not see the dark hand cross over the night light?"

"I saw nothing, Squirrel Tooth." Another of the Nez Perce spoke up. "Bah, you would whine and cry if you were given a fresh buffalo tongue."

"At least I am still alive." Squirrel Tooth glared at the warrior.

"Is being a coward, being alive?"

"I am no coward. When we return to our village, remember your words, then we will see who is a coward."

"Enough!" Many Feathers yelled. "Have we not enough problems without fighting among ourselves?"

The warriors shook their heads, watching as their leader had to jerk and kick his horse to get past Wilson's dead body. The heavy smell of blood and the grizzly was still on the air. Apparently, the bear had taken her cubs and returned to the depth of the mountains, as no sign or sound of her came from the woods bordering the trail as they passed.

"I fear he will get us all killed before this trail is over." Many Feathers kicked his own animal forward. "I agree with Squirrel Tooth; he has gone crazy."

"Black Robe said we could go home." Squirrel Tooth fought his horse past the dead body.

"You know as a Nez Perce warrior, if we abandon our leader on the trail, we would lose face with our people and could never return to our village with pride or honor." The last of the warriors spoke up. "I rather die first."

Squirrel Tooth nodded his head. "You will probably get your wish. I see bad things ahead for us, but you are right."

All three studied the bloody ripped body of Wilson as they rode their skittish horses past where he lay. "The redhead didn't have a chance."

"He deserved what he got." Squirrel Tooth kicked his horse into a lope to catch up with Black Robe, but mainly to get far away from the evil place and demon that lurked there.

"No one deserves to die like that, not even the redhead." Many Feathers shook his head.

"If it wasn't for the redhead, we wouldn't be here to begin with, and our friends would still be alive."

Many Feathers took one last look over his shoulder at the still form of Wilson covered in blood. "Perhaps you are right, but to be eaten alive, ugh."

Red Hawk was still sore from his wound but he was able to trap a few small animals in his snares. Coon, rabbit, and one turkey hen were all he had trapped, and it was enough to keep them alive. Never using the same trail twice, he always made sure to keep his tracks well hidden. Little Antelope recovered except for the bruising on her face from Wilson's rifle butt slamming her. Both took turns watching the river crossing and the trails leading down to the water.

Red Hawk looked over at the woman as she roasted a rabbit over a small fire. "If Crow Killer does not return soon, we must try to make our way back to our villages."

"Will you be able to travel that far afoot?"

"The longer we stay here, the more dangerous it is for us." The warrior turned his gaze to the river. "We have been lucky, but we could still be discovered."

"You are the great Red Hawk; the decision is yours."

"We have no choice. We must go."

"When?"

Red Hawk looked out at the great river. "Tomorrow or the next day, we must leave this place soon. I have a bad feeling."

Bow Legs pulled his horse in and studied the waters of the river from atop a small hill, overlooking the large waterway. It hadn't rained and the tracks still showed clearly in the sandy trail that Bow Legs and the Cheyenne sat on.

"The river is close. We will ride there and rest the horses before we cross."

"And me." One of the younger warriors rubbed his backside.

"And feed my stomach." A paunchy warrior chimed in.

Yellow Dog shook his head at his friends who came with him to help find Little Antelope. "Your bottoms and stomachs grow soft."

"The Great Yellow Dog has no feelings." The first warrior, Lame Horse, spoke up. "You show us no mercy."

"When Little Antelope is safe, then I will have feelings." Yellow Dog shook his head at his friends. "Then you can rest and eat your fill."

"They are just kidding. We remember Little Antelope when she lived with us as a child."

"I know you do, Crazy Cat." The paunchy Lame Horse laughed. "After Walking Horse won her heart, you didn't speak for many moons."

Turning red faced, the one called Crazy Cat frowned. "This is true."

"Then you lost the fight and black horse as she watched." Lame Horse teased the frowning warrior. "Twice you have lost face, in her eyes."

"Be careful, fat one." Crazy Cat touched his knife. "Maybe you will lose something."

"Enough, both of you." Yellow Dog growled at the two warriors.

"His mouth is as big as his stomach."

Lame Horse laughed, making his paunch jiggle up and down. "I have hit a nerve."

"I said, enough." Yellow Dog swung onto his horse. "We go!"

As the argument grew quiet, Bow Legs motioned forward and kicked his horse down the trail. The sun was almost full in the sky as the Cheyenne, with the Arapaho leading them, reined in several feet from the rotting carcass of the black. After examining the many tracks surrounding the dead horse, they rode on to the river's edge and slid from their horses. Watering and hobbling the tired animals on the lush grass by the river, the warriors took greasy pieces of jerked meat from the leather bags Bow Legs tossed them and reclined on the grass.

"Crow Killer's horse was killed by a warrior with a rifle." Bow Legs bit into the jerky. "It had to be the white man riding with the Nez Perce."

Yellow Dog nodded, the tracks they had found were several days old but they could still plainly read the tracks of a white. "The tracks of a large white man with turned out toes were with the Nez Perce warriors."

"But where is the body of Crow Killer?" Lame Horse looked about the riverbank.

"Perhaps, the young one was not injured and escaped into the woods." Crazy Cat muttered. "The rifle has only one shot, it killed his horse."

"Perhaps." Yellow Dog agreed with Crazy Cat. "If Crow Killer had been killed, the Nez Perce would have taken his scalp but not his body.

Bow Legs shook his head. "The tracks lead into the water. We have no time to look for him; we must ride."

Red Hawk watched the Cheyenne, with the Arapaho leading them, as they sat along the riverbank, talking. He knew they were letting their horses rest before making the hard crossing. Nudging Little Antelope awake, he pointed toward the river.

"Your people, they are here." Red Hawk nodded at the warriors.

Little Antelope stared across the expanse of the river's shore to where the warriors sat. She immediately recognized her brother Yellow Dog, Crazy Cat, Lame Horse, and Bow Legs. She could tell their horses had traveled fast, as all were covered in heavy sweat stains. They would need rest before crossing the wide river. "Yes, one of them is my brother, Yellow Dog."

"Five are Cheyenne and one Arapaho."

"Yes, we are safe now. They are between us and the Nez Perce."

"Go out to them." Red Hawk started to rise. "Warn them that many Nez Perce crossed the river in front of them."

"No, if they searched and discovered this place, they would kill you." Little Antelope watched the warriors. "They can read sign as well as a Crow. They know how many warriors are ahead of them."

"You could stop them from killing me."

"I'm not sure. You are the great Crow Warrior Red Hawk, the hated enemy of the Arapaho." Little Antelope kneeled undecided, staring out at the group of warriors. "No, we will stay hidden until Crow Killer returns."

"He could stop them from killing me?"

"Yes, they would do as he said."

"You are very proud of this warrior?" Red Hawk studied her face. "I can see it in your eyes when you speak of him. Perhaps, more than pride holds your heart."

Little Antelope blushed slightly from Red Hawk's words. He had guessed her feelings but that was all it was, a guess. "I love my husband, Walking Horse. We will speak no more of this, Crow."

Red Hawk laughed lightly and shook his head. "Okay woman, but the more you deny it, the more I feel it is true."

"One more word from you, Crow, and I will call out to them."

"Okay, okay, not another word."

Two hours passed as Yellow Dog let his horses rest before making the treacherous crossing of the swift river. Looking over at the far bank, he knew they would drift far downriver before coming out on the other shore. With his tired horses, he knew it was better to swim and drift with the current than try to swim straight across. The horses had to conserve what strength they had left, as there was no way to know how much further they would have to travel before they overtook the enemy.

Suddenly, a cry went up from Bow Legs as he rolled to his feet and pointed across the river. A lone rider on a sorrel horse, leading the spotted stallion, came into sight as he left the cover of the woods, riding out to the sandy riverbank at a high lope.

"It is Crow Killer and he has the stallion." Bow Legs hollered and jumped in the air.

"His horses are very tired. They have been ridden far."

"Look." Lame Horse pointed across the river. "Nez Perce."

"Only four." Yellow Dog watched as the four warriors came from the woods and sat their horses, looking out across the river. "Where are the rest?"

"Perhaps they wait in the woods, out of sight."

"What can Crow Killer do?" Bow Legs waded knee deep into the river. "He cannot swim the river, his horses are too tired."

Jed rode the two horses belly deep into the current, then whipped both of them hard with his bow before wading back to the sandy bank.

To be sure they wouldn't try to turn back; Jed threw stones at the swimming horses, watching as they struck out for the far bank. Across the river, Jed could plainly see the leaping form of Bow Legs and the Cheyenne warriors. Seeing the other horses across the river, the stallion struck out strongly for the far bank with the sorrel following.

"What does he do?" Crazy Cat watched as Jed turned and walked several feet from the river, then pushed his lance into the soft sand.

Yellow Dog watched helplessly as there was no way they could reach the far shore in time to help, even if they could, to be caught midstream by warriors with bows and deadly arrows would be a disaster for them all. "Crow Killer knew the horses were too exhausted to make the swim carrying him so he saved the spotted stallion. Now, he will stay and fight."

"Four against one." Bow Legs mounted his horse. "I go."

"You will not arrive in time, my friend, then there will be four against you, providing you get out of the river alive."

"I cannot leave him to die alone." Bow Legs started into the water.

"Wait." Yellow Dog held up his arm. "Look, only one comes forward to fight."

Bow Legs stared out across the moving water and shook his head. Yellow Dog was right, only one large warrior rode forward to where Jed waited straight and proud, with his lance planted firmly in the ground. The warrior was big, even bigger than Yellow Dog, and fierce looking. He was too far away yet to see the countenance of his face but Bow Legs knew it would be pure viciousness. "I should go."

"Wait, Bow Legs." Yellow Dog shook his head. "I know you want to help him but if you try to cross the river, they will all attack Crow Killer. This warrior has made it personal and challenged him to combat."

"I will wait, but I feel like a coward sitting here." Bow Legs frowned and dropped his eyes in shame. "A Lance Bearer does not hold back while a friend fights alone."

Lame Horse touched the warrior's shoulder. "All here know you are no coward, Bow Legs. Wait here; it is for the best. If you try to help, he will surely be killed."

"I do not understand why this warrior will fight Crow Killer alone when they have him outnumbered and caught against the river." Crazy Cat watched the far bank.

"Crow Killer has set his lance in the ground for all to see." Yellow Dog nodded. "The Nez Perce are a great people. If this warrior kills a Lance Bearer of the Arapaho by himself, his medicine will be strong."

"And if he loses?" Lame Horse questioned.

"He will be dead."

Bow Legs strained his eyes, trying to see the warrior plainer. "His bearing shows he is a proud warrior."

"Whoever this warrior is, he is probably a great warrior in his tribe." Yellow Dog looked across the river. "He is proud, very proud."

Black Robe rode his paint horse to the river's edge, stopping only feet from where Jed waited, staked to the ground by the lance. A long leather thong attached him to the lance, preventing him from moving too far in any direction. Jed glanced behind him, across the river. He knew Bow Legs and the warriors standing across the river were too far away to help him, and like them, he was curious why this warrior came alone to challenge him. The Nez Perce was huge with bulging muscles and thick torso. Power, strength, and confidence emitted from the warrior as he sat his horse, studying Jed.

"Why did you not cross the river, Arapaho?" Black Robe fingered his war axe.

Jed was surprised he could understand the warrior. "The spotted one was too exhausted to swim, dragging me across. I did not want to see him harmed further."

"You think much of my horse."

"No, but I think much of my friend's horse." Jed looked behind the warrior, trying to spot Wilson. "The horse now belongs to Walking Horse, Lance Bearer of the great Arapaho Nation."

"Bah, you lie, Arapaho." Black Robe raised his war axe. "The horse belongs to me, stolen from our village by you Arapaho dogs."

Jed smiled slightly. "Red Hawk the Crow stole him from you. I stole him from Red Hawk."

"And I stole him and your squaw back."

"And the white stole him and the woman from you as you slept like children." Jed watched the red rage creep deeper into the warrior's face. "A white made fools of the Nez Perce."

"The redhead is dead because of his theft of the spotted one." Black Robe smiled cruelly.

"You killed Wilson?" Jed was shocked. "Where?"

"No, a grizzly demon, who my warriors back there think is you, killed him." Black Robe jabbed his fingers in disgust behind him. "They are cowards, superstitious fools."

"A bear killed the redheaded one, is that what you are saying?"

"Yes. Now, Arapaho, demon, whatever you are, prepare to meet your ancestors." The big warrior slid from his horse and faced Jed. "You can meet the redhead in the other world."

"Where is his body?"

"Maybe a half day behind us." Black Robe looked back at Squirrel Tooth and the other warriors. "But tell me, if you are a demon, how do you not know this?"

Jed shook his head as he adjusted his war axe and skinning knife for battle. He couldn't believe it, Billy Wilson was dead, killed by a grizzly bear; that is if he understood the warrior right. "Turn away Nez Perce and live." Jed's face grew cold and hard. "Stay here and die."

"Turning away with my warriors watching is the same as dying." With his final words, Black Robe flung himself across the opening toward Jed with unbelievable speed.

Little Antelope almost screamed when she saw what her brother and the others were watching. Climbing from the entrance of the cave, she raced to the river where Yellow Dog and his warriors stood. Turning quickly, as they heard her approaching footsteps, the Cheyenne were shocked to see her.

"Why do you stand here? Go help him!" Little Antelope tore loose from her brother's hand as he reached out to her as she walked closer to the river. "There are too many enemies over there."

"Would you have us get him killed, Sister?"

"I don't understand." She looked at Bow Legs. "You are a Lance Bearer. You must help him, or lose face and honor."

"Little Antelope, he cannot." Yellow Dog quickly explained their predicament and why they couldn't cross the river. "We must wait."

As they watched the Nez Perce slide from his horse, Yellow Dog grabbed her tightly, preventing her from entering the water. The Cheyenne watched curiously as the warriors confronted each other and spoke. What did the two enemies, one Arapaho and the other Nez Perce, have to talk about for several minutes before the large warrior dismounted and started forward?

"I thought the Cheyenne and Arapaho were great, brave warriors." The words came from behind them. Whirling, they took in the form of the bloody and weak Red Hawk standing behind them. "You should go help him."

"Red Hawk!" Bow Legs pulled his knife and started forward. "Now, you die, Crow dog."

"No!" Little Antelope threw herself between Red Hawk and the warriors. "He has saved my life. He is the friend of Crow Killer."

"A Crow, the friend of an Arapaho?" Bow Legs was bewildered. "How can this be?"

"Red Hawk is my friend also." Little Antelope stepped back against Red Hawk shielding him. "He will not be harmed."

"Squaw, we will talk of this later." Yellow Dog held up his hand, stopping Bow Legs, and turning his attention back to the far bank. On the other side, none of the Nez Perce warriors had moved. Yellow Dog knew, for some reason, this combat was personal, only between these two warriors. "We will wait here and see what happens."

"Black Robe is a dead man." Squirrel Tooth shook his head as he watched the two men move toward each other. "He faces a demon with the spirit power of the grizzly."

Many Feathers scoffed. "He is but an Arapaho. He is no demon, no grizzly bear."

"The Lance Bearers of the Arapaho are great warriors, great fighters." Squirrel Tooth trembled. "I tell you now, the spirit of the grizzly is in the Arapaho. Black Robe is as a dead man."

"You are becoming as crazy as Black Robe." Many Feathers looked over at the trembling warrior. He knew he was only talking but even he was beginning to feel fear and anxiety.

"No, I am not crazy. I have seen the demon from the spirit world." Squirrel Tooth tried to calm himself. "He stands there in front of Black

Robe as an Arapaho but he is a spirit person; a demon from the other world."

"Squirrel Tooth may be right." The other Nez Perce pushed his horse closer to the worried and scared warrior. "Why would our chief fight this one alone, if he was not cursed?"

Squirrel Tooth shook his head. "This I do not know for sure. Perhaps it is the demon speaking to him, or it is because Black Robe is proud and wants to count coup on this one alone."

"Black Robe is powerful, much more than this puny Arapaho." Many Feathers raised his axe exhorting his leader. "He will kill the Arapaho dog."

"You are a fool, Many Feathers."

"I am not the one who is frightened of the unknown, my friend."

"I am no fool." Squirrel Tooth watched Black Robe sadly. "I tell you this, if Black Robe is killed, we will leave this place quickly and hope the demon does not follow us back to our lands to curse our villages."

Closing together, both warriors circled, feinting and slashing at each other, back and forth. Jed already felt the massive strength of Black Robe as they clutched and grabbed at each other's arms. Breaking loose from the powerful grasp of the Nez Perce, he used his speed to keep away from the huge warrior. Black Robe seemed obsessed, almost insane as he rushed and pushed forward, trying to come to grips with the smaller Arapaho. Only the speed and dexterity, Jed possessed, kept him from harm's way so far in this battle to the death.

Feeling the leather thong of the lance catching around his leg, Black Robe quickly cut it with his knife, releasing Jed to move about more freely. "You are free to run now, Arapaho. Your leash has been cut."

"I will only run toward you, warrior." Jed spat back at the warrior, knowing the Nez Perce had made a serious error in cutting the thong that bound him to the lance. "Tonight, I will hold your scalp, ride your great spotted horse to our lands, and brag of killing you."

"You talk big for one so young." Black Robe started to say more when he felt Jed's blade slice across his arm. The warrior facing him was fast, he moved with the speed of a shooting star.

"No more talk, warrior. Now, we fight."

Enraged, Black Robe sprang forward swiping with his own war axe, missing Jed's head by only inches. While the war axe missed its mark, the sharp knife of Black Robe sliced a path across Jed's left side, causing a small trickle of blood to flow. Whirling backwards and turning, Jed again swiped the warrior with his knife, this time causing a considerable amount of blood to flow.

Across the river, Little Antelope stood beside Red Hawk, watching as the two warriors lunged back and forth. Too far away to see the damage being done, Little Antelope unknowingly grasped Red Hawk's arm in a viselike grip. The Nez Perce warriors were closer, but they also were too far away and could not see the wounds being made or who was winning. Squirrel Tooth refused to move closer to the fight for fear of the demon he believed to be there.

Finally, Black Robe dropped his knife and grabbed Jed's wrist in a crushing grip, hanging on as the smaller man tried his best to wrench himself free. Pushing and shoving, the Nez Perce tried his best to club Jed as he swung his heavy war axe. Tripping over each other's feet, both men rolled apart as they hit the soft sand but quickly regained their feet. Black Robe swiftly scooped up his dropped war axe and leaped forward, swinging a wicked blow at Jed's left shoulder.

"What's the matter, old man, you tiring?" Jed laughed out loud. The watching Nez Perce could hear words being spoken but they were too far to understand.

Livid with rage at the younger and smaller warrior's words, Black Robe continued his bull rushes while swinging the axe with all his strength and might. Missing the evasive and nimble Arapaho, the Nez Perce fell to one knee, exhausted, just barely managing to regain his feet in time to evade the vicious downward strike of Jed's axe. The sand was deep along the river, causing both fighters to tire and slow down their attacks as they both fought the soft footing. Jed leapt forward, striking quickly, cutting a wide slice across Black Robe's belly, and retreated as the warrior lunged sideways holding his stomach. Confidence rising, Jed became more aggressive, rushing at the tiring warrior forcing him backwards, causing him to retreat. Again and again, the sharp knife found its mark but the Nez Perce was so powerful, so strong, he was still able to ward off the strike of the deadly war axe.

Stepping back, both men drew several long breaths into their lungs, trying to regain enough strength to finish the other man. Both warriors were cut and bloody. Their enraged bodies were full of adrenaline and neither thought of retreat nor backing away. Almost at the same time, both sprang forward simultaneously, their weapons springing forward with the last of their speed and power. The mighty war axe of Black Robe dislodged Jed's own axe, sending it flying harmlessly into the deep water of the river.

"Now, Arapaho, I've got you." Black Robe's erratic words came forth from the exhausted man.

"We'll see, big man." Jed held his knife ready while circling to his right, away from the war axe.

The Nez Perce held his axe, ready to strike the killing blow. "Yes, we will see."

"Black Robe has him now." Many Feathers saw the war axe fly from the Arapaho's hand and sail into the water. "He has only a knife to defend himself now."

Squirrel Tooth watched, his eyes aglow. "Black Robe is a dead man as we speak."

"But…" Many Feathers started again.

"Watch, you will see."

With his war axe raised high, Black Robe rushed forward, causing Jed to step back and trip over his lance that still stood upright, buried in the sandy ground. Falling backwards on the ground, as he tried to avoid the heavy war axe of the Nez Perce, Jed grabbed the heavy lance and pulled it in front of him. In his haste, trying his best to finish the downed man, Black Robe swung the heavy war axe down with all his massive strength, launching his heavier body on top of Jed. Everyone from both sides of the river watched apprehensively as the two men lay unmoving where they had fallen on the riverbank. Black Robe was atop the smaller Jed, and both men lay motionless, neither man moving for several seconds. The Nez Perce warriors moved forward a few feet until Squirrel Tooth raised his hand for them to halt. From across the river, seeing neither man moving and the Nez Perce warriors closing in on the two combatants, Bow Legs quickly mounted his horse, riding him into the swift current.

Watching in horror as Jed didn't move, Little Antelope turned her face into Red Hawk's chest and closed her eyes. She knew he was dead.

Looking over at his sister, Yellow Dog swung up on his horse, and with the other Cheyenne, followed Bow Legs into the river. "Take care of her, Crow." Yellow Dog looked to where they stood.

"Look." Red Hawk pointed across the river. "Something moves."

Jed, with the last of his strength, slowly rolled the larger warrior off from him and stood up shakily. Turning slowly, he looked to where Squirrel Tooth and the other Nez Perce sat their horses, with only a few feet separating them. Grabbing his knife and Black Robe's war axe, he turned, waiting for their charge. He knew he was in no shape to fight off three more warriors but there was no other choice, as he was too weak to contemplate swimming the river.

"Do we kill him?" Many Feathers questioned Squirrel Tooth as he looked out across the water to where Bow Legs was swimming hard toward them. "The others cannot reach us in time to save him."

Squirrel Tooth could only shake his head. His superstitions held him helpless as he feared a demon possessed this warrior. He had seen the demon's power, when he had killed Black Robe, as the Arapaho could not have done this by himself, and watched when the bear killed the redhead. Squirrel Tooth trembled, his superstitions were too strong. He was afraid to attack and infuriate the demon further. The warrior standing before them appeared weak from the battle with Black Robe, but Squirrel Tooth knew it could be a trick to lure them close so the demon could kill them.

"Kill him if you wish but I leave this place as fast as I can." Squirrel Tooth turned his horse. "If you value your lives, go with me before we are all killed."

"Our people will think us cowards."

"We will be alive, but if we attack this warrior, we will all surely die like Black Robe." The warrior argued. "Black Robe had this battle won but the demon with its powers helped the Arapaho."

"I am ashamed." Elk Runner spoke up.

"You are alive." Squirrel Tooth shook his head. "If you are so ready to die, Elk Runner, then go. I ride for home; we cannot help Black Robe now."

"No, I will not run from an enemy already beaten." Elk Runner screamed and busted his horse hard with the war axe he wielded. "Aiyee!"

Many Feathers, the remaining Nez Perce, only watched and shook his head in sadness as he listened to Squirrel Tooth. "He too is already a dead man and soon he will join Black Robe in the other world."

Jed braced himself for the onrushing warrior, then sidestepped the charging horse and swung the war axe in a deadly arc aimed for the screaming rider's stomach. Only a whoosh of air came from the man as he was knocked from the racing horse, dead before he hit the sandy ground. Looking to where the others were sitting their horses in shock, Jed let out a sigh of relief.

"He was a fool." Squirrel Tooth took a final look, raised his hand at Jed before kicking his horse hard, wanting to rid himself of this place. Never, as long as he lived and fought as a Nez Perce, would he believe or let anyone tell him that a demon had not set upon them in this place. Never would he return here; never.

"A fool perhaps, but he was a brave man and we are cowards." Many Feathers could only shake his head.

"You could join him if you wish." Squirrel Tooth was disgusted and tired of being told he was a coward. A demon was from the ones down under, and no warrior could fight one and win. "All you have to do is turn around."

"No, I have seen enough."

CHAPTER 10

Red Hawk and Little Antelope caught the spotted stallion and Red Hawk's sorrel horse as they waded out of the river further down the bank. Across the river, Bow Legs was the first to reach the far bank and ride to where Jed stood spraddle legged, exhausted. What was left of the enemy was two Nez Perce riding hard up the mountain trail, back the way they came.

"Are you okay, Crow Killer?" Bow Legs looked at the many rips and streaks of blood on Jed's clothing. "You bleed much."

Jed looked down at his torso which was drenched in blood, then over to where Black Robe lay. "It is not all mine, most of it is his."

"You killed him with your lance?" Bow Legs looked dismayed to where the dead Nez Perce lay with the lance protruding from his body.

"He fell on it in his haste to kill me with his war axe."

The warrior shook his head. "That is not what I have seen. You killed him with your lance, Crow Killer."

"You are mistaken, my friend." Jed shook his head tiredly. "I was beaten. He killed himself when he tripped and fell on it."

Yellow Dog and his warriors emerged from the river in time to see the two Nez Perce racing away from the river at a hard run. After the long swim, their horses were too tired to give chase. Dismounting beside Jed, Yellow Dog examined the many small knife cuts that shredded his shirt.

"It was a good fight, at least what we could see from over there." Yellow Dog smiled at Jed.

"It wasn't so good from over here." Jed smiled tiredly, even more so now that the adrenaline left his body, leaving him completely spent.

"Why did the others not help him?"

Jed shrugged. "That I do not know. If they had, I would be dead now."

Bow Legs shook his head. "I do not think this, the spirit people of the lance watched over you this day. The Nez Perce knew if they had attacked you, they would have been killed, the same as this one."

"This was Black Robe, of the Nez Perce." Jed looked at the dead warrior.

"He was a great warrior."

"He was big alright."

"Can you cross the river, Crow Killer? My sister, Little Antelope, and the Crow, Red Hawk, wait for you there." Yellow Dog looked across the river and raised his great arm. "Red Hawk says there are many more Nez Perce and they may come back."

"They won't be back; most are dead."

"You killed them?"

"No, they fought with some warriors, Blackfoot I think, many days back. Many were killed."

"No other warriors but the Blackfoot would dare fight the mighty Nez Perce." Yellow Dog nodded his head. "The spotted horse and my sister have cost these Nez Perce much."

"Much."

"What happened to the white that was with them?" Bow Legs remembered the tracks of a large white around the black horse's body.

Jed nodded over at Black Robe. "That warrior said a bear killed him, back there."

"A bear!" Yellow dog suddenly understood why the Nez Perce held back. Some of them may have thought Crow Killer was a demon or he had the help of the grizzly on his side. Yellow Dog knew how superstitious some tribes could be. "For a bear to attack is bad medicine and many think they are possessed by demons."

"Can you ride?" Bow Legs asked again.

"I can ride." Jed nodded. "But first I must see the body of the dead white before I can return to our village."

"This could be very dangerous, my friend."

"I will go alone." Jed looked across the river. "Yellow Dog must take his sister back to her husband."

"And the Crow?"

Jed nodded slowly as he studied the faces surrounding him. "He is my friend. I ask you to ride with him, as far as his hunting grounds, and see that he gets there safe."

"This we will do." Yellow Dog agreed. "You have our word."

"The spotted stallion is his. Let him ride him back to his people with pride." Jed once again looked across the great river. "Give me your word on this, Yellow Dog."

The Cheyenne frowned slightly. "You ask a great deal, my friend. The horse of the Nez Perce is a great coup to bring home to my people, but you have my word; the Crow will have the horse and his life."

"And you, my friend, have your sister back safely. It is more than an even trade." Jed spoke tiredly. "Much more."

Yellow Dog laughed. "My brother-in-law, Walking Horse, might not think so."

"If she was my woman, I wouldn't trade five horses like him for her."

"I know." Yellow Dog had watched Little Antelope's face as Jed battled alone across the river. He knew her feelings for Crow Killer were strong. "You should come back with us to your people."

"No, I must see the dead body of this white." Jed shook his head.

"You don't need me to get back." Bow Legs looked across at Yellow Dog. "I will ride with Crow Killer. I wish to see this huge white that was killed by a demon."

Crazy Cat laughed out loud. "Be careful, Bow Legs, the demon might eat those scrawny little legs of yours."

Bow Legs did have about the skinniest legs in the whole Arapaho Nation and that was exactly how he got his name. "The women love my legs, perhaps the demon will too."

"I don't see how." Crazy Cat shook his head and laughed. "They look like two twigs with moccasins tied to them."

Jed stared once more across the water where Little Antelope and Red Hawk stood, then gathered the reins of Black Robe's paint horse. "We go."

"I believe my sister would like to speak with you before you go."
Yellow Dog stepped near the piebald paint, that Black Robe prized, and
whispered up at Jed. "She cares for you very much."

"Tell her I will return, then we will speak." Jed shook his head. "I
care for her but she is the wife of my friend Walking Horse, and I would
do nothing to shame him."

"I will tell her, Crow Killer." Yellow Dog nodded. "I understand you
are an honorable warrior and I am honored to have you for a friend."

Looking down at the tall Cheyenne, Jed placed his hand on the
broad shoulders. "Thank you, my friend, and tell Red Hawk, we will
hunt the shaggies together when I return."

"This I will do also." The Cheyenne shook his head. "Remember,
my friend, you are still a Lance Bearer of the Arapaho and he is a Crow."

Jed nodded thoughtfully. "This is true, but now we are brothers by
blood. He is my friend."

"As I am, Crow Killer." Crazy Cat extended his hand which Jed took
in his own.

From across the river, Little Antelope and Red Hawk watched as Jed
waved to them, turning his horse back to the west and north, following
the same trail the Nez Perce had taken. Her small face stiffened as she
realized he wasn't crossing the river. Fighting to hold back her tears, she
turned away so Red Hawk could not see.

"He leaves. Where does he go?" Her dark eyes followed the fading
figures of the two warriors. "He rides away with Bow Legs. He is not
coming across."

"He takes a warrior with him." The Crow also watched as Jed
disappeared. "I do not know where he goes but it must be important."

"He rides to the north." The girl sniffed slightly. "I feel he will never
return to us."

"What will you do if he doesn't return?"

Composing herself before the others made it back across the river,
she shook her head. "I told you, Crow. I have a husband."

"I hear what you say, little one." Red Hawk smiled. "Perhaps you
feel a little something for another too."

Yellow Dog and his warriors waded from the water and slid from their dripping horses, letting the tired animals catch their breath from the long swim back across the river. He studied the small face of his sister for several seconds, then turned to where Red Hawk held the spotted stallion. Running his hand over the well-muscled neck and back of the Appaloosa stallion, he nodded in approval.

"Crow Killer says the horse is yours. We are to take you back to your hunting grounds like a lost child." The Cheyenne stood proudly in front of an age-old enemy. "To let one such as this spotted one go is a hard thing to ask."

"Crow Killer said this?"

"Yes, this was his wish."

"And?" Red Hawk was too proud to ask their intentions since they were his enemies. He knew they wanted to kill him and take the horse, but they had given their word to Crow Killer.

"The horse is yours, Crow, but someday, I might come to steal him away from you." Yellow Dog laughed. "Be alert and do not sleep."

"No one will steal this horse, ever again." Red Hawk smiled. "But, the first spotted horse colt from this one and my best mare will be yours, Yellow Dog. A great Cheyenne leader needs a great horse."

Little Antelope could not stand the suspense any longer and stepped in front of her brother. "Where has Jed, I mean Crow Killer, gone?"

"After the white man that took you from the Nez Perce."

"Why?" She looked up at him confused. "We are all back."

"You should ask him when he returns." Yellow Dog shrugged. "Perhaps, he wants revenge."

"I will ask him one day." Her chin was firm. "He will return."

"Good, now let's take this Crow home before his mother starts to worry." Yellow Dog just had to get in one more jab at Red Hawk. "If he has a mother."

"I do Cheyenne, do you?"

Yellow Dog laughed, tossing his sister aboard the sorrel Jed had been riding. "My mother was a lobo timber wolf and my daddy was a wolverine. Watch out, Crow, I'm a bad Cheyenne warrior."

"I believe, Yellow Dog." Red Hawk smiled weakly, then mounted and followed the small caravan back to the east.

Jed didn't have any idea how far back up the trail Wilson's body might be. He figured if the bear hadn't come back, covering it with leaves and dirt, it wouldn't be hard to find. He really didn't even understand why he was looking for Billy Wilson, the man who had brought him so much grief for years. He remembered a fondness for Ed Wilson, and the way the man had treated him and his mother so well. Billy didn't deserve burying but Jed figured he owed Ed Wilson at least that much. Pushing the paint down the trail at a pretty good clip, Jed thought back on the form of Little Antelope, standing so small across the river. He knew he should have crossed the river to say good-bye, at least tell her where he was going, but he didn't trust his feelings and didn't want the others to see them together. This way was best, and he would explain to her when he returned to the Arapaho. The way Yellow Dog had whispered to him, he figured the warrior already knew the feelings he carried for his sister. Jed liked and respected the warrior too much and if Walking Horse ever discovered what they felt, there could be many problems, and he didn't want that.

"How far do you figure the white will be?" Bow Legs rode slumped on his horse, riding like a man half asleep, but the sharp eyes missed nothing in passing.

"The warrior didn't say, but I figure we will find him before the day is out." Jed tossed back over his shoulder.

"Maybe the bear ate his body and there will be nothing to find."

"Billy Wilson was a mean one. I doubt the bear could have chewed him."

For three hours, they rode at a slow pace; saving the already tired horses that had been used hard for two solid weeks. The paint was broad and powerful, more powerful than even the black given to him by Yellow Dog, but he too was tired. The day was beginning to heat up and Jed could feel the stickiness of the sweat from the horse's bare back seeping through his leggings.

"The sun will go down soon, Crow Killer." Bow Legs shaded his eyes from the western sky. "We don't want to pass him in the dark."

"I figure the horses will smell him out for us."

"Maybe, but not if the bear drug him far back into the brush."

"You think we should camp for the night?"

"Yes, I do." Bow Legs folded his hands across his pony's withers. "If it was a grizzly that killed him, a grizzly will protect their kill, sometimes for days. My skinny self sure doesn't care to run into one in the dark."

"Tell me, why?" Jed grinned. "You're not scared, are you?"

"Simple, I do not want him to eat us." The warrior laughed. "I told you, a grizzly will hide and guard his kill from any enemies that might try to get it, that just might be us if we are so foolish to ride in the dark."

"Sounds like good advice. We'll camp at the next water." Jed looked back down the mountain trail. They had covered almost ten miles since leaving the river's edge, and both men and horses were ready for a good night's rest.

Bow Legs suddenly stiffened, reining in his snorting horse. "We may not have to camp. I think we found what we are looking for, Crow Killer."

Whirling the paint, Jed turned to look at whatever Bow Legs saw. "You see something?"

"No, but my horse smells something, listen." The dark thin face was frozen, his every sense tuned in, keen as a sharp knife to the many sounds lingering on the clear air. "There."

The unmistakable sound of metal striking on metal came from the deep underbrush, only feet from where they sat their horses. Slipping to the ground, both men notched arrows and moved quietly toward the sound. Again, as they stooped to pass under low hanging limbs, the sound came from in front of them. The sound was barely audible but it was metal hitting against metal, there was no mistaking the sound. Bow Legs motioned with his hands for Jed to separate slightly as they closed in on whatever was making the noise. The underbrush was dense, making the notched arrows and bow useless if it was a bear ahead of them. Sweating slightly, not from the heat as much as from the tension of stalking what might be a grizzly in close quarters, Jed wiped his face. All his life, he had heard stories of the ferociousness of the huge grizzlies living in these western mountains. Now, he just might be fixing to find out if they were true.

Looking over to where Bow Legs pointed, Jed strained his eyes but he could see nothing in the undergrowth. Cedar, heavy oak, and brush, along with matted waist high grass, covered the slight slope that started upward from where they stood.

Moving back to where Jed waited, Bow Legs pointed at the ground. "Something has been dragged along here."

The two drag marks and blood were clear in the dead leaves and matted grass, covering the ground where they stood. "Look."

A pair of bloody feet, one still wearing a moccasin, the other bare and almost chewed off, lay before them, covered by grass. "We should leave this place quick, Crow Killer. This is the work of a grizzly and he could be watching us now."

"You go back with the horses, my friend. I must see." Jed motioned Bow Legs back.

The warrior shook his head whispering. "No, Crow Killer. Once already today, I have let you fight alone, not this time."

Jed smiled and looked at the bow held in his hands. "If it is a grizzly, I don't think these things are going to do us any good in this brush."

"We will only have time for one shot each, so make it good." Bow Legs grinned.

"Then what?"

"Run fast and find a big tree." Bow Legs laughed lightly. "Every man for himself."

Jed looked about him, doubting that any of the small mountain trees would suffice to get them high enough out of reach of a bear, providing they could reach one in time. He knew grizzlies were ferocious and very fast afoot, much faster than a man. He had always been told to run downhill if a bear was chasing him, but right now the tree sounded like better advice.

Slipping quietly through the brush, both men could hear the slight wheezing and gurgling sounds coming from slightly ahead of them. Bow Legs shook his head worriedly, grabbing at Jed, as he knew it could be the sound of a bear feeding on the white man. Jed shook him off, as he had to know, and he had to be able to tell Ed Wilson if his son was really dead. Pushing ahead stealthily, Jed rose slowly from his crouching position and looked at the dark spot in the deep grass.

"Help me." The sound was almost inaudible, coming from where the redhead, that was once a man, lay torn and bloody. "Help me, whoever you are."

"I'm here, Billy." Jed knelt beside the bloody body. "We'll help you."

Bow Legs could only look at the bloody body and shake his head. Turning, he surveyed the surrounding brush piles carefully. "The bear might still be close, Crow Killer."

"How did you get here, Billy?"

The sound coming from the torn face was just a squeak, barely discernible. "The bear, it drug me here, then left me after the Nez Perce rode away."

Jed studied what was left of the torn up body of Billy Wilson. Even if they were where a doctor could help, there was no use. The damage the bear had done was too severe, and Jed wondered how Wilson could still be alive. Blood soaked the ground all around him. His ribs stuck through what was left of the leather hunting shirt. Only one eye was visible as dried skin hung down from his ripped away scalp, covering the other.

"You seem familiar." The voice rasped out as the lungs fought for air. "The voice."

"I am Crow Killer, an Arapaho."

"You're the one we're after, ain't you?"

"Yes, don't try to talk."

"What happened to Black Robe and the rest?"

"Dead, now lay quiet."

"I'm already dead, you know that." Wilson tried to raise his ripped arm. How come you speak English, if'n you're Arapaho."

Jed dropped his eyes. "Jesuit priests."

Grimacing in pain, his one eye studied the face above him. "I need a favor, whoever you are."

"What favor?"

The one good arm felt for the leather shot pouch hanging across his chest. "My pappy and brother got themselves a farm north of here, this side of the Wallowa Valley."

The voice gave out and hissed causing Jed to think Wilson had passed. "Wilson, Billy Wilson."

"I'm still here." The voice was weaker, barely discernable. "I stole this. My pa doesn't even know I've got it. It's his, take it back to Ed Wilson. Tell him I'm sorry, and I've gone under."

Jed looked at the diamond wedding band the bloody fingers held, the same wedding band that his mother had worn for a short time. "Where did you get this? It was buried, on my mother's finger."

The body stiffened as the one eye widened. "Jed, is that you?"

"It's me, Billy. You're just plain no good."

"How, where did you come from?" The one eye opened wider. "You're dead."

"How did you get my mother's ring?"

"I dug her up and stole it."

"You and Seth?"

"No, just me." The bloody hand grabbed at Jed feebly. "Seth knew nothing about it, don't do him harm."

"Did you push me from the wagon, Billy?" Jed leaned down to hear. "Did you? Don't lie."

Only a gurgle and a whisper came from the ripped mouth as the head turned slowly sideways. "Jedidiah."

"Is he dead?" Bow Legs leaned over the dead body.

"He'll never get any deader." Jed grasped the ring in his hand. He knew Billy was mean but to steal a wedding ring from a dead body already in the ground. "He's one critter that deserved killing, if any ever did."

"We will be dead too, if we do not run." Bow Legs looked frantically up the hill. "Listen, the brush pops. The bear has not smelled us yet, but it comes."

Racing across the short distance to the horses, neither man worried about the noise they were making. Once the bear got their scent it would charge, and noise at this time didn't matter. Springing on the startled horses, without slowing their pace, the two warriors raced their horses up the trail without looking back until they reached the crest of the hill. Below them, standing on its hind legs in the middle of the trail, stood the grizzly and her two cubs that were just emerging from the brush.

"She almost had us, Crow Killer."

"Almost, but you were safe."

"What do you mean?"

Jed laughed. "Those legs, my friend, no self-respecting bear, even a grizzly, would be hungry enough to bother with them."

"This is not funny. We were almost a meal for that one."

Jed suddenly grew serious. "She's got a meal, I reckon."

"Where do we go now, Crow Killer?"

Jed watched the bear as it lumbered back into the brush, out of sight. "You, my friend, will go back to the Arapaho Village."

"And Crow Killer, where does he ride?'

Opening his hand, Jed looked down at the ring. "I have something to deliver."

"And then, will you return to us?"

"Time will tell, my friend." Jed reached and untied the leather thong that held the gold nugget White Swan and Lame Wolf had presented him along with the name Crow Killer. "Give this to Little Antelope and tell her to hold it for me."

"But, it is your medicine charm, it protects you." Bow Legs reached out hesitantly for the nugget. "I do not like this but I will do as you ask, my friend."

"Ride safely back to Arapaho lands, Bow Legs. We will hunt the shaggies again, soon."

Bow Legs turned his horse with a low whisper coming from his voice. "I do not think this will ever be, my friend."

Jed watched as Bow Legs quickly passed by where the bear had disappeared back into the brush, only minutes before. Seeing the warrior was safely past, Jed turned the paint horse and kicked him down the trail leading north. He didn't have any idea where the Wallowa Valley was located, but he knew it was north and west of where he was. He had heard Lige Hatcher and Chalk Briggs speak of it many times on their way west. Hopefully, he would run into trappers or a trader who could tell him exactly where and how far it was. He would have to be careful. Now, he was in enemy territory, riding a dead Nez Perce warrior's horse, one he knew would be very recognizable in the Nez Perce Nation. Also, he looked down at his bloody clothes, easily recognized as Arapaho.

Somewhere ahead, as he pointed the piebald down into the lower valley, he knew he would eventually run across some settlements, hopefully white, not Indian. The next few days as he passed into the lower lands, he noticed it was still fertile soil, not near as beautiful or wild as the upper mountain valleys he had ridden through. Jed knew he would never find another land, as breathtaking or abundant in game, as he had passed through during the last three weeks. He could feel the pull of this great mountain land on his heart already. Someday, he knew he would return; he had to. Whether a man wanted to be a farmer, hunter, or trapper, the upper valleys and mountains contained everything a man could ever need or want. During the passing days, several rabbits, squirrels, and quail were killed as he rode, and cooked over small fires at night, enough to keep his belly filled. The piebald too was no longer gaunt, filling out and regaining his strength as Jed let him graze his fill as they passed through the rich deep grass of the lower lands.

Late in the afternoon of the fourth day, since leaving Bow Legs and dropping down into the flatlands, Jed saw the smoke from a fire, lower in the valley he was passing through. Riding slowly toward the smoke, he dismounted and hid the paint in the shelter of some cedars, then slipped quietly toward the unsuspecting camp. Jed had to use caution, he was white but any white seeing him would see an Arapaho Indian, cut up and bloody, and they wouldn't know his intentions. Worse yet, any Indian discovering him in these lands would see him as an enemy warrior, or an intruder here to steal or count coup. Either way, Lige Hatcher had repeated to him many times as they hunted, riding in on any unsuspecting camp could be dangerous, even fatal. Out here people were always ready to shoot first and ask questions later.

Peering into the camp, he watched as two whites moved about their small fire, oblivious to the fact they were being scouted. Jed watched as one man made camp and the other tended their horses. Moving closer, Jed slipped behind a large oak and raised his voice to the camp.

"You in the camp, I am a white man; don't shoot."

Instantly on hearing the voice, both men sprang for their rifles. "Who you be, pilgrim? Come out so's we can eyeball you."

"Jedidiah Bracket, I was a member of Chalk Briggs' train and a friend of Lige Hatcher."

"Step out from behind that tree, where we can see you." The smaller man ordered again. "And keep your hands where we'uns can see them."

"Don't shoot." Jed stepped cautiously from behind the tree. "I ain't armed."

Both men advanced slowly to where Jed stood with their rifles ready for trouble. "Hey, I do remember you, pilgrim. You're one of Ed Wilson's boys, the oldest. We thought you drowned crossing the Platte."

"Almost did."

"Why you dressed in that get-up and where did all the blood come from?" The second hunter looked Jed up and down, staring at all the blood covering Jed. "You hurt bad?"

"I was taken in by the Arapaho Tribe." Jed shook the question off. "And I am Ed Wilson's boy; stepson."

"You escape, did you?"

"No, not exactly." Jed felt of the ring in his small pouch. "I've news for my step-pa and figured you fellers would know where to find him."

"We was on the wagon train ourselves, split off when we reached this side of the Wallowa Valley. Me and Vern Gray here started doing a little trapping and trading with the Nez Perce and the Blackfoot." The older of the men lowered his rifle. "We been doing pretty good. Sure beats grubbing in the dirt like your pa and brother Seth are doing."

"I remember you, Abe. Sorry, I forgot your last name. You rode some with Lige Hatcher." Jed nodded. "You didn't like working then either."

"Abe Reed. Yep, I did work with old Lige some." The bigger trapper grinned. "And you're right; I ain't particularly fond of hard work."

"Where is Lige now?"

"We seen him last year, down by the settlements in Baxter Springs, resupplying." Reed looked back at their camp. "You look tuckered, come on over to camp. We'll fix you a bite to eat."

"Where is he now?"

"Couldn't say for sure. Last we heard he was hunting Billy Wilson."

"Wilson?

"Yep, your stepbrother." The one called Vern spat. "Orneriest varmint in these parts, bar none."

"I'll get my horse." Jed was curious, why would Lige be hunting Billy?

Leading the piebald paint of Black Robe back to the fire, Jed was surprised when both men turned their full attention on the horse, seeming to forget him. Running their eyes and hands over the horse, they shook their heads curiously.

"This is the piebald that Black Robe the Nez Perce rides." Vern looked at Jed's bloody shirt closer. "How did you come by him?"

Jed didn't like the hardness that came into the trapper's voice as they studied the animal. "I needed a horse to ride, he didn't."

"Black Robe is dead?" Reed was shocked. "Are you telling us you killed one of the greatest fighters in the Nez Perce Nation?"

"Look!" Vern pointed to the quiver of arrows that hung from Jed's back. "If I ain't missed my guess, Abe, that's an Arapaho Lance sticking out of that quiver."

Reed studied Jed's clothing closer, looking him up and down, from his ripped bloody shirt, to his blood flecked leather leggings and moccasins. "You be one of them Arapaho Lance Bearers or did you steal that carved up stick with the feathers?"

Jed ignored the question. "Tell me why Lige Hatcher is hunting Billy Wilson?"

"You speak first, and be quick about it." Vern looked again at the horse, raising his rifle, and glaring at Jed. "Black Robe was a friend of our'n."

"You mean you traded with him?" Jed remembered the fight with Black Robe. "I don't think that Nez Perce was a friend of any white."

"The way you speak of him, you knew Black Robe well?"

"Nope, I didn't know him at all." Jed watched the one called Vern closely, knowing he would be the one to challenge him. "He challenged me to fight, and I killed him."

"You!" The trapper smirked, looking Jed up and down slowly. "Why you're not much more than a tadpole. How much help did you have?"

"Just me is all it took, but he had warriors with him. Why don't you ride back to their village and ask them." Jed looked over at the fire. He couldn't figure why this white was so concerned about one Indian. "You said something about food."

"Listen to him, Abe. He takes the food from our mouth and now wants us to feed him." Vern shook his head in disgust.

"Pay no attention to him, Jed." Reed motioned at the fire. "It was just that Black Robe was our meal ticket and it sounds like he ain't no more."

"That's the truth if I ever heard it. He was our friend, like Abe says, our meal ticket." Vern thrust his chin forward. "And you stand here with a straight face and tell us you killed him. That piebald and your scalp, boy, would sure go a long way to get us back in good with the Nez Perce."

"Shut up, Vern." Abe motioned at the fire. "Grab you some meat out of that cook pot, young feller."

"I'm much obliged to you fellers." Jed moved to the fire, all the while keeping his eyes on the trappers. "I could use a bite to eat."

"Don't you be obliged to me, runt." Vern shook his head. "You can thank old Abe there for your vittles, not me."

"Why, Vern." Jed grinned as he knelt over the fire. "A little old runt like me ain't gonna eat much."

"Your smart mouth could land you in trouble, boy." Vern laid aside his rifle and fingered the large skinning knife on his side.

Dropping the wooden spoon he had picked up, Jed slowly stood up. "You ain't man enough, Vern, so don't push your luck."

Abe laughed lightly. "Think about it, Vern old son, if he did for Black Robe what chance would you have against him?"

Cussing over his shoulder as he walked back toward the horses, Vern had to have the final say. "Ain't worth the effort, ain't nothing to thrashing a kid."

"Eat up, Jed." Abe shook his head. "Pay, old Vern, no attention. He's always on the prod."

Nodding, Jed knelt and dished himself up a plate full of meat and dried potatoes, food he hadn't eaten for many months since falling into the Platte. Letting his eyes rove the camp as he ate, Jed noticed the bundles of furs, buffalo hides, beaver, and many trade goods stacked close to the picket rope where the mules stood placidly. He knew these men were doing well, prospering from the help of leaders like Black Robe, trading with them. Many times, he had seen trappers like these come into the Arapaho Village to trade cheap trade goods for valuable furs, a very lucrative business if they kept their scalps. What he couldn't understand, if Black Robe was their benefactor, why was Abe taking the killing of the Nez Perce leader so easily, Vern sure wasn't. He studied the older trapper and something was on his mind, but what?

"You never told me why Lige was out tracking Billy Wilson."

Looking to where Vern sat mending some britching on a mule packsaddle, Abe shrugged slightly. "Well Jed, we don't rightly know, only what he told us."

"What was that?"

"Told us he owed Wilson something."

"What?"

"He didn't say, but he was after him for sure." Abe shrugged. "You know how tight-lipped old Lige can be."

Jed set the empty plate beside the small blaze and nodded. He knew Abe was holding something back. "Well, if you'll just point me toward my step-pa's farm, I'll head that way."

"Why don't you stay the night?" Abe stood up. "This be dangerous country to travel at night, all alone."

Jed looked to where Vern sat. "It might be more dangerous right here. I best be moving on."

"Well, okay, but you're welcome." Abe pointed off to the northwest. "You're pap and brother has set up his trappings about a week's hard ride or more, due north and west of here."

"I'll be riding on then."

"When you reach the Snake River turn north, and you'll find someone who can steer you the rest of the way to Baxter Springs."

"Due north at the Snake." Jed nodded. "How will I know the Snake?"

"You'll know, from here it's the only big river this side of the Wallowa."

"Thank you Abe, for everything."

"Before you go, you better change shirts." Abe pulled out a leather fringed doe skin shirt. "Bloody like you are some folks here 'bouts might just shoot first and holler hello second."

"I can't pay for it now."

"Consider it a gift. Maybe I'll collect from your pap."

"Well, thank you." Jed quickly changed shirts.

Abe took in the scabbed over scars Black Robe's knife had left. "Looks like old Black Robe got in a few licks on you."

"Yeah, reckon he did at that." Jed agreed. "He weren't no coward."

"Hard to believe he's gone under." Abe shook his head. "He was tough as an oak."

"Believe it, your oak is dead."

Jed rode the piebald from their camp, stopping to wave as he crossed a small stream, then passed from the trapper's sight, behind a line of trees. Vern didn't even look up as the piebald passed him by, causing a shiver to go up Jed's spine, a natural result he couldn't stop. The smaller trapper had a cold, evil eye. Jed knew the way he focused on him, the man hated him for killing Black Robe. He would have to be watchful, always on guard as he rode west, passing through the rolling mountains and wide valleys where places of ambush were abundant. Vern and Abe knew this land like the back of their hands, including shortcuts and many passages through the mountains.

"Why did you let him go, Abe?" Vern walked back to the fire. "If we had taken that paint horse of Black Robe back to the Nez Perce along with that kid's scalp, we could have bought our way back in with them."

"How do you know we're out?"

"Don't be a fool. Black Robe was the only one in the village that wanted to trade with us. He made the others trade for our trinkets and worthless blankets instead of taking their pelts to the settlements for real cash."

"Sure, he was the only one." Abe agreed. "And why was he the only one?"

"You know perfectly well why he done it."

"Exactly, he was getting well paid for keeping his tribe in line." Abe grinned. "The rest of them Nez Perce were the ones losing."

"Now, thanks to this kid, we've lost him." Vern shook his head. "Maybe our scalps too, if we try to push our way back in with them."

Abe nodded thoughtfully. "Maybe you're right for once."

"With that horse and kid's scalp, we'd be welcomed back with open arms." Vern looked to the north. "Providing he did kill old Black Robe."

"He killed him all right. I believe the lad's truly a Lance Bearer of the Arapaho."

"Then I say we kill him."

"Well, we know where he's heading." Abe laid some wood on the fire. "Let's study on it tonight. We can always cut across the rim rock and catch up with him in the morning."

"I say go now." Vern threw up his hands. "He's riding maybe the fastest and strongest horse in these mountains."

"So?"

"So, pulling these mules along behind us, we'll never catch up to that paint horse, shortcut be danged." Vern waved his hand at the picket line. "We sure can't leave them here, all alone to be plundered."

"What are you suggesting, Vern?"

"I'll go after him alone."

"Alone?"

"He ain't armed with nothing more than a bow and that war axe." Vern held up the rifle. "Mister Jedidiah and that little old war lance of his will never know what hit him."

Abe looked over at the grazing mules, pelts, and trade goods, which would produce a considerable fortune when they rode into the settlements. He grinned to himself; either way, if Vern was killed or did the killing, what did he have to lose? He studied the youngster as he ate. A young man with the skill to kill Black Robe should not be taken as lightly as Vern was doing. If Vern went and got himself killed like a dang fool, he would have everything to himself. If Vern managed to kill Jed, then with the piebald paint, they would be able to get back in the good graces of the Nez Perce.

"All right Vern, you go right ahead. I'll wait here and guard the camp." Abe reached for the coffeepot. "But, you be careful, you hear?"

"Careful, what for? He's just a wet nosed kid." Vern spat, grabbing his saddle and striding cockily to where the horses were picketed. "Careful, ha."

Abe watched as Vern saddled, then disappeared from his sight, following the same trail Jed had taken, then shook his head. "Good-bye old pard, be seeing you, maybe."

Vern turned in his saddle and looked back at the campsite. Now, out here alone, he wasn't so confident and his bravado was quickly ebbing. He remembered Abe's words of warning about Jed. He wanted to catch up quick, ambush the kid, and get back to Abe as quickly as he could. Vern was one of those individuals who found bravery in numbers or in the corn whiskey he liked so much.

CHAPTER 11

As he rode north, Jed recalled the words of Walking Horse about watching warning signs from his horse and paying heed to them. Several times, he noticed the piebald twitching his ears, turning them to the rear, listening. Someone was following, and whoever or whatever it was, wasn't far behind, causing the piebald to react nervously. The piebald sensed another horse or perhaps a bear. Jed remembered Walking Horse's words as he looked down at the sandy soil where his own tracks were plain to see. Riding the Piebald into a tall stand of trees, Jed dismounted and held the horse's nose so the horse couldn't nicker or call out. A rider was coming fast, running hard, Jed could hear its hooves drumming on the soft trail. Looking down, he cussed, as he made his first mistake by not wiping out his hoof prints, showing where he departed from the trail.

Jed watched, straining his eyes as the rider and horse neared his place of concealment, coming at a hard lope. He couldn't figure Abe or Vern chasing after him in such a manner, if they intended to do him harm, but he couldn't be sure. He saw Vern's eyes when he rode from their camp, and for some reason, the man hated him. Was his hate strong enough for the man to want to kill him? The piebald's ears pricked forward as the bay horse came into sight, racing along the trail. Jed immediately recognized the small figure of Vern, leaning forward in the saddle, his eyes focused down the trail for any sign of Jed instead of reading the signs plainly showing in the soft dirt.

The trapper's rifle was across his lap, not slung on his back, telling

Jed the man was ready to use the weapon. Swinging upon the piebald, Jed slapped him across the rump with his axe and rode out onto the trail as Vern passed without even a sideways glance at the charging horse. Finally, hearing the hard pounding hooves of the piebald, Vern looked back in terror as he discovered the hard running horse close on his tail. Swinging the long rifle, he fired almost point-blank at Jed, but in his terror and hurrying the shot, his ball went wild. Pushing the piebald faster, Jed quickly caught the smaller bay horse. He grabbed the terrified Vern by his leather shirt, pulling the small trapper sideways from the running horse. Reining the piebald to a sliding stop, Jed rode back and circled the downed man, almost stepping the horse onto the shaking Vern.

"I didn't know it was you, boy." Vern whined, his voice breaking. "I thought you were an Indian attacking me."

Dismounting the piebald, Jed approached the fallen trapper. "Get up."

Composing himself, Vern pulled himself together as he stood slowly to his feet to face Jed. "You play kinda rough, boy."

"I'm fixing to get a lot rougher." Jed tossed down his bow and quiver. "Why did you try to kill me?"

"What you aiming to do, boy?" Vern still held the empty rifle.

Slowly pulling his skinning knife, Jed smiled. "I'm gonna gut you like a fish, Vern, that's what I'm fixing to do."

"Big talk for a boy, don't you think?" Vern drew back the rifle like a club.

Vern rolled onto his side gasping for air as Jed's right foot caught him hard in the chest, knocking him down and knocking the wind from him. Crawling across the sandy trail as he gasped, trying to regain his wind, Vern ignored Jed, who was following him as he crawled.

"You forgot to duck, Vern."

Finally regaining his air, Vern raised to his knees. "You kick hard."

"I'm fixing to kick you all over this valley unless you start talking and quick."

"What you want me to talk about?"

"Billy Wilson for one, and why are you following me?" Jed stepped closer to the shaking trapper. "And you best not lie this time."

"What makes you think I'd lie to you, you being a white man?"

Ignoring the whining trapper, Jed raised the war axe. "Why is Hatcher after Wilson?"

Vern looked up at the deadly axe and shuddered. "You've done turned Injun, ain't you boy?"

"This is your last chance, Vern."

"All right, all right." The trapper raised his arm to protect his head. "Wilson killed a good friend of Hatcher's last year, then dismembered him."

"Where you reckon Lige is now?"

"How would I know that?" Vern cringed as the axe rose again. "Man, I ain't lying. We stay away, as far as we can, from Billy Wilson. He's crazier than you are, that one is."

"Now, why were you following me?"

"Abe wants the horse and your scalp to appease the Nez Perce." Vern lied. "Without Black Robe, the others won't trade their plews to us."

Picking the rifle up, Jed quickly stripped the trapper of his shot pouch and powder horn, laying them beside the piebald. Grabbing the trembling Vern by the scruff of his neck, Jed dragged him to the bay horse.

"What you fixing to do?"

"Why Vern, I'm just gonna give you a ride, that's all." Jed motioned at the horse. "Get aboard."

"You're gonna kill me, ain't you?"

"It's a thought."

Tying the pleading man to the horse, Jed wrapped the reins around the saddle horn. Vern's feet were hobbled underneath the horse's belly with his hands tied to the horn. Turning the bay back, the way he had come, Jed looked up into the hate filled eyes.

"If I fall off, he could drag me to death." Vern pleaded. "Give me a chance."

"Well then Vern, old boy, I wouldn't fall off if I were you." Jed shrugged. "That's your chance."

"You've turned into a stinking heathen, just like your Arapaho friends." Vern cussed Jed. "Billy Wilson always said you were an Injun of some kind."

"You hear me now Vern; hear me well." Jed pulled his skinning knife. "The next time I find you in these mountains, I will skin you bare. You understand?"

The shaggy head nodded slowly. He mumbled under his breath as Jed slapped the horse hard, back down the trail. "If we don't skin you first."

Jed watched the bay horse with its helpless, trussed-up rider pass out of sight, then turned the piebald back to the north. If the bay horse headed back to where Abe and the mules waited, Vern would probably survive, if not, oh well. Jed shook his head, perhaps Vern was right, maybe he was a heathen. Turning his attention back to the trail, Jed remembered Abe had said the Wallowa Valley was more than a week's ride to the north and west. Abe probably figured that would be the time needed while leading pack mules and taking their time, as men in no hurry were prone to do. Kicking the powerful piebald into a trot, he pushed the horse faster, intending to cut the days as much as he could.

His thoughts turned momentarily to the two trappers he let live. He knew what Walking Horse would say, by letting Vern live, he showed weakness. Now, the two trappers would be out there, somewhere in the mountains, maybe waiting to ambush him. Perhaps, by Arapaho standards, he showed weakness. No matter, despite what Vern said, he was still part white, and to kill in cold blood was still hard. He remembered the sleeping Nez Perce and Red Hawk's orders to kill them as they slept, and he didn't like it, but for Little Antelope's sake, he would have killed them all.

For three days, Jed pushed the piebald hard, warily watching the narrow mountain trails and flat meadows with tall grasses and flowers. He was aware Abe and Vern knew these mountains and shortcuts through the passes, but leading a string of pack mules would slow them too much to catch up with him, if that was their intention. He still wanted to hurry, to find Ed Wilson, and be on his way from Wilson's farm as quick as possible. The two trappers knew where he was heading and if their plan was to ambush him, they would know exactly where to look. Four days later, after many days hard riding, Jed forded the Snake River. For five days and into the night, when possible, he pushed the piebald hard. The powerful animal seemed not the worse for wear, as he had taken the trail well, keeping up his ground-eating jog trot, mile after mile.

Daybreak, on the eighth day, found Jed topping out over a small mountain range looking down into a valley. He could see far-off smoke drifting across the valley below as he sat the piebald. Studying the valley, he knew it was a white settlement. The smoke was too heavy, probably coming from chimneys, much heavier than the Indian fires would produce. Further to the north, he could see what looked like an immigrant road, snaking its way across the valley, heading toward the smoke. Pulling Vern's nasty leather hat from under his leg, he quickly tucked his long hair up under the hat, pulling it down snug. Sitting the paint with his dark skin, long hair, buckskin clothing, and riding the piebald bareback, he didn't want to be mistaken for an Indian before he had time to speak. The old, beat-up hat would at least hide his long black hair.

Studying the trails leading down the mountain, he decided to intersect the wagon road before it entered the settlement. At least out on the open road, people would see him plainly and not get spooked. He had no way of knowing the mind-set of the whites or how they got along with the local Indian tribes. He remembered how the wagon train immigrants would just as soon shoot as talk, if they were surprised. Kicking the piebald forward, he wound his way down the heavily wooded mountain slopes, twisting and turning before coming out on the level road. Turning onto the well-used road, he reined in at the first log cabin he came to and hallowed the structure. A tall man carrying a long rifle warily exited the barn and lean-to that sat alongside the cabin.

"Who be you, and what do you want?" The voice was rough and unfriendly.

"I'm looking for Ed Wilson's farm." Jed studied the hard face. "I was told he lives here in Baxter Springs."

"What you be wanting him for?"

"I'm Jedidiah Bracket, his stepson."

The rifle lowered slightly as the man squinted up at Jed. "Heard something about him losing a boy on his way out west. You be him?"

"I'm him."

"We came here a year later." The bony chin motioned down the road. "You could be taken for an Injun the way you're skinned out there in that giddup."

"Y'all have trouble with Indians around here?"

"Noo, can't say we do, not around these parts." The farmer shook his head. "Could have some soon though. The Nez Perce ain't happy with the way we're pushing in here, that's for sure."

"The whites taking their hunting grounds?"

"Yep, they don't cotton to it much."

"Ed Wilson?"

"Oh yeah, he lives about ten miles west along the Pennybrook."

"Pennybrook?"

"Small tributary of the Snake. Ride straight through Baxter Springs, cross the Pennybrook, first farm on the north side of the road."

"Much obliged." Jed started to turn the paint.

"I've seen that piebald before."

"Yes, sir. He's hard to miss the way he's painted up."

"And the rifle."

"You know it?" Jed was surprised. The farmer had a sharp eye.

"Yep, ain't too many rifles all fancied up with them copper tacks like that one be."

"You know the owner?"

"I do." The big Adam's apple bobbed up and down in the long skinny neck. "Vern Grey, he runs with another trapper named Abe Reed; rough pair of boys."

"Well, thank you kindly. Reckon I'll be moving along."

"Sit a spell and water up if you like." The farmer looked the horse over. "Looks like you been riding a spell."

"Reckon I best be moving along."

"Vern dead?"

"Wasn't the last time I seen him." Jed turned the horse. "By the way, you seen Lige Hatcher around these parts?"

"Nope, not lately." The bony head nodded. "Last we heard, he was after Billy Wilson."

"Thank you, sir."

"Ain't you gonna ask about your brother?" The Farmer asked curiously, still looking at the rifle Jed held across the withers of the paint.

"Stepbrother, nope, don't care."

The farmer stepped closer. "Vern set a lot of store by that gun. How did you get it?"

Jed looked over the man's shoulder at the windows of the cabin that seemed to be filled with children of every size. "You might say he gave it to me. His hands were all tied up and he couldn't hold onto it at the time."

"Tied up, with what?"

"Oh, he was holding onto a lot of rawhide strips."

"And he gave you the rifle for some rawhide."

"Something like that, I reckon." Jed kicked the horse. "Be seeing you."

The small settlement of Baxter Springs lay peacefully in the midday autumn sun as Jed rode the piebald boldly down the middle of the main street. Eyes looked out at the tall, dark-skinned rider with the bow and arrow quiver strung across his back, trying to figure out if he was white or Indian. Curious people stepped from the doorways, to get a better view of the rider and prancing piebald, as both cut an imposing figure. Jed's dark eyes took in the storefronts, reading the lettering, identifying each establishment. Two general stores, one saloon, two fur trading emporiums, one livery stable alongside a blacksmith shop, and a two-story building with rooms for rent above the door. Baxter Springs wasn't much of a town to look at, although there appeared to be a splattering of every business a town would need. Jed wasn't sure, but the town couldn't be very old, maybe five years. The one fur trading post was quite a bit older looking than the other buildings and probably traded with the Indians, then the rest of the town sprung up around it. Not a boomtown for sure, but still it held what the local farmers needed to run their farms.

Jed felt his stomach rumble as it was awhile since he ate breakfast, and the scrawny little rabbit didn't keep his stomach full long. He looked at the general store hungrily, but with no money and a stranger to these people, there was no use stopping. Kicking the piebald, Jed hit a jog trot and with his broad shoulders straight, he rode proudly through

Baxter Springs. He halfway smiled, remembering Little Antelope's words. "Walk proud, Crow Killer, proud."

At the edge of town Jed passed near where a tall, slender young woman stood with her eyes glued to his face.

"Pa, look." The woman called to an older man who was leaving the blacksmith shop, and pointed to where Jed was passing.

"What, gal?"

"That Indian reminds me of Jedidiah." Her face was in shock. "It looks like him only maybe older, and that scar on his face."

The older man beside her shook his head. "Ah lass, it can't be, that's an Indian. Look at the way he sits his horse and the bow across his back."

Stepping into the street, she felt the man's strong hand grasp her arm. "Pa."

"Let it go, lass. Don't embarrass yourself, that's an Indian."

Sally Duncan stood silently beside the wagon with her eyes glued to the back of the Indian riding away on the big paint horse. She would have sworn it was Jed. They had been close on their trip west, and many times she daydreamed of being his girl. Once, he had defended her honor by soundly whipping Freddie Abbott, an older boy, for calling her ugly. She recalled his handsome face, thinking, could two young men of different races look so much alike?

"It's him, Pa." She leaned forward, shielding her eyes from the sun. "It's Jedidiah Bracket, unless I'm stone blind."

The man beside her nodded. "Well lass, if it is him, he'll be headed for Ed Wilson's place. We'll know soon enough."

Stopping the piebald in the middle of what he figured to be the Pennybrook Tributary to let him drink, Jed sat the horse, studying the cluster of buildings and corrals. According to the farmer's directions, this had to be Ed Wilson's farm.

"Well, at least you got your stomach full, old man." Jed patted the sleek neck, then kicked him forward, splashing onto the far bank.

Two men worked on a wagon in front of the barn, their backs to him. Only the loud barking of a large bluetick hound gave away his presence. Jed easily recognized both men, as their red hair and ruddy complexions hadn't changed in the least. The younger of the two had matured since Jed had seen him last. He had grown heavier, but the look of his face was still the same, and he was definitely Seth Wilson.

Reining in near the men, Jed slid easily to the ground. "Hello, Pa."

Both men studied the figure before them in total shock, their eyes taking in everything about the man. "Jedidiah, is that you son?"

"It's me all right, in the flesh."

"Jedidiah." The older of the men rushed to Jed, taking him in a bear hug. "My son, you're alive."

"I'm alive."

Holding Jed at arm's length, the farmer studied the face closely. "We gave you up for dead, boy. Lige looked for you at least a year."

"Well, I'm here now."

The younger of the men stepped forward and extended his hand. "It's good to have you back, Brother."

"Seth."

"Come, no more work today boys." Ed Wilson took Jed by the arm. "First, we will eat, and then you will tell us of your adventures since we last saw you."

"Three years, isn't it?" Seth looked at the long scar on Jed's cheek. "You must have many things to tell us about."

Jed walked slowly beside Wilson as they approached the cabin, his eyes studying everything. The farm showed the hard work they had put into it. Everything was built strong, able to withstand the heavy storms and rain that would soon come. Wilson motioned to the long, split-log table, and placed a boiling coffeepot on the table.

Seth entered the cabin and closed the door quietly. "I put your horse in the corral and gave him some hay."

"Thank you, Seth." Jed took the extended coffee cup. "It has been many years since I have had coffee."

"Why?" Seth pulled up a chair and looked at Jed.

"Arapaho don't drink coffee."

"Arapaho?"

"I've been with them since I fell into the river."

"It was an accident, Jed." Seth looked across the table. "Me and Billy were rough on you, but we would have never intentionally pushed you into that river, and I hope you know that."

"I know." Jed sipped on the coffee. "The wagon lurched and I fell."

Ed Wilson studied Jed's face. "We're glad you're back, son."

Seth stared into his own cup. "You planning on staying, Jed?"

"I don't know yet."

"Of course you're staying, boy." Ed spoke up, smiling. "We'll all be back together again."

"What would Billy think of that?" Jed watched their faces.

"Billy's not here." Ed's eyes dropped to the table. "Last we heard Billy was headed for the Bitterroots to trade."

"We also heard Lige Hatcher was hunting Billy for killing another trapper." Seth grinned. "That old gray beard will have to hurry to catch Billy."

"Shut up, Seth." Ed Wilson's face was strained and his voice was hard. "Don't you have one little bit of respect left."

Jed looked at the older man's sad face. He knew he had to tell him about Billy, but at the same time, he hated to. Billy Wilson was no good, but he was still the man's son and he was special to his father, even if he didn't deserve it. Sipping slowly on the coffee, Jed looked at each man.

"I heard Lige was hunting Billy too." Jed nodded.

Ed studied the dark face before him. "You know something you ain't speaking of, Jedidiah, tell us."

For several seconds, Jed hesitated, not knowing exactly how or what to say. "I have bad news for you."

"Billy?"

Seth watched as Jed nodded his head. "Did Lige Hatcher do for him? I'll kill him if'n he has."

"I said shut up, boy." Wilson stood up abruptly. "You ain't killing anyone. Ain't Billy done enough killing for this family?"

"No, he was dead before Lige caught up with him."

Ed Wilson's big hands clenched hard. "How, where?"

"Grizzly bear attacked him, back on the Yellowstone, maybe ten days ago."

"You sure, Jed?" Seth's face turned red.

"I'm sure." Jed nodded. "I buried him."

"Billy was a wild one." Seth shook his head. "He was bound to get it one way or another, but killed by a grizzly."

Jed felt into the small pouch that held the ring but removed his hand empty. Billy Wilson died a terrible death and there was no need to bring further grief to Ed Wilson by showing him the ring.

Ed Wilson's voice choked. "Yes, Billy was wild, but still he was your brother."

All three men sat motionless saying nothing, just sitting as the moment turned awkward. The mood in the small kitchen of the cabin was now subdued, instead of the joyful reunion of a few minutes past. Suddenly, the quiet was broken as the big hound bayed at the sound of a wagon pulling up in front of the cabin. Rising to his feet, Seth peered out a gun port in the front door.

"It's old man Duncan and Sally Ann." Seth frowned. "You remember Sally Ann don't you, Jed?"

"The young girl from the train?" Jed nodded. "Yes, I remember Sally Ann."

"You and her were kinda sweet on each other, weren't you?" Seth stepped aside as Ed Wilson opened the door. "I know she was sweet on you, Brother Jed."

Jed shook his head. "I swear Seth, you ain't changed a bit."

"I know what I know, and that girl hasn't looked at another man since we settled here and believe me, she's been asked many a time."

"Asked what, Seth?"

"You know, asked to go to dances, church socials, and even marriage. She turned them all down, stone-cold she did." Seth started for the door. "You're gonna be shocked. She really bloomed as she got older, a real looker."

"Why would she do that?"

"What?"

"Why won't she court men?"

"Still carrying a torch for you, I figure." Seth shrugged. "Sally Ann, she's an odd one for sure."

Exiting the cabin, Jed blinked in the afternoon sunlight as he looked up at the tall girl sitting in the wagon seat. Seth didn't lie, Sally Ann Duncan had matured and blossomed into a beautiful young woman. Thick raven hair framed brown eyes with the cutest little nose that turned up with just the right tilt to make any man's heart twitch. He knew this was the same Sally Ann, but she had changed so much, he couldn't believe it.

Seconds turned into a minute as Jed and Sally Ann stared deeply into each other's eyes. Finally, breaking away and turning her attention to her father, Sally Ann smiled. "I told you it was Jed we saw in town, Pa."

"Yes, you did, Sally Ann." The older man smiled. "And you were right."

Stepping down from the wagon with her father's help, she looked over at Jed and smiled. "I knew someday you would come."

Breaking the awkward moment, Ed ushered everyone back into the cabin and closed the door. "I'm sorry Duncan, you and Sally Ann have arrived at an unfortunate time to have a reunion with old friends."

"Is something wrong, Mister Wilson?" Sally Ann looked across the room.

"Jedidiah has just brought us distressing news about Billy." Wilson, almost in tears, cut off her next question. "My son is dead."

"I'm sorry, Mister Wilson." Sally Ann never liked Billy and never liked being around him, but she did like Ed Wilson and she was truly sorry for his grief. "So sorry."

"Come, Sally Ann, we must be going." Duncan could feel the awkwardness in the room. "We will pay our respects another time, Ed."

Jed followed them out to their wagon and helped the young woman up onto the seat. He wanted to say something to her but his tongue was tied. Had he forgotten how to talk with a white woman, especially a woman he had talked with so much on the wagon train? Looking up at her, he smiled and touched her hand.

"Will you be staying here, Jed?" The brown eyes pleaded with him.

Jed looked off toward the east, where the Arapaho lands were. Now, after seeing her again, his feelings were mixed. "No, I brought news for my pa about Billy. Now, I must return to my people."

"Your people?" Sally Ann was confused. "I thought we were your people, Jedidiah."

"No longer, Sally." Jed remembered his words to White Swan many moons ago. "My people are the Arapaho now."

"That's preposterous, Jedidiah Bracket." The little nose turned red. "You're white, and we are your people."

"I'm sorry."

Composing herself, she smiled. "Will you come see me before you leave?"

"I will do that, I promise."

"Our place is about four miles down this road." Sally Ann pointed. "Don't forget, you promised."

"I won't forget."

Reaching out, as her father slapped the work team, she let her fingers touch his face lovingly, running her hand over the scar lightly. "I'll be waiting, Jed."

Inside the cabin, Jed found Ed Wilson and Seth sitting at the table in silence. The room was uncomfortable to him now, it felt sad. Maybe he shouldn't have come back, but Ed Wilson deserved to know what had happened to his son. Billy Wilson wasn't worth the effort to grieve on, but his father had always been blind to the faults of his son. Walking back out to the corral, Jed pitched the piebald some grass hay and a few ears of corn. He smiled to himself as the paint horse grabbed at the yellow corn several times. Never having eaten whole corn straight from the cob, the horse didn't know exactly how to get a bite of the corn.

"A good night's rest and solid feed will do you good, old son." Jed spoke soothingly to the horse as he shelled the corn. "We'll head back come morning."

Jed never felt comfortable or at ease living with Ed Wilson and his sons, not that his stepdad made him feel that way. Since his mother's passing, he just didn't feel at home anymore. Sitting against the barn wall, he looked up at the quiet cabin, turning his attention up the road where Sally Ann and her pa had disappeared. Seeing the young woman again, awoke old feelings he had for her back on the wagon train. Little Antelope came into his thoughts; he also has feelings for her. His thoughts were always with the Arapaho woman, but she was another's wife and he has no right to think such things. Walking Horse had become his good friend and never would he betray the warrior in any way, but even his thoughts shamed him. Jed thought of the Arapaho people, Slow Wolf and White Swan, and he obtained a deep respect for all of them and missed their peaceful way of life. He was happy for the first time in his life and wanted to return to them. Again, Little Antelope crossed his thoughts, perhaps it would be better for all if he stayed away.

Standing up, as Seth beckoned to him from the cabin, Jed patted the paint. "We'll decide which way we ride before the coming of the morning, old son."

"You must be hungry, Jed." Ed spoke up from the wood stove, where he was busy cooking as Jed entered the cabin. "We forgot our manners."

"Yes, sir. I could eat."

"Sit down, boy, sit down." The older man placed a cast iron skillet with fresh baked cornbread on the table. Beans, potatoes, and squash from the garden filled their plates along with glasses of buttermilk. "Dig in."

"Thank you." Jed smiled.

Seth watched Jed as he looked down at the eating utensils. "Something funny?"

"No, it's just been a while since I sat at a table or ate with a fork."

"What do them people eat with, their fingers?"

"Mostly wooden spoons and their hunting knives." Jed nodded. "And yes, sometimes with their fingers."

Ed Wilson pulled himself up a chair and sat down. "Tell me Jed, are you remaining here with me and Seth?"

"No, sir. I'm not." Jed looked over at his stepdad. "I'll be pushing on with the new sun."

"You even talk like an Indian, Brother." Seth shook his head. "Reckon Brother Billy was right."

"About what?"

Seth shrugged sadly. "He always said you were part Indian."

"That'll be enough of that, Seth." Ed interrupted. "Jed, I have a favor, no a wish, I would ask of you."

"Yes, sir."

"One day, I would ask for you take me to Billy's grave, the place where he died." Ed Wilson choked up and turned his face from the table. "Someday."

"Yes, sir." Jed nodded. "You know all you have to do is ask."

"How will we find you, Jed?" Seth spooned a mouthful of food. "Billy spoke of the Arapaho but he said their land was far away."

"I will keep in touch." Jed turned his eyes from Wilson. "I will come to visit from time to time."

"This is your home, Jed, always."

Jed pointed the piebald away from the Wilson farm, long before the sun started to rise in the east. The light from a coal oil lamp came to life inside the cabin as Jed left the corral behind him. He heard his name being called from the cabin doorway, but he didn't return the call or pull the piebald up. Words of farewell had been spoken the night before and there was no need for more. Now, he only had one stop, he promised to make, before turning back to Arapaho lands.

The sun was barely peeking in the east when Jed spotted the Duncan farm as its dim structures showed themselves in the early morning. Smoke drifted over the cabin as Jed reined in and slid from the piebald. Looking about, he noticed the place was almost a duplicate of the Wilson farm. Jed knew all the new settlers pulled together and helped one another build so all the cabins were laid out in almost the same manner.

"You did come."

Jed watched as her tall form materialized from the porch swing. "How long you been out here, Sally?"

"I've been waiting for you awhile."

"You should be in bed."

"I can sleep anytime, Jed. I can't talk with you anytime." Sally stepped to the edge of the porch. "Don't ask me to, please."

Taking her by the arm, he turned her toward the swing. "I'll not do that."

"You want some coffee?"

Shaking his head, he looked into her eyes. "No, not now."

"You've changed, Jed." Sally touched the scar. "Did this hurt?"

"I've got older." Jed shrugged. "I reckon it did some, but I don't remember many things when I got hurt."

"You've lived with the Arapaho ever since you were lost in that awful storm?"

"Ever since." Jed nodded. "The Arapaho found me, nursed me back to health, and have been good to me."

"And now you're returning to them?"

"I came here to see my stepdad and tell him about Billy." Jed thought of the ring which he hadn't mentioned. "I left people I care about behind. There had been a fight, and some were hurt."

"A girl?" The brown eyes looked at him expectantly. "Was one a girl?"

"Yes, one was a girl."

"You cared for her?"

"Very much. She is the wife of my good friend, Walking Horse, who had been badly wounded before I left." Jed looked at the beautiful face before him. "I have to return and check on them before I can decide what I will do in the future."

"What do you wish to do?"

"I thought I knew exactly what I wanted to do." Jed stared straight into her eyes. "Now, I'm not so certain. You have come back into my life."

"Is that bad?"

"Seth says many have tried to court you."

"Many have." Sally took his hand. "Years ago, I set my heart on one man. I will wait for him."

"For how long?"

She shrugged, then cut her eyes up at him. "I hope not long but I will wait for you, Jed Bracket, as long as it takes."

"I don't understand, on the train we were friends but that was all."

"Maybe that was all it was to you, Jedidiah." Sally frowned slightly. "You don't know women at all do you?"

"No, I reckon that's a fact, I don't." Slightly embarrassed, Jed smiled. "I believe I'll take that coffee now."

"Okay."

"Miss Sally, you're not exactly bashful or shy about speaking your mind, are you?"

Rising, she looked down at him and smiled. "No, Mister Jed, I don't have the time to mince my words or be bashful, as you put it."

After a quick breakfast, Sally walked with Jed to where the piebald stood alongside the cabin. Handing him a flour sack full of biscuits and jerked meat, she let her hand linger on his arm. The dark eyes looked softly over at him, showing her feelings. Standing this close to her, Jed was surprised he hadn't remembered her being so tall. Maybe she had grown taller in his absence, as the girl before him was only an inch or two shorter than he was.

"I'll be waiting." She seemed to pout. "Hopefully not for long, I'm almost twenty."

Looking over at her, he accepted the sack. "I'm not promising anything. Where I ride it is very dangerous."

"Maybe it is too dangerous for you here?" She smiled. "Women can be dangerous, you know."

"We will see what the future brings for both of us."

"I'll be waiting." Her voice was soft, inviting. "However long your business takes, I'll be here."

"You are a determined young lady and a mighty beautiful one."

"You finally noticed." Sally smiled. "And yes, Jed, I'm very determined. There is only one man for me, and I decided that a long time ago."

"I never knew."

"Most men are blind as bats in the daylight, they don't know women at all." Sally stepped closer to him. "The sooner you get going, the sooner you will return."

Touching her face gently, he smiled down at her. "Then I better ride."

"Kiss me first."

"Sally Duncan!" Jed stammered and looked at the cabin window. "You wanna get me shot dead? Your dad is just inside."

"It's okay, Pa's seen a woman kissed before. Besides, he's still having his morning coffee."

His face, beet red from the kiss and missing his first attempt at mounting the horse, Jed finally swung on the horse, nudging the big piebald into a hard lope back to the east. This was his very first kiss, actually his second, he had barely touched her lips and pulled back when she jerked him to her and held him for a long embrace. Never has he been kissed by a woman. His heart still skipped as he felt the heat rush across his face. Just before passing from her sight, he pulled the horse in, then turned and waved back at her.

Ed and Seth Wilson did not show themselves as Jed passed their farm and forded the Pennybrook. As he rode east, his thoughts returned many times to both Sally Ann and Little Antelope, making him shake his head in confusion as thoughts of both women raced through his mind. He knew he had feelings for the little Arapaho woman. Was it because she had nursed him back to health and taught him the Arapaho tongue, or was his feelings for her what a man felt for a woman he truly cared for? He didn't know anything about women and now he was confused. He couldn't help himself as his thoughts jumped back and forth from one woman to the other. The kiss from Sally Ann both startled and tempted him, urging him to turn the piebald and return to her, and forget anything else. On the train coming west, he had befriended her, even came to her defense when she was insulted by Freddie Abbott. Sally was very young back on the train and he thought they were only friends. Now, she has blossomed into a full-grown woman, a beautiful woman. Jed knew Little Antelope was Walking Horse's wife, and he knew she was not for him, whatever he or she felt. He shook his head, as women were truly complicated. Although, his mind was set, he knew it was his responsibility and his choice as a man with honor to do what was right. Whatever else he did, he owed it to Slow Wolf to return to the Arapaho and find out how Walking Horse and the Arapaho people were.

Jed left the cumbersome rifle of Vern's at the Wilson cabin until his return. Riding bareback, the Arapaho way, he had no way of carrying the rifle, sack of food, and his own bow and weapons as an Arapaho warrior and keep one hand free. White trappers had a saddle with bags to hold their belongings, leaving their hands free to carry a rifle. Lige Hatcher had taught him to load and fire the long gun of the whites, but it had been so long since he used one and the bow was just more comfortable for him.

Again, as he passed through the settlement of Baxter Springs, he could feel the eyes of the townspeople following his passing, watching him as he rode down the main street. He knew their thoughts were well founded, as he could just imagine what he looked like as the piebald pranced proudly through the settlement. Baxter Springs was a small community, and he figured someone already spread the word that he was Ed Wilson's missing son and that would make them even more curious. A few waved as he passed but none tried to stop or speak to him.

The piebald was fresh, eager to hit the trail out of Baxter Springs. Very little urging was needed to push the horse into a slow, easy, ground-eating lope that he could hold for miles without tiring. The land he passed, following the road from Baxter Springs was familiar, as he recognized the many landmarks he had passed coming to the northwest. Near midmorning, Jed spotted the small trail leading off to the east, his tracks still visible on the trail he had followed off the mountain only two days before. Reining the piebald from the wagon road, Jed turned onto the trail. He studied the trail closely and figured the Snake River should be two days ride from the crest of the mountain ahead. His mind carefully thought out the trail, remembering both the bear further east that had killed Billy Wilson, and the pair of trappers, Abe and Vern. He didn't want to run into either of them unexpectedly since riding head first, unaware into a trap laid by either the men or bear, could be deadly.

The teachings of Walking Horse, his words and wisdom, rushed through Jed's thoughts as he pushed the piebald east, over the mountain trail, warily watching everything around him. The bear and her cubs would still be many days away, nearer the big river, but Vern and Abe were another matter. Encumbered by the pack mules, they would be slowed, somewhere ahead, and he knew there was a possibility the two trappers could be waiting to ambush him. If they were indeed waiting, Jed would need all the teachings of Walking Horse to survive. Heavily laden with furs and trade goods, the trappers would be heading for the settlements the fastest way they could, to sell and get drunk. The trail he was following might be the one they were riding, and he remembered the hate in Vern's eyes. He also remembered Vern's words that they would need the piebald and even his scalp to get back in with the Nez Perce Tribe.

Sweat formed on the black coat of the Piebald as the big horse climbed slowly up the mountainside in the midday sun. The small gravel pebbles, covering the narrow game trail, rolled downhill, disturbed by the black hooves of the piebald as the horse made his way along the rocky trail. Passing through stands of cedar, spruce, and small oaks, Jed stopped at every turn of the trail to study the passage that seemed to lead steadily upward without end. He couldn't remember the trail being so long on his downward trip. Switchback after switchback passed as he watched warily, his eyes alert at every turn. He could have enjoyed the flowers, beautiful scenery, and the sweet, fresh smell of clean air if the fear of ambush by the trappers wasn't possible.

Finally, topping out the crest of the mountain, Jed could see the sheen of the Snake far below in the valley, so far away it made the mighty river look like a small ribbon. The piebald picked up his speed, his powerful haunches bunched up under him as he slid on the steeper parts of the gravel trail. Jed's inner leg muscles began to quiver from the task of gripping the horse's wide back, as he made his way down the steep, grueling trail. At last, the trail flattened and widened at the same time, causing Jed to rein the horse in. Only the mountain grasses and flowers moved as the wind blew its soft breath along the trail, nothing else stirred, causing Jed to kick the piebald into motion. This far up, the narrow trail would make it difficult for the trappers to hide the mules and heavy packs they carried. Jed knew the whites and he figured there was no way the lazy trappers would leave the valuable pack train unguarded long enough to climb far up the mountain to wait for him.

Almost three full days later, after letting the piebald have a short rest before descending the mountain, Jed finally rode out onto the flat ground leading to the shallow crossing on the Snake. Through the huge sycamores, willows, and normal growth of shrub bushes, Jed could see the flowing ripples of the river from where he sat the horse. This was a dangerous place, he could sense it, as the mules could be hiding anywhere in the dense woods. The path leading to the crossing was a perfect place for Abe and Vern to lay in ambush, if they were waiting. For several minutes, he sat the piebald, waiting to see if the horse would locate any hidden animals, or if the mules would sense him and bray. If the two trappers intended to ambush him, this would be the place. The Snake River was deep and swift in most places, but this was the only crossing Jed knew of.

Suddenly, the small ears pricked forward, nervously twitching as the soft muzzle sniffed, searching out the riverbank for whatever he sensed there. Black Robe had trained this great horse almost like a watchdog, making the animal so valuable, as nothing could stay hidden from his sharp nose and ears. Jed eased the horse back into the shadows of a stand of cedars and slid to the ground. Tying the horse, he glided forward, working his way soundlessly from one tree to another. He didn't see or hear anything, only the uneasiness of the piebald concerned him, causing him to scout out the crossing before showing himself. Walking Horse's words came back to him as he stalked forward, "It is better to take your time and see for yourself, rather than hurry and be seen by the enemy."

Nothing moved in the trees, only the sound of a squirrel barking down near the river. Jed squatted under a large cottonwood, listening and watching as the current moved slowly over the shallower rocky parts of the crossing. Again, the squirrel scolded from the high branch of a willow tree, hanging over the river, and Jed turned his full attention toward the sound. The squirrel saw something, perhaps a coyote or hawk, but he was definitely upset about something. Easing forward slowly, Jed suddenly fell to his stomach as he heard the faint sound of a breaking limb further along the riverbank. Sniffing the air, he could definitely smell the faint acrid smell of cured hides on the air. The squirrel barked angrily again, causing Jed to pull three arrows from his quiver and string his bow.

Quietly, slithering forward on his stomach, he crawled soundlessly along the sandy ground, slipping from tree to tree. The underbrush along the river was thick, which was a great help, allowing Jed to move closer without being seen to where the squirrel perched, angrily scolding a warning from time to time. Peering around a great tree, Jed could plainly see the legs and forms of the horses and mules through the heavy brush. Low voices came to him on the air as he crept as close as he dared to the mules which would smell him out, as the piebald had smelled them.

"He should be getting close, Abe. I spotted him earlier coming down the mountain." The voice of Vern was recognizable across the flat space. "I'll bet you a bottle when we reach Baxter Springs, a bottle that I get him through the left eye with one shot from here."

"Just get him your first shot." The heavier voice of the older trapper came to Jed. "Last time you two met, it didn't turn out so well."

"He surprised me, that's all."

From where he lay, Jed could hear the voices of the two trappers but he couldn't see them. He needed to get closer for the bow to be accurate. Only fear of the mules smelling his scent kept him from moving closer. Holding the bow in his left hand, he started forward. He had no choice, to stay where he lay was dangerous, as he would be discovered if a mule snorted or stamped his foot. Abe and Vern were veteran Indian fighters and trappers, and they knew their mules, investigating any alarm sounded by their animals.

Busy bragging about what they were going to do when they got Jed in their sights, neither man heard a mule stamp his foot in warning, as Jed worked his way closer to the picket line. The camp was laid out less than sixty feet from where Jed lay scanning the piles of hides, saddles, and the tied animals. From the look of the horse droppings and heaped ashes of the campfire, the two trappers had been camped here waiting on him for at least three days.

"Well, don't let him surprise you this time, old hoss." Abe hissed. "We need to kill him and get these hides to the buyer soon. I'm dry as a dead fish."

"It's less than sixty yards to where he'll cross the river." Vern cackled lightly. "Even you couldn't miss at that distance, Abe."

"I don't like killing him, Vern." Abe shook his head. "But, we need that piebald."

"And the scalp and lance of an Arapaho warrior sure wouldn't hurt none."

"We'll have them both, old hoss, then we'll be back in the good graces of the Nez Perce."

"It's a shame old Black Robe, gone and got himself dead. Without him, we couldn't trade them Injuns a thing unless maybe we have that horse." Vern sounded worried. "Even then, I ain't sure of them heathens."

"You're right, Vern." Abe agreed, not knowing his every word was being heard. "And the scalp; don't forget the scalp."

Both trappers were lying comfortably on buffalo robes with their attention focused fully on the river crossing. Jed listened and watched the actions of the two men, and he knew they had no intentions of warning him before they fired. Cold-blooded murder was what they were about, and Jed knew it. He remembered Red Hawk's words back at the Nez Perce camp about sometimes having to kill without honor. He knew, armed only with the bow and arrows, he was definitely at a disadvantage. His chances of killing two veteran trappers, both crack shots, armed with rifles, without getting killed himself was slim, but he had no choice, he had to kill. It was only right, as these trappers intended to kill him, to kill a man just for a horse.

Jed watched the men closely as he moved to within forty feet of the trappers, an easy shot for the stout bow Walking Horse had given him. Vern was the closest, his body turned sideways to Jed with his eyes focused solely on the river crossing as he talked with Abe. Jed could see the fingers of the trapper, nervously tapping the stock of the Hawken. He could see the cold face plainly as the trapper anxiously waited, wanting to kill. Abe was twenty feet distance from Vern, his attention focused too on the crossing. Jed looked out across the river and this was the only crossing he knew of. Given the choice, he would ride to another place to ford the deep river, but being new here, he knew of none. Jed had no choice; it was his life or the two trappers. He knew both men were dead shots with their Hawken rifles and the crossing was easily in their range. There would be no way he could cross the river without them getting off at least two shots. Notching an arrow, he rose to his knees and looked at Vern's exposed side. Red Hawk's words came back to him as he hesitated momentarily.

"Vern, Abe." Jed called out across the open space separating them. "Drop them rifles."

Whirling, Vern tried to bring the rifle to bear as the hissing arrow penetrated his side, knocking him sideways. Jed heard Vern scream out in pain, watching as the trapper collapsed, and then ducked back as Abe's rifle discharged, harmlessly hitting a tree. Rising to his feet, Jed charged across the opening, trying to reach Abe before he could reload. Only feet separated the two men as Abe brought the rifle again to bear on the charging Jed. Only a click came from the rifle as Jed slammed into the trapper, knocking the rifle away.

"Seems you forgot to prime your rifle, Abe." Jed pulled his skinning knife. "Bad luck."

"Maybe for you, Jed." Abe grinned, pulling his own knife. "I'm not Vern."

Both men faced each other with their knives ready as their sharp points searched, flicking out, trying to bring blood on the other. Lunging across at Jed, Abe slashed several times, finding only thin air where Jed stood seconds before.

"You're fast, Jed." Abe pushed forward. "Real fast, but you're soft."

"We'll see." Jed stalked the trapper patiently, waiting for an opening.

"How could the likes of you be an Arapaho Lance Bearer? That just beats me, Jed." Abe growled. "I'm gonna open you up like a ripe melon."

Both knives clashed several times as the men sprang forward, raking the air as they tried to finish the fight. Abe was slowing, tiring, and the mad rushes were taking their toll on the older man. Jed's knife began to find its mark as Abe retreated slowly across the clearing. Lunging together, both men took hold of the other's wrist and struggled, trying their best to force their knives forward. Exhausted, his endurance finally gone and unable to defend himself, Abe lowered his knife as Jed advanced.

"I'm done in, Jed, finished." Abe leaned back against a tree. Suddenly, as Jed advanced toward him, the trapper lunged forward in one last desperate attempt to sink his blade into his elusive foe.

Only the sound of air exiting Abe's open mouth sounded as Jed drove his sharp blade into the trapper. "Now, you're done, Abe."

Looking down at the blade, Abe groaned slightly. "I reckon you are an Indian, you didn't even blink, Jed."

"Would you have, Abe?"

No sound came from the trapper as he slowly slumped to the ground. Retrieving his bloody knife, Jed wiped it on the trapper. Hearing a noise, Jed stood up and turned to where Vern was lying on the ground, watching him.

"You've killed us both, boy." Vern groaned and slowly rolled face down with his final word. "Both."

CHAPTER 12

Looking around the camp at the dead bodies, Jed shook his head in disgust, then retrieved the piebald. Before mounting the horse, Jed released the animals of the trappers from where they stood on the picket line. After taking one last look around, he started across the Snake River. Stopping midstream, Jed reached into his small leather bag and pulled out the small ring. The beautiful face of his mother seemed to appear as he dropped the small band from his hand, watching as it disappeared beneath the current. Yes, she was beautiful, not only her looks, but in her sweet and kind mannerisms as well. He had no regrets for not returning the ring to Ed Wilson. Now, with the killing of the two white trappers, he didn't know if he would be able to return to Baxter Springs. Even though they tried to kill him and it was self-defense, the whites would hang him if they found out who killed them. An Indian wasn't allowed to kill a white, and even though he was white, Jed knew they would look upon him as an Indian.

The piebald took his time, alternating between walking and trotting as Jed worked his way back through the beautiful mountains and valleys as he passed back to the east and south. Again, the grandeur and beauty of these mountains left him in awe, breathless. The grass along the trail was plentiful for the horse, and the bow killed him plenty of small animals as he passed along the trail. Only the bear remained in his thoughts, as the bear could be a man killer now, after killing Billy Wilson and tasting man's blood. Somewhere ahead, as he neared the big river, the grizzly could be waiting. Reining in the piebald on the ridge of a large valley, Jed blinked as he noticed what appeared to be a piece of metal or mirror shining brilliantly from across the grassy floor. Never, has he seen anything as bright in full daylight, almost like a shooting star, beckoning him. Curiously, he kicked the horse down into the flats, making his way across the valley floor, trying to keep his eyes on the beckoning light as he passed through the tall grass. Several times, he retraced his steps to locate the bright beam of light in the valley. He was amazed, the beam was only visible from certain angles or distances, and the slightest variation would cause him to lose sight of it.

Jed sat in the middle of the valley, knowing he was close, and at times it was as if he could almost reach out and touch whatever he was seeing. Slipping to the ground, he led the piebald, searching on foot for the beam. He knew it was not his imagination, because he saw it, something bright and shiny. For two hours, Jed walked the valley, amazed at how such a strong signal could just disappear, then reappear. Disgusted, he mounted and rode back to where he had first seen the shiny signal. Nothing, whatever he had seen was gone. Straining his eyes, he looked from every angle, but to no avail. Looking up at the sky, Jed studied the sun, and perhaps only with the sun at a certain zenith would the shiny signal show itself. Maybe it was only his mind playing tricks on his tired eyes. Perplexed, he wanted to spend the night in this spot and wait on the morning sun for another look, but he couldn't wait any longer, he had to find out about Walking Horse. Marking the exact spot and the valley in his mind, Jed turned the piebald back toward Arapaho lands.

The Arapaho Village had moved, but Jed finally located it closer to the Yellowstone after following the drag marks of the many travois used for transport. The village was near where the buffalo herds gathered to feed, fattening on the ample grasses of the flatlands before the first snows fell. Riding unchallenged into the village, he nodded as the villagers stopped whatever they were doing and surrounded the piebald, all trying to touch him at once. Sliding from the horse, Jed turned to where Slow Wolf and White Swan stood.

"You have returned to us, my son." Slow Wolf smiled and embraced Jed.

"Yes, Uncle, I have returned."

"You have traveled far." White Swan stepped forward. "I have seen you at the great river in the smoke."

"Yes, Grandfather, I have traveled far."

"Is your journey finished?"

"I do not know yet. I have come back to see Walking Horse and the people."

"We are glad you are here with your people, my son." Slow Wolf smiled. "Go, your lodge is prepared, and Walking Horse waits in his lodge."

Jed wanted to question White Swan about what he had seen, but seeing Walking Horse and Little Antelope came first. "I would talk with you later, Grandfather."

"I know, my son. The old medicine man nodded. "You have seen what is not to be seen."

Completely flabbergasted that the old medicine man already knew of what he had seen, Jed nodded his head and turned in the direction Slow Wolf pointed. "Yes, later, Grandfather."

The small frame of Little Antelope stood beside the fire as Jed led the piebald across the village, turning the horse in with the herd before continuing toward her. The dark eyes looked up and smiled as he approached. In his eyes, she was still the same beautiful woman, but Jed knew he now looked at her differently. Smiling, he embraced her and stepped back.

"It is good Crow Killer has returned to his people."

"It is good to see Little Antelope again. She has been missed."

"You could not say good-bye at the river?" Anger sounded in her voice. Jed nodded. "There was no time."

"Even for me?"

"I have come to see my friend, Walking Horse." Jed didn't want to argue with her. "How is he?"

"He is inside his lodge, very weak." Little Antelope stepped aside.

"May I go in?" Jed looked into her dark eyes. "May I speak with him? Is he strong enough?"

"An Arapaho Lance Bearer does not ask the permission of an Arapaho squaw to speak."

"Little Antelope knows she is more than an Arapaho squaw to me."

"You say this now, but I remember when you turned from me at the river and rode away."

Shaking his head, Jed turned and started for the lodge. "I knew you were well protected."

"Men always know so much." She frowned. "I didn't need protection that day, I needed you."

Walking Horse lay propped up on a pile of buffalo robes in the back of the lodge. The once-fiery dark eyes were now with heavy lids. Jed could tell he was very weak and thought he seemed weaker than he should by now.

"How are you, Walking Horse, my friend?"

Opening his eyes slowly, the warrior smiled slightly and motioned for Jed to take a seat beside him. "I am worthless as a three-legged horse."

"It is good to see you alive."

"It is good to see my friend, Crow Killer."

"I have returned to the people."

Walking Horse nodded slowly. "Did you kill the redhead?"

"No, a bear killed him." Jed quickly told the warrior everything he had done since his journey to the north. Nothing was omitted, except the ring.

"The scout, Lige Hatcher, was here just one sleep ago."

"Lige Hatcher?"

"He said he was riding back to the white settlements." Walking Horse tried to straighten himself. "This is a bad thing, if he follows the trail you rode, he will find the white trappers."

"I did not pass him on the trail." Jed shrugged.

"Lige Hatcher is smart. If he did not recognize you, he probably kept out of sight and let you pass unseen."

"You're right, I was watching for the bear, and he could have let me pass without being seen." Jed nodded. "Do you think he will find the trappers?"

"He misses nothing. He will find them if he rides that way."

"Why was he here?"

"He says he follows the trail of the redhead." Walking Horse grimaced in pain as he moved. "I do not think he knows of you."

"Did he find Wilson's bones?"

Nodding his head, Walking Horse answered. "Rolling Thunder is a great tracker and scout, one of the greatest. He found the bones of the redhead."

"Rolling Thunder?"

"It is the name the Arapaho gave Lige Hatcher long ago"

"I did not ask, how is the meat taking going?"

"Slow, the herds are across the Yellowstone." Walking Horse flattened his hands. "We must go deeper into Crow lands to kill what we need."

"Where are the warriors?"

"Some guard the village, others hunt for the shaggies." The warrior frowned. "And here I lay, a cripple when my people need me."

"I will take the hunters out, tomorrow. The Lance Bearers will take the lead."

"It will be very dangerous. The Crow will be watching, they know we need meat." Walking Horse rolled his head. "They know the big herds have not crossed the river."

"Someone told me once, no Arapaho fears a Crow." Jed smiled at Walking Horse.

The warrior nodded his head. "Yes, now that one lies here like a buffalo calf, helpless."

"You rest now, I will speak with Bow Legs and prepare for tomorrow." Jed touched the warrior on the shoulder. "Rest easy, my friend. We will have meat for the cold times."

"I hope so. I will rest now."

Little Antelope stood beside the fire as Jed exited the lodge. Turning, she walked off to where the piebald stood grazing. She knew he would follow her toward the horse.

"You have changed toward me, Jed." The dark eyes grew soft. "You look at me, but you do not see me as you once did."

"You are the woman of my friend, Walking Horse, who lies helpless in his lodge." Jed frowned down at her. "We are friends and it is not right for me to have any feelings for you, other than friendship."

"And if we feel more?"

"No one must know, no one."

Little Antelope dropped her eyes. "I know."

Jed looked across the village making sure they weren't being watched. "Tomorrow, I lead the hunters after buffalo, maybe into the land of the Crow."

"You change the subject, Crow Killer."

"No, Little Antelope, there is no subject. Your husband is inside, and never will I betray or insult him." Jed pointed at the lodge. "You will go to him, now."

Turning back to the center of the village, Jed sought out the lodge of Bow Legs. He wanted to get away. He wanted the warriors ready for tomorrow's hunt. People smiled and spoke as he walked by, but no one tried to stop him to talk.

"You tread on dangerous ground, my friend." The familiar voice of the bowlegged one came from behind a lodge. "She is the woman of Walking Horse."

"There is nothing."

"It does not look like nothing when she speaks to you with calf eyes, Crow Killer."

Exasperated, Jed frowned. "Ready the warriors, we hunt tomorrow."

"I watched her eyes as you walked away." Bow Legs looked around to be sure no one was listening. "Are you sure it is nothing, my friend?"

"You have my word, Bow Legs. It is all I can say."

"I will ready the warriors." Bow Legs nodded. "Your word is enough, Crow Killer."

White Swan nodded to Jed as he finished talking with Bow Legs. Walking to where the old one sat in front of his lodge, Jed took the seat across from the medicine man. White Swan seemed older than Jed remembered him, frail and bonier.

"Are you well, Grandfather?"

"Yes, my son. I am well." The grey head nodded slowly. "I summoned you here to speak of what was seen, and never seen."

Jed nodded, the old one was right. He had seen something but did he? "Will you tell me of what we spoke of a long time ago, a thing I don't understand?"

"Yes, the smoke has spoken." White Swan held up his bony hand.

"You are Arapaho now, but the valley where you were summoned will be your new home. You will always be near your people so you can help them if needed. Now, circumstances prevent you from staying here among the people. Once, we spoke of you leaving the people, soon perhaps this will have to be."

Jed knew what the old one was talking about. "I have seen this coming too."

"I am sorry, my son, you are a great Lance Bearer of the people."

"I will always be ready to help my people." Jed looked into the eyes of the old one. "When the hunt is over, I will return to the valley of the bright light."

The old head nodded. "This will be for the best. Walking Horse has found a friend in you. There is no reason to put temptation in front of either of you."

"Yes, Walking Horse is my friend and so is Little Antelope, a friend." Jed nodded.

"I know, Crow Killer, it will be hard but it will be for the best that you leave the village, at least for a time."

"Tell me, Grandfather, does anyone else know of what we speak?"

"No my son and we will speak of this no more."

Jed stood to leave and smiled at the old one. "I have been happy here."

White Swan nodded. "From what the smoke tells, you will be very happy in your valley with the dark haired woman."

Walking back to his lodge, Jed shook his head, bewildered. Was White Swan speaking of Sally Ann, but how would he have known? He knew he would never understand the old one, the valley with the glowing light, and now Sally Ann Duncan.

Lige Hatcher had watched from hiding as the Indian riding the piebald horse of Black Robe passed him on the trail, one day ride from the Snake River. He didn't know the Indian but he knew the horse. Any trader or trapper in the northwest knew the big black paint horse only the Nez Perce warrior rode, and there was only one like him in all these mountains. He was curious how the Arapaho warrior got him, but for now, he needed to push on to Baxter Springs and report to the constable about Billy Wilson's demise. He had been commissioned by the town fathers to bring Wilson in for the killing of local trader, Eli Kaine. Now, all he could report was Wilson had been killed by a bear. There was no doubt, what he found of the man was the bones which had been gnawed and chewed by powerful jaws, the jaws of a huge grizzly. There had been signs of two Indians found on the sandy trail around the bones, but Wilson had been killed by a bear. Anyway, he was dead.

As the unsuspecting warrior passed from sight, Hatcher kicked his horse and started for the crossing on the Snake. It was a long, hard day's ride on to the river, and if he pushed hard, he would be in Baxter Springs in four days. The bay horse was tired and worn out as Hatcher neared the sandy banks of the Snake. The scout stopped the horse, letting him drink in the knee-deep water of the river. Suddenly, his curiosity was aroused again as he noticed a small herd of mules and horses grazing in the meadow across the river. Nudging the bay, he let the tired horse pick his way slowly across the rocky bottom, splashing out on the far bank.

Even from across the meadow, Hatcher recognized the mules and horses that belonged to Abe Reed and Vern Grey. Turning downstream, he rode into the visible, quiet campsite of the trappers. Unslinging his Hawken, the scout eased down from the bay. Already, he found the bloated bodies of the two trappers by the vultures and the smell. The grey eyes surveyed the dead fire, furs, and many trade goods that most traders carried with them, but nothing looks as if it had been disturbed. Looking down into what was left of the staring eyes of Vern Grey, a man he knew well, he could plainly identify the arrow protruding from the trapper as Arapaho. The warrior, he had watched on the trail, was no doubt the killer. Hatcher had followed the warrior's tracks all the way from where he had seen him and the tracks of the piebald were plain in the sand around the camp. Hatcher shook his head, as nothing had been touched, not even the rifles that were so valuable to an Indian. The scout was confused, as he had seen many men killed, but never had he seen nothing touched, not even a scalp or horse was taken.

Picking up both rifles, Hatcher started to sort out the story of the camp. Both Abe and Vern had fired their weapons but how did they miss? Carefully following the tracks, it slowly dawned on Hatcher; the Indian he had seen on the piebald was a white. The toes of the killer were turned out, not turned in as most Indians were. Finally sorting out what had happened, the old scout stopped to build a fire for coffee as he was satisfied. He didn't know why the trappers were killed, but he had most of it figured out.

Hatcher shook his head in confusion as the coffee started to boil over the small blaze. A white dressed as an Arapaho. His mind thought back to the figure he had watched passing him on the trail, thinking it could have been Jedidiah Bracket. Too far to be certain, Hatcher knew he would have to find out, and that meant returning to Slow Wolf's village and not going on to Baxter Springs. Wilson was dead, and his report could wait. Now, the killing of Abe and Vern was far more pressing.

The trappers were not particularly his friends but they were white men killed by an Arapaho arrow, and he had to have answers. Could this Arapaho be Jedidiah? What reason would Jed have to kill Abe and Vern, then casually ride on toward Arapaho Country? Hatcher was curious and had to find out before returning to Baxter Springs. If this was Bracket, did he turn lobo like Billy Wilson?

Thirty warriors sat their horses behind Jed as they waited on the banks of the Yellowstone before crossing into Crow hunting grounds. Five of the warriors were Lance Bearers, the rest were all younger, but all were experienced hunters and fighters.

"If we cross the river, we may have to fight." Bow Legs looked at Jed's set face.

Nodding, Jed kicked the piebald forward, then slipped from the wide back as the horse hit swimming water. The water encircling his body was still warm as he held onto the horse's mane, kicking hard to help the big animal swim. Focusing his eyes across the river, Jed watched as a lone rider rode from the far bank, racing his horse out of sight. Riding from the water, Jed didn't stop to let the horses blow from their long swim, but pushed them further into the heavy timber, out of sight, away from the banks of the great river.

Slipping from the piebald, Jed looked into the faces of the gathered warriors. "We have been sighted, my friends. We have come for buffalo, but perhaps we will be challenged by the Crow."

"What will we do, the Crow outnumber us?" Little Weasel asked as his eyes searched the far timber.

Looking at the nervous warrior, Jed shook his head. "Any who wish to return to the village, without winter meat, may go."

"What will Crow Killer do?" Another huge warrior spoke up.

"I came for winter meat, Big Owl. I will not leave with nothing." Jed watched their faces. "Is it not better to die here fighting, then to let our people starve this winter?

"I am with you."

Bow Legs shook his head sadly. "My poor legs, it is said the Crow women like a man's legs."

"Those are not legs. They are sticks, like a deer has." Crooked Mouth laughed.

"They are beautiful." Big Owl spoke up. "They remind me of my horse's legs."

"You are both crazy." Shaking his head, Jed had Bow Legs lead out, following the small trail to where the buffalo herds were reported being seen by two Arapaho scouts. This was a dangerous place, the Crow lands were across the Yellowstone and the Crow would defend it with their lives. Two hours passed as the column of warriors rode steadily to the north.

Riding out onto the flat grasslands, Bow Legs raised his arm and pointed. "There, the shaggies." The warrior grinned widely. "Even enough to fill your huge stomach, Big Owl."

"And the Crows." Crooked Mouth pointed.

Jed watched as the Crow warriors spread out in a long line and advanced, straight to where they sat their horses. The Crow warriors numbered at least twice as many as the Arapaho hunters with Jed.

"My friends, will we fight and feed our families in the cold times, or will we run home and let them starve this winter?"

Bow Legs shook his head sadly again. "My legs say run but my stomach says fight."

Nodding, Jed pulled his lance from the arrow quiver on his back. "Wait here, my friends. I will speak with our friends who are coming."

"Friends? I rather be friends with a rattlesnake." Crooked Mouth spat.

Jed rode forward and stopped the piebald only feet from where the Crow sat their horses. Raising his arm, he called out to an older warrior, he figured was their leader. "We have come for meat. We do not wish to fight."

The Crow warrior laughed. "Neither would I, if you had me outnumbered two to one."

"We must have meat for the cold times." Jed argued. "My scouts tell me you have finished your hunts already."

"These are our lands, Arapaho." The warrior pointed to the north. "Leave now, or die."

Jed studied the formation of Crow warriors before him. Most were older, experienced warriors but some were young, still old enough to fight. There were too many and he knew if they fought, they would probably lose. If they won, their warriors could be wounded, useless for the hunt and they needed meat not hurt warriors. He had to save face, but if they retreated, the Arapaho would be laughed at and have no pride left.

"We do not wish to fight and see our young men killed." Jed shrugged. "But, we have no choice."

"You are a fool, warrior."

"My name is Crow Killer." Jed turned the piebald and rode back halfway to the waiting Arapahos.

"I have heard this name." The warrior watched as Jed dismounted and plunged his eagle-feathered War Lance, deep into the ground. "At least you are a brave fool, Arapaho."

Raising his huge arm, the Crow looked up and down the line of warriors, then started to motion them forward.

"Wait, our Chief comes." Another warrior yelled out as he watched a large group of warriors riding toward them.

Jed swore softly to himself as he watched a huge warrior on a sorrel horse coming toward him with another group of warriors. His eyes squinted as he took in the full eagle-feathered headdress the warrior was wearing, and this had to be Plenty Coups himself. They were outnumbered and couldn't win. Jed wanted to spare his warriors, but he knew they would not leave him staked to the ground. He looked down at the lance, then at the approaching warriors. He would not shame the Lance Bearers of the Arapaho by pulling the lance from the ground.

Jed readied his war axe, as Plenty Coups was almost upon him. The big warrior pulled in his sorrel horse and looked across at the waiting Lance Bearer. Jed held his hand up to stop his warriors from advancing.

"Young one, you must be Crow Killer." Plenty Coups looked across at Jed.

"I am Crow Killer, my Chief."

"You know me?"

"Every warrior knows the great Crow Leader." Jed nodded. "Your son, Red Hawk, told me of you."

"You saved my son's life in the fight with the redhead."

"And he saved mine."

"Do you think this will save your life?"

"No, I think Plenty Coups will do whatever he wishes."

"You are on Crow lands."

"My people need meat." Jed shifted slightly. "The cold times come soon."

"Are there no shaggies on your side of the river?"

"We have found none." Jed shrugged. "They stay on this side."

Plenty Coups' big head nodded. "This means we will have a hard winter. A very hard winter."

"Tell me, before we fight, how is Red Hawk?"

"Why do you ask?"

"He is my friend, I wish to know."

"You are Arapaho, he is Crow."

"So?"

Plenty Coups dismounted and walked to where Jed waited, uncertain whether the chief was going to fight him alone or motion his warriors forward. Jed was tall, but Plenty Coups was at least six inches taller. Astride the sorrel, he made the huge horse he rode seem small. Stopping at arm's reach away from Jed, the chief stepped forward and pulled the lance from the ground. "You have given my son his life. You have also given Red Hawk the spotted horse and his pride back." Plenty Coups examined the lance carefully. "You may bring your village here to hunt the buffalo this one time, no more."

"For this, the Arapaho thank you, my Chief."

"You are a brave warrior, Crow Killer." Plenty Coups smiled. "I would be proud to have a son such as you."

Jed nodded. "You are a great Chief and you have Red Hawk, the bravest of all Crow warriors."

"Red Hawk's wounds heal. He could not come here to greet you." Plenty Coups held out the lance. "Perhaps Crow Killer could come visit him. He would like that."

"And I would like that."

"Then it is settled." Plenty Coups removed a painted bear necklace out to Jed. "This is for you. It gives you safe passage through our lands."

Jed held the necklace, admiring it. "Thank you, it is a thing of beauty."

"It is not for Red Hawk's life." Plenty Coups smiled. "It is because you gave me back my headdress."

"I did not know it belonged to the great Plenty Coups, Chief of the Crow people."

The big warrior mounted his sorrel horse nimbly. "Come to my village, Crow Killer. Now, go hunt your winter meat. Your people will be safe."

As Plenty Coups raised his hand and turned the sorrel, a war cry went up from the Crow lines. An older warrior raced his horse forward and challenged Jed by throwing down his war axe.

Plenty Coups looked at the warrior, then over at Jed. "He challenges Crow Killer to fight."

"Why?" Jed was confused.

"He is Wounded Bear, the father of Wild Wind, the one you killed many suns ago."

"I do not want to kill this one."

Plenty Coups rode to where the older warrior sat his horse. Jed could not hear what was being said, but he could tell by the warrior's actions, he paid no attention to his chief. If the man wanted vengeance for the life of his son, he would have to fight.

"His pride and loss of his son will not permit him to ride away, while one of you lives." Plenty Coups shrugged. "I am sorry, my son."

Jed rolled up the rawhide rope that attached him to the lance and replaced it into his arrow quiver. Laying the bow and quiver beside him, he turned to where the warrior waited.

"Tell him I tried to talk his son out of fighting but he would not listen." Jed lifted his war axe. "The young one wanted to count coup on me."

"The warriors with his son said different."

"They lie. I did not ask for the fight." Jed's temper started to show. "I do not wish to kill this one."

"I cannot stop this fight. It is a personal thing between you and him."

Turning his horse, Plenty Coups rode back toward his warriors. As he passed the warrior, he swiped his hand down and shook his head. Jed watched as the Crow dismounted and started toward him. He did not want to kill the warrior and to do so could mean they wouldn't get their winter meat. Both sides watched as the older warrior rushed at Jed swinging his war axe. Dodging the swinging axe, Jed kicked into the air, catching the warrior with both heels on his face, knocking him senseless. Pulling his knife, he straddled the unconscious man and looked across at Plenty Coups.

"I took a life, now I give him his." Jed stood and gathered his bow and quiver, then walked to where the piebald waited ground tied. "I will fight no more with him."

Plenty Coups nodded in awe of the swiftness of the Arapaho's flying feet and the ease in which he defeated a great warrior. Pointing at the Crow, who was trying to rise from the ground as he held his head, the chief barked at the warrior. "It is finished."

Bow Legs, Crooked Mouth, Big Owl, and the rest all stared at Jed in awe and disbelief, but said nothing as the piebald passed them in a trot, heading back to the south. Silence prevailed as they crossed the Yellowstone, then the small river beside the village, and as they entered the village. Jed was tired; having ridden far in the past days, all he wanted was rest. As the warriors passed through the village, Jed looked at no one, spoke to no one as they slipped from their horses. The dreaded Lance Bearers of the Arapaho, even the normally talkative Bow Legs, had not spoken a single word on their way home. They were still in awe and could not believe Crow Killer had defeated the Crow so easily and somehow got Plenty Coups' permission to let them hunt in Crow hunting grounds, without a fight.

"Have the village prepare to move with the coming of the new sun." Jed turned the piebald loose into the horse herd.

"It is for Slow Wolf to give the order to move." Bow Legs warned.

"Go tell them, I will speak with Slow Wolf." Jed tiredly assured. "It will be okay, my friend."

"You are a great warrior, Crow Killer." Crooked Mouth spoke over at Jed. "We will follow you anywhere."

"No, my friend there will be no fighting tomorrow." Jed shook his head. "We will hunt buffalo, that is all."

"With you leading us, we can defeat any tribe or people."

Jed shook his head. "I have fought enough. Now, I wish to rest."

Slow Wolf and White Swan listened closely as Bow Legs told of the meeting with the Crow, Plenty Coups, and what they had witnessed themselves. Both of the Arapaho elders nodded their heads as they listened to the warrior.

"He is the greatest of all Lance Bearers." Bow Legs bragged on Jed. "Alone, he defeated the Crow and gained us permission to hunt the shaggies on Crow land."

Slow Wolf nodded slowly. "The prophecy is fulfilled. Tomorrow, we move across the Yellowstone to hunt."

Bow Legs' chest swelled. "Plenty Coups himself was afraid of Crow Killer."

"This is so, my Chief." Big Owl, a Lance Bearer of great respect, nodded. "I watched and there is none like him."

The great river, the Yellowstone, was wide and deep with a swift current, still the whole village, men, women, children, and everything that walked, crossed safely as they moved on to the Crow hunting grounds. Many Crow warriors watched the village pass as they sat on the ridges of the valley. Most of the warriors didn't like the Arapaho in their hunting grounds, but their chief had given his permission and none dared dispute his word.

While the squaws quickly set up the village, the main body of Arapaho warriors prepared their arrows and horses for the big hunt with the coming of the new sun. Horse's tails were tied up, paint of each individual warrior decorated their horses, and the warriors themselves tied up their hair and prepared their medicine.

Bow Legs stopped his horse before his chief's lodge. "Do we keep warriors back to guard the village?"

Slow Wolf looked over at Jed. "What does Crow Killer say?"

"Send all the warriors tomorrow." Jed looked around the bustling village. "Let's get our meat and return to our lands quickly."

"Do you not trust Plenty Coups?"

"I trust him, my Chief, but still I urge the people to leave this place quickly."

Jed ducked through the entrance of Walking Horse's lodge and looked down at the warrior. "How are you today, my friend?"

"Thanks to Little Antelope, I am getting stronger."

"She is a good wife." Jed smiled over to where she sat.

"Perhaps one day you will have one such as her."

"If I am lucky."

Little Antelope did not speak. Only her eyes moved slightly as she worked on a new pair of moccasins for Walking Horse.

"Tomorrow, you take the warriors for the big hunt."

Jed nodded. "White Swan says the big snows come soon. We must hurry and return to our protected valleys."

"I wish I could ride with you."

"Next year, my friend." Jed looked at Little Antelope. "Next year, we will hunt them together."

"I would have liked to have seen you defeat the warrior from the valley."

"I felt sorry for him, Walking Horse." Jed shrugged. "He was a sad old man."

"I know, my friend. It is a sad thing to lose a son." Walking Horse looked at Little Antelope. "Or anything you love."

Following Jed from the lodge, as he departed, Little Antelope handed him back the gold charm White Swan had given him to ward off the evil ones. "Tomorrow, you will need this, Crow Killer. Good luck."

Nodding, Jed took the nugget from her hand. "Thank you, Little Antelope. You will always be in my thoughts."

"And you mine." She smiled sadly. "But, as a friend only."

Slow Wolf took Jed's words to heart, and the hunt started early the next morning. The warriors were lucky, as enough shaggies had been killed the first two days to feed the village during the cold times. The women and young people skinned and cut up the buffalo that fell in the valley, until they were exhausted and had to rest for the night. The next morning, another herd was located and the hunt began again. Jed pushed everyone hard, almost to the limits of their endurance. He wanted to leave the Crow lands as quickly as possible. The Crow kept their word, never attempting to interfere with the Arapaho. As the village lined out, preparing to depart back across the Yellowstone, a lone Crow warrior appeared close to the village.

Mounting the piebald, Jed rode out to meet the warrior. "My chief wishes for the great Crow Killer to come to our village."

"It is agreed. Wait here and I will go with you."

Walking Horse watched from where he lay on a travois, waiting to leave for Arapaho lands. "What did the Crow want?"

"Plenty Coups has sent for me to come to his village."

"Is that wise, my friend?" Walking Horse shook his head. "To ride alone into the bear's lair could be deadly."

"One day, I will rejoin you on the other side of the river." Jed smiled down at the warrior. "Then we will hunt the shaggies again and you can continue my training."

"Good hunting, Crow Killer." The warrior smiled and extended his hand. "My friend."

"I will return soon."

Little Antelope handed Jed a leather bag filled with dried berries. Looking up at him, she smiled. "I am proud to have one such as you as my friend, Jed."

"You understand, little one, it wasn't meant to be." Jed asked. "You are not mad?"

"No, I care for my husband and I was being a stupid jealous woman."

"I will always be your friend." Jed turned the piebald. "If you ever need me."

"And I yours." The little woman smiled. "Walk proud my warrior, always walk proud."

"You have taught me much, Little Antelope, very much." Jed smiled as he took the bag. "Thank you."

Her small hand rested lightly on his arm as she spoke. "If only we could have met sooner."

Jed looked over to where Walking Horse lay on the travois. "You have the greatest husband any woman could wish for, far better than I."

"We won't see you anymore, will we?"

"You will see me if I am needed."

The Village, during the day, seemed much larger than it did when Walking Horse had brought him across the river alone to raid the Crow. Sliding from the piebald, Jed waited as the warrior he followed entered the large lodge, then motioned him inside.

Red Hawk was seated against a backrest as he entered. Smiling, the warrior motioned Jed to a seat before the small fire. "It is good to see you, my friend."

"It is good to see Red Hawk." Jed sat back against a backrest. "How is your wound?"

"Thanks to you, it is good."

"And the spotted one?"

"Come, we will walk to where he is." Red Hawk gained his feet slowly. "He is a thing of beauty."

"It is said you promised his first horse colt to the Cheyenne, Yellow Dog."

Red Hawk frowned, but then laughed. "If I had not, I wondered if I would have gotten out of there with the horse."

"He is a temptation, that's a fact." Jed laughed. "He is a great horse."

For two days, Jed stayed with Red Hawk and enjoyed the food and good times with the Crow as they celebrated their victorious buffalo hunts with feasting and dancing. Jed danced with the many young women of the village as he had become very popular. His tall, good looks, plus the praise and friendship that Red Hawk piled on him, made them all want him for a dance partner.

"Crow Killer should stay here with the Crow." Red Hawk laughed from where he sat. "You could have many wives."

"It is a thought." Jed smiled. "Thank you, my friend. Tomorrow, I must leave."

"To the Arapaho people?"

"No, I must return to a place I have found."

Red Hawk straightened a little and smiled. "You will leave the Arapaho people and the woman?"

"She is the woman of another."

"This may be true, my friend." The warrior nodded. "But, I have seen the way her eyes search for you, not the way a married woman does."

Jed looked hard at the warrior, first Bow Legs, White Swan, and now Red Hawk. Did Walking Horse also know Little Antelope's heart? "Her husband is my friend, and this is why I leave the Arapaho."

"Then stay here with us. We don't have Lance Bearers, but we do have many pretty unmarried women." Red Hawk laughed. "We will ride east and fight with the Pawnee, Paiute, or anybody else we find that wishes to fight."

"Thank you, my friend, it is tempting. Perhaps, someday, if this place I find doesn't work out, I may return here."

Two days after saying his goodbyes to Red Hawk and Plenty Coups, Jed rode the piebald onto the banks of the mighty Yellowstone River and looked out across the broad current. It was a beautiful river, with clear, cool, inviting water. Looking down at the beautiful buckskins he carried across the back of the piebald which were a gift from Red Hawk, he nodded thoughtfully. After crossing the river, he would bathe and change into the new hunting shirt and leggings which was of Crow workmanship but he knew he would be recognized by the Arapaho if he was seen wearing them. He knew, across the Yellowstone was Arapaho country, dangerous country to ride for anyone encroaching on Arapaho lands. Slow Wolf always kept scouts out to watch for any enemy raiders.

As he was about to kick the horse forward, he hesitated as a rider emerged from the trees across the river. As the horse and rider moved down the slight incline to the edge of the water, Jed straightened on the piebald. If his eyes weren't lying to him, the rider waiting on the other side was the old scout, Lige Hatcher. Raising his arm in greeting, he waited and watched until the other rider raised his own. Scanning the banks for any other riders and finally satisfied there were none, he kicked the piebald forward into the water. Jed felt the strong current pull at him as he entered the river. He slipped from the powerful animal, letting the horse pull him across where both man and horse waded ashore, stopping ten feet from the old scout.

"Well now, youngster. It's been awhile." Hatcher studied Jed's face. "We thought you a goner, back on the Platte, boy."

"I almost was." Jed looked at the man. The scout hadn't changed, maybe a little older. "What are you doing here?"

"Looking for the Indian that did for Abe and Vern."

"Why, you planning on taking him into the settlements?"

"If'n it was cold-blooded murder, I just might."

"You think it was me?" Jed looked at the rifle resting in Hatcher's hand. "You following me?"

"I know it was you, Jed." Hatcher fingered the rifle. "I ain't blind, I can still read sign. Tell me, why did they try to kill you?"

Jed studied the scout for several seconds. "I killed Black Robe. He was their meal ticket to the Nez Perce. They thought if they had this piebald horse of his and my scalp they might worm their way back in with the tribe."

"Sounds like them alright." Hatcher nodded. "Peers it didn't work out too well."

"Nope." Jed studied the woods behind Hatcher. "Who told you where I was?"

"Walking Horse."

"You found me quick enough."

"Yep, me and you crossed paths back this side of the Snake, but I didn't recognize you that day."

"Um huh." Jed nodded thoughtfully. "Walking Horse said we'd meet."

"He sets considerable store by you, Jed." Hatcher thumbed back over his shoulder. "I know they're over there watching this little play."

Whistling at the unseen riders, Jed watched as Bow Legs and several other Lance Bearers rode out from the shadows of the woods. Racing their horses toward the river, the warriors rode up and encircled Hatcher.

"Crow Killer was not eaten by the Crow." Bow Legs grinned. "We have been watching this one."

"Thank you, my friends." Jed smiled. "He is a friend as you are."

"It seems like you have many friends here." Hatcher studied the warriors. "I have known most of them since they were babies."

"And we know you, Rolling Thunder." Bow Legs frowned. "Tell us, do you come here after Crow Killer?"

"We still have a problem with the two white trappers I found dead."

Hatcher frowned, ignoring the warriors. "They were done in by an Arapaho arrow."

"Tell me, Lige, are you the law out here?"

"Kinda, I work off and on for the appointed constable in Baxter Springs." Hatcher shifted in his saddle. "He's gonna have to know about this."

"Tell him." Jed eyes narrowed. "Self-defense, they shot at me first."

"You willing to ride back with me and tell him yourself?"

"No, sir. I've got business somewhere else." Jed shook his head. "But, I'll ride partway with you."

Shaking hands with the warriors, Jed bid them all good-bye, promising to return to the village in the spring. Bow Legs wanted to follow him to the west, but Jed refused the warrior's offer. A wave of loneliness hit him as he watched them turn and ride off, disappearing back into the woods. Nodding at Hatcher, Jed kicked the piebald and turned back west, toward the beckoning light.

Two days hard ride, east of the Snake, Jed reined in at sundown and picketed the piebald on the banks of a small stream where the grass was knee high on the horse. Hatcher removed the saddle from his roan horse and piled it beside the creek. Quickly building a small fire, the old scout placed his beat-up, fire-blackened coffeepot atop the flames to boil.

"Is this where we part company, Jed?" Hatcher looked out across the beautiful valley.

"It is. Tell your constable, I'll be in, come spring thaw and explain things to him."

"You've come a long way, Jed. The Arapaho sing your praises, and even the Crow call you friend." Hatcher handed Jed a tin cup. "I doubt the constable will be wanting to see you."

"I hope not, Lige."

"You coming to Baxter Springs for anything in particular, Jed?" Hatcher grinned as he had already heard about Jed and Sally Ann's visit.

"I am. Tell her I'll be there for her with the spring melt off." Jed looked over at the older man.

"I'll tell her." Hatcher nodded. "What you gonna do till then?"

Jed looked around the beautiful valley as the sun lowered in the western sky. Whippoorwills called along the small stream, doves sang their songs, calling for their mates, and several small herds of elk grazed out on the meadows. His dark eyes searched for the elusive shining light, he had first spotted on his way east, but nothing caught his attention. Shrugging his shoulders, he knew he had all the time in the world to search for White Swan's shining light. He was home and no man could ask for anything more.

"Well Lige, I've got me a cabin to build, meat to get in for the winter, and a lot of exploring to do."

"That should keep you busy enough."

"It will, until she gets here."

Shaking hands with the old scout, Jed watched the roan horse pick his way along the mountain ridge, through the late summer flowers and grasses. Turning, he looked out across the beautiful valley and smiled. The blazing flash or whatever he had seen did not show itself again, but Jed knew this was the place White Swan had spoken of. Looking down at the new axe Hatcher had given him before he left, Jed smiled happily. He was home and when Sally Ann got here it would be more of a home.

THE END

Ingram Content Group UK Ltd.
Milton Keynes UK
UKHW020114090323
418239UK00014B/846